*The Third Harmony*

# OTHER BOOKS BY MAWI ASGEDOM

*Of Beetles and Angels*

*The Code*

*Win the Inner Battle*

*Beyond Character Education*

*Mimic the Devil*

For individual or bulk purchase, please visit
MawiBooks.com or email info@MawiBooks.com

# THE THIRD HARMONY

## Book One of HARMONY WARS

# MAWI ASGEDOM

*To my brother Hntsa,*
*who has always shared my love for adventure stories.*

# ACKNOWLEDGMENTS

Special thanks to Bonnie Nadzam and Tim Clinton who read countless drafts and provided detailed feedback that had a transformative impact on this book. Victor Kore also made major contributions to all aspects of *The Third Harmony*.

Big thanks to all my Eritrean and Ethiopian brothers and sisters for sharing many of the stories and proverbs used in this book. I'm also indebted to the following people for the generosity of their time and insights:

Sue Maylahn and her 8th grade class of real-life Jignas: Angelo, Molly, Hunter, John, Roy, Sean, Cole, Edwin, Eric, Mathew, Juan, and Megan.

Jeannine Nyangira, Mary Stec, Pat Martin, Paul Veldhouse, Lynn Veldhouse, Hntsa Asgedom, Tsege Asgedom, Mehret Asgedom, Sarah Nun, Sam Mullin, Kristina Eschmeyer, Griffin Clinton, Mezgebe Gebrekiristos, Kristin Barrett, Elly West, Linda Washington, Sewit Amde, Marcie Garcia, and Glenn Austin.

Big thanks to Alyssa Force for the cover and interior design; to Rebecca Peed for creating the map and the cover symbol of the eagle; and to Clint Hamilton for his preliminary sketches.

And finally, the biggest thanks to my wife Erin for her patience during all my writing sessions and for her invaluable insights. And of course, to my 1-year old son, Sawyer Tewolde Asgedom.

# PROLOGUE

Blood drenched the chamber, soaking the walls, the floors, the yellow straw-woven cots. Wood debris large and small littered the floor. Honey wine, escaped from shattered oak casks, cast a sweet scent over the otherwise chaotic room.

The air shimmered in the chamber's center. A tall, imperious woman appeared. She instantly drew both swords and backed into a wall. Blood! Everywhere…blood!

Her long blond dreadlocks swung as she surveyed the carnage. Lines furrowed into her head; her blue eyes narrowed.

What had happened? Who had done this? Where were her friends!

From a corner, a tall, foreboding shadow appeared. His long, angular face jutted like a wolf snout. Fresh welts and lacerations lined his body. His black staff gleamed.

The woman's soft voice rattled as she spoke. "Where are my companions?"

"I gave them a choice and they chose war."

Faster than any eye could see, the woman sped, thrusting with both swords. But the man ducked under one sword and parried the other with his staff.

The woman reached within for Aura power and cast fiery red beams at the man's head. But instead of ducking, the man extended his hands and absorbed the flames.

The woman lowered her swords. How…?

He smiled. "I can do things now, Tirhas, that you never dreamed of."

He released his hands and a hundred flames screamed toward her. Tirhas jumped high above the flames and landed on a ledge.

The man clenched a hand and the ground shook. An oak wine cask rattled. A sword fell from the weapons rack. He spoke in a steely voice. "Tell me where the last Book of Harmony is and you will live."

Tirhas trembled. It was impossible! His whole body was Aura!

She shouted, "Fool! What have you done to the Harmonies?"

He attacked. His staff blurred. She parried low then stabbed through his leg. He screamed and hurled another flame. She ducked. Flames singed her hair.

Something hissed. A steel throwing star ripped her jaw, taking a clump of flesh. Pain erupted. Another star sliced her right eye. Black dots clouded her vision. She summoned Aura but could not concentrate. What was happening? Darkness swirled and with it, the distant realization that she was going to die.

The man's voice boomed, "Where is it?"

His staff shattered her mouth, carrying her off the ledge. Her arm snapped against the ground. The pain sharpened her senses, cut through the darkness. She crawled and forced herself to stand.

"You can kill me. You can destroy the last Book of Harmony." She spat. A bloodied tooth fell from her mouth and rattled to the floor. "But the Harmonies are Truth. And while the rod of truth may grow thin, it will never break."

The man jumped down. He limped forward until he was inches from her face, "Your armies have lost. Your companions are dead. And all you can do is recite some tired proverb."

He jabbed her with his staff. "It's a new world, Tirhas. That's what you could never see. No one will need to restore the Harmonies because the Harmonies will still be here. Your rod of truth will thicken, not thin."

He pointed to four crumpled bodies in a far corner. His voice hardened. "The others died. You can live. I won't ask again. Where is the Book of Harmony?"

They were....dead. Her companions were dead. Tirhas crumpled. Blood splattered from her right eye, her chin.

Dimly, she watched as the man strode to a massive wine cask.

He pushed the lid aside. The sweet scent of honey wafted out. The man pointed at the four corpses and summoned Aura.

The bodies rose from the corner and floated until they hovered above the gigantic cask. After hanging in the air for a moment, the four bodies plunged into the cask, spilling wine over the sides.

Tirhas levitated. Her coiled hair slashed across her bloody face like an axe. It couldn't end like this! No! What had happened? Had she failed the Harmonies? Had the Harmonies failed her?

When the man spoke, his voice carried a tinge of regret. "Farewell, Tirhas."

Tirhas plummeted into the cask and the lid slammed shut with the finality of a tombstone. Red beams shot from the man's hands and circled the cask. An explosion rocked the chamber. Lightning flashed.

Where the cask had been was air. The debris that had covered the room was gone. The man exhaled. It was done.

Blood spurted from his leg as he stepped forward. There was no one left to challenge him now. He could usher in a new Age of Harmony far greater than any the world had seen.

Only one thing troubled him. The red fox. The fox had escaped in the earlier battle. No matter. The tall man adjusted his cloak, stepped through the chamber's wall and disappeared.

The Harmony Wars were over.

※ ※ ※

The wine had not yet dried on the chamber floor. The sound of claws ripping against wood reverberated through the air. Above the chamber door, a large fox bounded from a hidden ledge. The red fox swung his claws where the wine cask had vanished. But there was only air.

The fox howled, the only dirge Tirhas and her four companions would receive. As the howls echoed, the fox bent its legs,
leapt through the nearest wall and disappeared, melting into the
forest outside.

# PART I
## The Tree

❊ ❊ ❊

*"The twine of truth may thin but it will never snap."*
Tirhas the Light

# One

*"Do not come back unless you bring food."*

The words dripped in Twid's head like the *tib tib* of rain on his neck. A flicker of sunlight lit Twid's brown face, revealing jutting cheekbones and soft eyes. Dark, curly hair sprouted in every direction.

*"Do not come back unless you bring food."*

Those were strong words from Twid's adopted father, Zeru. But Twid could hardly blame Zeru. The orphanage where they lived was out of food and as the oldest son, Twid had to hunt.

Locusts had devoured the orphanage's grain and ravaged its garden. If Twid didn't catch any meat, the orphanage would have to kill one of its five goats.

Killing a goat for meat would mean less goat milk. Less goat milk only increased the likelihood that the orphanage would have to kill the next goat. And so on until the orphanage had neither goat milk nor meat. Then, when they ran out of grain… Twid couldn't imagine Zeru begging.

Twid bent his lanky frame under a protruding branch.

What a disaster! Zeru wouldn't care that Twid had hunted the Adwa Forests for eight straight hours. Nor would Zeru consider that darkness and the coming storm would make it impossible to continue hunting. No. To old Zeru, failure was just another word for laziness. Zeru would…

A movement in the trees! Twid craned his neck and tightened his grip on his spear. The branch jerked again. Twid was about to call out to his little brother, Him Too, who walked a few feet ahead, when a small animal darted up a tree.

Twid exhaled and kicked a branch. A squirrel. That's what happened after a day of fruitless hunting. Squirrels became deer; rabbits, moose.

Twid's adopted brother, Him Too, was in one of his quiet moods and nothing could pry his mouth open. You could poke fun at Him Too's crooked nose. You could call Him Too a midget. You could laugh at the way Him Too's stubby feet waddled in the forest. Nothing.

Twid had first seen Him Too ten years earlier, not too long after Twid started living at the orphanage. Even back then, Twid had a long list of daily chores: Milk the goats, wash the chicken coop, weed the garden, fetch the water.

One summer night, the sheep outside the orphanage had bleated madly and the goats had joined them, creating a clamor that could have roused a deaf man. So Twid had started his morning chores early by grabbing a wooden bucket and heading to the well.

As Twid stepped out, he had stumbled over what he thought was a baby. But Him Too was five years old at the time, just two years shy of Twid. Him Too's mother had abandoned him outside the orphanage door.

Thunder boomed in the distance; raindrops slashed past the forest's thick canopy. Twid groaned as a cold drop smacked against his neck.

Him Too cleared his throat. He spoke in a screechy voice that made the forest seem haunted. "Twid, I had a dream last night where I heard a legendary joke."

A faint smile crept over Twid's face. Him Too's jokes never made sense.

Him Too gestured with his bow. "What is the fastest way to cook a side of lamb?"

Twid's eyebrows rose. Yes, this sounded like a typical Him Too joke gone awry; this one even sounded more like a riddle. But Twid forced himself not to smile or laugh. It was important to humor Him Too or Him Too might descend into silence for another hour. "I don't know. A blacksmith's forge? A mountain fire? A hearth?"

Him Too leapt over a mud pile. "No. A lightning bolt. If you could hold the lamb inside the bolt, the meat would char before it even cooked."

Twid stopped walking. "What?"

Him Too stared at his friend. "You don't think it'd be hot inside a lighting bolt?"

Twid stamped his spear. "How could you get inside a lightning bolt, Him Too? Even if you could get inside, what makes you think it'd be hot?" Twid spat at a puddle. "Even if lightning was hot, wouldn't *you* yourself burn while cooking the meat?"

Him Too looked at Twid as if Twid were a monkey. "I didn't ask if I would burn; I asked, where is the hottest place for a side of lamb to cook. You've spoiled the joke."

Twid climbed over a log. "If that's a joke, then I'm a Dream King." Twid lowered his voice. In the rare event that they found an animal bigger than a squirrel, they would scare it away with all this pointless arguing.

*"Do not come home unless you bring food."*

Two dozen arrows. Him Too had started the day with two dozen arrows. Now, after a day's futile shooting at rabbits, he had only two arrows left. Zeru's black arrows.

Twid could already see the look of disappointment on Zeru's wrinkly face; that look was worse than ten lashes. Feeling another drop of cold rain, Twid glanced up again at the storm clouds. Thunder pounded. Him Too asked, "How's your stump?"

Twid's left arm ended in a stump where Twid's wrist should have started. Twid winced as his arm trembled—the stump always ached before a fierce storm.

Suddenly, Him Too gestured. "Twid! Look to the right of that slanted aspen."

Twid fell back and caught himself against the nearest tree. Atop a small mound, a gigantic red fox towered! Muscles bulging, head held high, the fox had the imperious bearing of a lion. Twid whispered, "The Creator spare us! That thing could eat us both."

Him Too pulled his small bow into position. "Not if we kill it first."

Twid nodded, forgetting the ache in his stump. They could sell the fox's red fur for at least 100 birr. Maybe more. Yes. With this kill, the orphanage would feast for a month. Old Zeru might even allow them to abandon their endless chores and just hunt.

Twid adjusted his spear. He rarely missed with his sling shot, but foxes were skittish creatures, and the wind-up motion could send it fleeing. As they crept closer, the fox grew in size until it looked bigger than most wolves. For a moment, Twid found himself hoping that the fox would scurry away.

It was too late. Him Too had already pulled the two black arrows from the now empty quiver. The black arrows, whittled by Zeru himself. Twid swallowed as he recalled Zeru's hunting mantra, even when the orphanage had food to spare: "Come back empty-handed or with an empty quiver, but never both."

Putting the second arrow between his teeth, Him Too notched the first and drew. Twid readied his spear. They fired together. Him Too's first arrow raced towards the fox's neck; a second arrow toward the body. Twid's spear sped toward a front leg.

But the giant fox, or wolf, or whatever it was, dashed left and the arrows missed. The spear planted in a small tree's trunk.

Zeru's name! Twid cast an incredulous look at Him Too and found his friend's brow furrowed.

"Twid, have you ever seen an animal do that?"

Twid shook his head. Late at night, when he was in a good mood, Zeru sometimes told them stories of talking animals. Of rabbits who could sing, antelopes who could talk, tigers who could dance.

But those were only stories. And none of them featured a fox who could sidestep arrows or spears. The fox stared at them for a moment, as if rebuking them, then disappeared into the trees.

Twid retrieved his spear and they raced after the fox. Looking ahead, trying to keep the darting fox in view, Twid said, "Hyenas take us, Him Too! Is this one of your crazy dreams?"

"Hold your tongue, Twid."

Twid didn't respond. If there was one quality his friend had, it was stubbornness. Wouldn't talk if he didn't want to. Wouldn't fight if he didn't want to. And he certainly wouldn't back down from a fox.

Thunder boomed again.

"I have a bad feeling about this, Him Too. It's getting dark. You don't have any arrows left. My spear only works in close range. And even if I hit the fox with my slingshot, I won't kill it."

The two friends stopped. They had entered a circular clearing. Dark splotches riddled the trees surrounding the clearing. Skeletal branches rustled like deadwood in a cemetery.

Him Too asked, "Have you ever seen a clearing without grass?" Twid squinted at the ground then looked across the clearing. Him Too was right. No grass. No weeds. No bugs. Nothing but shiny black dirt.

The fox had stopped in the clearing's center. Its long snout curved up as if it could summon companions with a short howl. Him Too's grunt could have been mistaken for laughter. "By my father's grave, I think it's mocking us."

An aching sensation rocked Twid's arm. His nose itched. As the two friends crept closer, the itch spread to his ear. Another raindrop splotched his neck.

Twid blinked then rubbed his eyes. He blinked again.

Hyenas take him! It was impossible! Twid glanced over and found Him Too's equally incredulous face.

The red fox had vanished. Gone like a cresting fish returned to the ocean or a bird disappeared into clouds. Except there was no ocean or cloud to disappear into – the fox had vanished into air.

Rain obscured Twid's vision. Twid heard Him Too curse and wondered again if they shouldn't just return home, even without food. The two friends circled the clearing, searching for any signs of the fox, wondering if it was all a dream.

Him Too groaned. "What are we going to tell Zeru? That a lion-sized red fox led us to a lifeless clearing, sidestepped both black arrows, mocked us, then vanished into nothing?"

Twid would have laughed if he didn't know Zeru. Old Zeru
allowed no mistakes. Mistakes were excuses, alibis for the truth.
And mistakes were always punished.

Well, it wouldn't be the first time he and Him Too were punished together. When Him Too first joined the orphanage, Him
Too didn't talk for two full years and everyone thought him
mute. Because he never talked, no one knew his name; he was
simply the runt that followed Twid around.

One day, Zeru caught Twid and Him Too pilfering white crystal honey from the cupboard. Zeru dragged them by their ears to
the other brothers and sisters and decreed: "Twid will be doing
all the chores at the house for the next week."

Not having a name for Twid's co-conspirator, Zeru simply
pointed and said, "And *him too*." And that was the naming cer-
emony for Twid's red-headed, diminutive friend.

The rain intensified. Twid bit his lip as he looked across the
clearing. Regardless of what Him Too said, they would have to
head back. It was getting dark and there were many dangerous
animals in the Adwa Forests. Snakes. Wolves. Hyenas. Even
plant eaters could be dangerous if startled.

Pulling out a narrow piece of long cloth, Twid folded it in
half, and placed a smooth stone inside. With ease, he spun the
slingshot and felt the stone speed with each flick of his wrist.

"The fox was right THERE," he said, and released the stone
with a jerk of his wrist. The stone flew to the spot and disappeared into a gigantic tree, taller and wider than any tree Twid
had ever seen.

Yellow and green leaves shimmering, scintillating in the rain
like light racing across a puddle, the colossal tree radiated life,
like it could pick up and walk. Gigantic branches curved in every
possible direction. Deep roots circled the trunk like a moat. And
the tree's massive trunk could have housed ten adobes.

Twid took a step back, his heart pounding. Shivers coursed
throughout his back. He tried to talk but couldn't manage any-

thing. He tried again, and in a hoarse whisper asked, "Him Too – did that tree just appear out of nowhere?"

Him Too shielded his face with his hands, as if the rain could explain him missing the massive tree. He nodded.

Twid asked, "How could we miss it? You could fit half of Adwa in that trunk."

Him Too blinked again. Was it even a tree? The trunk looked too square, like the side of a house.

Lightning flashed and the drizzle intensified into downpour. Twid frowned. Maybe they were supposed to miss the tree. Maybe they were supposed to miss the fox.

He thought of the Old Ones' saying: "The coward gets home safely to his mother." The saying had always struck Twid as uninspired. But Twid found himself with new appreciation: Bravery was admirable, but survival had its own virtues.

It was obvious. They should forget the fox and tree and head home. They still had several miles, and with the worsening storm, the walk would take longer than usual. What if the strange tree somehow attacked them? As the oldest, Twid would be held responsible if anything went wrong.

The friends stared at each other, each thinking the same thing. Old Zeru would skin them alive if they came back empty-handed, with a story about a gigantic fox and a massive yet invisible tree. *Do not come home unless you bring food.*

But it wasn't just their fear of Zeru. The strange tree glimmered, rendering them unable to look away. The shimmering leaves and the branches beckoned. Somehow, the two friends found themselves inches from the trunk.

Then, without quite knowing why, Twid put his good arm on his friend's shoulder and touched the grey bark. A bright light flashed like lightning! The friends cried out. When they opened their eyes, they found themselves in a large, dim chamber. They could see no dust, mold, or signs of decay, but the air felt dank, as if no human had visited the chamber in years.

Twid tasted wet saltiness and realized he had bitten his lower

lip. *We're not supposed to be here.* He pushed against the wall to
see if they could leave the tree as easily as they had entered. But
the wall was solid wood. And there was no door in sight.

"Stay close, Him Too."

Him Too was already moving.

"Look here, Twid."

Him Too stood in the nearest corner next to five wooden cots
with beddings made of tightly-woven yellow straw. Twid walked
over and sat on the nearest cot. He winced as the hardened
straw cut into his thigh. Even the beds at the orphanage were
more comfortable.

Looking up, Twid saw that the chamber's ceiling stretched so
high he could not make out the top. Though the chamber had
no windows, the walls themselves radiated a reddish glow that
cast an angry tone.

Twid walked to the next corner where he found the remnants
of a kitchen, with several pots, a cauldron, ladles, and spoons.
Two gigantic wine casks towered next to the cauldron. Twid
walked to the cask and pushed against the lid. He sprang
back as the sweet, biting odor of over-fermented honey wine
flooded out.

On the next wall hung enough weapons to outfit a small
army: swords, staffs, daggers, maces, spears, Nishan throwing
stars, and more. Twid's cheeks scrunched, causing his eyes to
crinkle. What was this place?

"This had to be a secret barracks for someone," said Him
Too. "Someone was hiding here."

Twid's eyes ran across the weapons, resting on a long thin
sword that hung in the center, hilt up. With his hand trembling
for a reason unknown to him, Twid pulled the sword off the
wall. The scabbard had faint outlines of drawings. Twid held
the scabbard closer and saw a rolling landscape that featured
hills and bridges, caves and what appeared to be sand dunes. A
mountain loomed over the landscape. Twid turned the scabbard
and saw the same design on the other side.

Taking a breath, Twid drew the sword and swung. Like wind whistling through tall grass, the sword made a weeping sound, combining with the angry red walls to raise hackles on Twid's back. He lifted the gleaming blade close to his face. "They may have been hiding, but I don't think they were weak."

Twid strapped the sword across his waist. He looked at the wall again. There was still no door in sight. What would happen if they couldn't find a way out of the tree? They couldn't live on honey wine. Twid cursed. Their crazy sister, Iwala, was known for acting without thinking. But Twid? Twid had always been the responsible one. And now, he had led Him Too into this trap.

In the middle of the room, Him Too jumped, fighting an imaginary foe with a small staff. "Take that!"

Twid smiled. Whoever lived in the tree must have used the middle area for sparring. Twid walked to the final corner. The Creator be thanked! Twid called out. "Let's go, Him Too. I found the door. We can sell this sword and buy enough meat to last a mo..."

A menacing shape jumped from a hidden ledge and blocked the door. Long, jagged teeth lined its narrow snout. Muscles rippled like red stone reflected in a mountain creek. A piercing howl echoed.

The red fox.

Twid fell back and shouted. Howling again, the fox thrust its snout, its fangs now reflecting the room's bloody hue. Twid scrambled to pull his dagger, knowing it was too late. The fangs sliced inches from him...but somehow, missed!

Him Too soared past. Before Twid could move, Him Too smashed the fox with his newfound staff. The fox slammed into the door.

A sharp clicking echoed, then a rushing like a hail of arrows. Five thick spears slammed down from above, piercing the fox and blocking the doorway. The fox's red blood spurted toward Twid.

Twid crawled back. The spears…the door was a trap! They had almost died!

Him Too stumbled to the chamber's center and tried to steady himself with the black staff. What had happened? He had thought to save Twid from the fox but the fox had saved them both.

Suddenly, a deafening crack shook the chamber and the roof flew off, revealing a raging storm. Lightning flashed. For a split second, Twid looked up and saw a gigantic wooden cask suspended in mid-air, high above them.

Before Twid could wonder how the cask could hang in air, lightning flashed again, striking the cask. The entire chamber shook; the cask exploded.

Twid screamed. "MOOOOOOOVE, Him Too!"

But it was too late. The gigantic cask exploded and nails, wood, and orange-red liquid avalanched Him Too, obscuring him from view.

Twid ran to the pile and dug through the mountain of debris covering his friend. Nails cut Twid's good hand, and his stump bled as he tried to clear the debris. Splinters sliced. Lightning flashed again. Thunder boomed. Rain soaked Twid. He kept digging. The smell of honey was everywhere.

Twid stopped. There were…. There were…human bones, human skulls mixed in with the debris!

A cold sensation froze Twid as he touched a gooey liquid that smelled like honey wine but looked like blood. JIGNA. The word JIGNA exploded in his head. JIGNA! THE FIVE HARMONIES! JIGNA!

Twid lifted his sticky fingers. Blood. Bones. Bodies. There had been bodies in the cask. Bile rose. Twid retched. The voices screamed in his head again. THE FIVE HARMONIES! JIGNA!

Twid forced himself to ignore the voices. Him Too! He had to reach Him Too. Twid kept digging. Then recoiled. Nails dotted Him Too like needles on a porcupine. Rivulets of blood flowed from his cracked head. The honey blood substance had seeped into his cuts, causing his pale skin to glow and his red hair to darken. Too shocked to cry, Twid put a hand on Him Too's neck – there was a faint pulse.

Twid lifted his unconscious friend from beneath, making sure he touched no nails, grateful for his friend's childish stature, grateful that they didn't need a door anymore – lightning had destroyed an entire wall.

Adrenaline pounding, Twid ran, his wounds and fatigue forgotten. Two miles. Him Too was his brother and sister, his mother and his father; his best friend. Two miles. Good thing you were wrong, Him Too. Two miles. Good thing lightning isn't hot or the falling liquid would have burned you like a lamb. Two miles!

JIGNA. THE FIVE HARMONIES. JIGNA.

# Two

The hunched man sat atop Adwa's hill, ignoring the red ants that crawled along his dark legs. Nestled above chiseled cheekbones, his eyes shone with the intensity of onyx hewn into crystal. But below, the teeth on the left half of his mouth had all fallen out, causing the left side of his face to droop like a half-shaved mustache.

Zeru wobbled to his feet. Everyone in Adwa considered him an unforgiving taskmaster. Even the town drunk had dressed Zeru down: "When your kids are old enough to judge your harshness, they will disown you."

Now, after the last month's tumultuous events, Zeru's only regret was that he hadn't pushed his kids harder. Looking down from the hill, he surveyed the four orphans in his care as they circled Adwa. They had all done at least ten laps around Adwa.

Not that circling Adwa was a hard task. Only out here, in an endless, barren wilderness, could 200 straw-and-mud adobes separated by a miserable dirt road be called a city. Zeru's eyes ran from the south, where the shopkeepers had already set up their wares, to the north, where the goat herders met each morning. If this was a city then Zeru's adobe was a Dream Mansion.

Zeru considered again the last month. Four weeks had passed since Twid had carried Him Too's broken body from the Adwa Forest. Everyone had thought Him Too dead. The witch doctor had even led a midnight procession through the village, as customary for all who heard death's knell.

When Him Too recovered, the witch doctor declared it a divine miracle and ordered the town to sacrifice a young goat. Of course, the doctor received all the best parts, including the intestines and stomach.

After Him Too recovered, Twid led the village elders back to the forest, and they searched for a full day. But they found no signs of the mysterious tree or the red fox. Most of the towns-people concluded that Twid and Him Too had made up the story to cover something up. Some townspeople blamed Iwala, the town troublemaker, even though Twid swore that Iwala did not go with them.

Zeru continued down the hill. He alone believed Twid and Him Too. But he still didn't know how to tell them *why* he believed them.

All these years, Zeru had felt like a dog scratching his hind leg—scratching, but not knowing why. Living in Adwa, but not knowing why. Until now. Zeru didn't pretend to know why the tree mattered—only that it did. Still, Zeru almost wished his children hadn't found it. He thought of the Old Ones proverb, "You pray for rain but complain when your sandals become muddy."

Zeru stopped as he heard a noise, then realized it was his own molars grinding. He didn't like to think about what might happen next. What if someone came asking about the tree? And not just any someone, but someone who knew what he was asking about?

# Three

The dead rattlesnake felt cool and hard in Iwala's hands. She reached into the snake's slippery mouth and yanked it open. She had already cut out the fangs.

Bending low, Iwala grabbed a small hunting dog that was trapped between her legs. The frantic dog kicked as if it were in water. Iwala had no rope, just a short strand of cow intestine she had removed from a guitar. Iwala pinned the dog against a silver maple tree and with a twist, tied the dog's tail into the snake's head.

She smiled. Father Gebre had always complained that his dog's short tail made his dog look like a rabbit. After tonight, Father Gebre would not complain again.

The snake rattled, causing the dog to squirm and bark, which only caused the dead snake to rattle again. Iwala hoisted the small hunting dog with one hand and steadied the snake rattle with the other. As she stepped forward, her tightly-wound braids swung past her thin shoulders. The dog's left foot slid through a hole in Iwala's tattered shirt.

Tonight's "rattledog" would surpass anything Iwala had ever accomplished in Adwa—other than the rats, of course. Yes. Tonight's story would be told and retold by villagers for years.

Iwala approached from behind. Outside the adobe's front, Father Gebre sat on a short stool, talking with three neighbors. His daughter brewed coffee over the open fire. They were telling stories as villagers often did in the evening.

Father Gebre was speaking, "The poor husband was beside himself at his wife's lack of sense. He sat her down and implored her, 'Woman, will you not think? Please! For once, just think! Think of our family! Think of our future! Think of important matters!'" Father Gebre sipped his coffee. Iwala massaged the dog's neck to keep it from barking. "In the middle of the night, the wife awoke her husband. 'I've taken your words to heart, dear husband,' she said. 'And I've had an important thought.'"

Iwala grinned. Father Gebre continued, "The husband was overjoyed, expecting to hear something profound from his wife. Something related to improving their home or livelihood, or raising their children. But the wife said to him, 'Yes, I had an important thought that's kept me up all night: *The mice that are in our village, where do they get their drinking water?'"*

The friends roared at the poor husband's fate. Suppressing her own laughter, Iwala moved to take advantage of their revelry. She reached into a small pouch, and drew a goat bone. Before the dog could snatch it, Iwala tossed the bone behind Father Gebre.

The hunting dog leapt toward its master. The sharp rattling caused an immediate commotion. Two of the guests fled. Father Gebre's daughter screamed. Coffee splattered.

Father Gebre leapt to his feet and scurried across the fire, his old limbs exhibiting surprising agility. The dog rattled after its master.

"MY DOG. MY DOG! IT'S BEING EATEN BY A RATTLESNAKE."

The dog leapt again after its master, but Father Gebre soared onto a tall clay container next to the adobe. Iwala bit her tongue. If only Twid and Him Too could see this. One moment more and Father Gebre would scale the adobe itself!

Sudden laughter erupted from the one remaining guest. Father Hagos called out, in a fit of hysteria. "Hyenas take me!" He dropped to the ground. "Hyenas take me!" Father Gebre looked bewildered as Father Hagos's laughter drowned out even the rattle.

Father Hagos pointed, "Someone has tied a dead rattlesnake to your dog's tail!" Father Gebre squinted. What? It couldn't be true. No. No. Not to he, Father Gebre. He let out a soft moan. It had to be Zeru's miserable daughter. Iwala.

If only Father Hagos had fled with the others. Now he would tell and retell this story. Father Gebre drew himself up, "Fool, even a blind man can see that there's a rattlesnake on his tail. While you were scurrying like an apronless maiden, I was positioning myself in front of this adobe to prevent the dog from starting a fire. One spark on this adobe and the whole village would have burned."

Father Hagos cast a skeptical look. Iwala bit her lip so hard she drew blood. She had to remember Father Gebre's exact words: "MY DOG. MY DOG! IT'S BEING EATEN BY A RATTLESNAKE."

Iwala forced herself to tip-toe away. If she laughed any louder, she'd give her position away. Avoiding the main road, she walked behind a row of adobes and then let loose laughing. The best part was that Father Gebre was trapped. If he went crying to Zeru, Father Gebre would only bring more attention to the matter.

*Twik. Twik. Twik.* Revelry forgotten, Iwala spun. Over the years, she had learned to trust her ears. Noises that were out of place were often the only clues before disaster. *Twik. Twik. Twik.* It sounded like quick, rapid footsteps. Iwala bent behind a chicken coop and scanned the mud-thatched adobes, the tomato gardens, the gigantic clay containers that villagers filled with homemade beer.

Father Gebre couldn't have found her already. Her gaze turned to the hill that led into the Adwa Forests. She turned suddenly to her left.

Shadows. Shadows and more shadows. She crept toward the orphanage. Maybe Twid and Him Too's new paranoia was rubbing off on her.

A fox bigger than a ram. An invisible tree. A wine barrel suspended in air. At first Iwala didn't believe Twid. But Twid had insisted, as had Him Too once he recovered.

Zeru surprised her, too. Zeru, who would lecture you if you left one bowl out of place. Zeru, who considered explanations nothing more than crutches. Zeru hadn't come out and said that he believed Twid and Him Too, but he hadn't denied them either.

Iwala reached out to a low-hanging branch and broke off a small twig. She rubbed the twig against her teeth. It tasted like an under-ripe crab apple but she liked the way the twig massaged her gums. Zeru claimed twigs kept one's mouth clean, but Zeru had lost half his teeth. Iwala tossed the twig.

The strangers. That was another thing. No one visited Adwa. On rare occasions like weddings or baptisms, they would get a visitor or two from Axum or Lemlem. Now there were a dozen visitors in Adwa.

No children. No women. Just grim-looking men with swords who trickled in one at a time, a couple each week, until today, when Ran's makeshift inn ran out of room.

What were they doing here? Adwa was at the edge of the world, as Zeru liked to say, "Not just under the stone, but the stone under the stone under the stone."

She tiptoed closer to the orphanage. She had promised Twid an update.

Twid sat outside the adobe, a pot boiling before him. An outbreak of diarrhea had struck Adwa and all the villagers now boiled the well water before drinking or bathing.

Most people would have moved the pot as soon as the water started boiling. But not Twid. Iwala could hear the water churning, could see the sweat cascading down Twid's bony face like water down a mountain. Iwala smiled. Given a chance, Twid would boil half the water away. That was Twid for you, though. Careful to a fault. Always had to do everything right.

Iwala took a soft breath and whistled, making sure Twid couldn't hear. A small animal jumped from a nearby shrub and crept toward Twid. The rabbit-size animal jumped onto Twid's shoulders, claws digging.

Without moving to touch the animal, Twid barked, "Iwala. Get your flea-covered monkey off me."

Iwala stepped out. Her brown skin blended into the adobe wall behind her. "Remember what the Old Ones said, 'Fleas attract fleas.'"

"Funny coming from you," Twid retorted. Twid pointed. "In this pot is water. Believe it or not, some people use water to bathe."

"Sorry, I already jumped into the river last month," Iwala replied.

"Fine, then have your monkey pick the lice out of your hair. Just get Kwee off me."

Smiling, Iwala whistled, and Kwee leapt onto Iwala's shoulder. Iwala wasn't upset. There was an unspoken rule between Twid, Him Too and Iwala. Make fun of each other. Call each other ugly. Compare each other to chickens, goats, hyenas. But never be nice. That was when you had to flee, when people starting telling you how great you were, or how much you meant to them. Shortly after the niceties, you were sure to be told that a band of roving Hyeks had eaten your mother.

Iwala sometimes wondered why they bantered as they did. Was it a natural byproduct of their harsh lives in the midst of the wilderness? Had Zeru's critical style of childrearing set the tone? She could hear Zeru's favorite saying, "Life is a pack of rabid hyenas that ambush you in the wilderness. The sooner you accept that reality, the sooner you can prepare."

Thinking of Zeru, Iwala surveyed the exterior of the Ald Nald House and peered inside, a mouse scouting the cat. Twid reassured her. "Zeru isn't here."

Iwala had lived at the Ald Nald house years ago, but Zeru kicked her out, claiming he didn't want her teaching the younger brothers and sisters her vices.

It was the rat fiasco that had been the last straw.

Iwala didn't mind – it was a great excuse to leave the dream-forsaken town. She had wandered the Three Lands for three years. Only after she was imprisoned did she come home.

Twid explained, "Father Markos broke his leg and Zeru is

spending the night with him. Zeru took the kids along."

Iwala sat on a rock. "Where's Him Too?" As if on cue, a small wail emerged from the adobe.

Twid slapped a mosquito too late. "He still can't sleep more than a few hours. Still has the nightmares."

Iwala didn't say anything for a moment. When she spoke, her voice was soft and sweet. "Well, I've been talking to everyone for you. Asking them about the strange voices you and Him Too hear in your heads."

Iwala frowned. "Still no luck on Jignas. And two different people threw their coffee grinders at my head when I asked them about The Five Harmonies."

Twid said, "I'd be lucky to get something thrown at me — the whole town avoids me like I have yellow fever."

Iwala nodded. Asking for five Harmonies was like asking for five eyes. Two. Everyone knew that there were just *two* Harmonies.

Iwala grunted. "How about old Zeru? What's he saying now?"

Twid shook his head. "He's worse than anyone else."

He stood and motioned with his left arm, his lanky frame bent in imitation. "Remember, Twid. You are the oldest. The oldest has a special, but tough responsibility to care for the younger siblings. If those younger than you fail, you have failed. If they excel, you have excelled."

Twid had heard these words for years, but Zeru now spoke them with renewed intensity. Surely Zeru wasn't blaming Twid for Him Too's accident?

Twid had been certain that Zeru would want to sell the sword and staff from the tree. Twid reached down to his waist and touched the sword. It would have fetched enough to feed the Ald Nald House for months.

But Zeru had insisted they not sell it. "You and Him Too almost gave your lives for these. Remember what the Old Ones said: 'Barter not away gifts bought with blood.'" Gifts...?

"What's that?" Iwala interrupted Twid's thoughts. On the dirt next to Twid, someone had scrawled lines and words. "Zeru still making you do the nightly Giiz lessons?"

For years, Zeru had forced all his children to read and write the ancient language of Giiz. Zeru claimed that if one could read Giiz, one could read any other language.

Iwala walked closer. Scrawled into the dirt was a detailed map of Nisha, Wirba, and Ras — the Three Lands. In the middle was the capital, Dream City, where the three Dream Kings reigned along with the Dream Council.

Twid answered, "Zeru drew it. He spent most of today quizzing me on every goat pen in the Three Lands." Twid kicked dirt over the map. "I need to forget about all this, at least for one night." He motioned to the pot. "Want to help me carry this water to Mother Scale's?"

Mother Scale lived near the shopkeepers. No one knew her real name. Actually, no one needed her real name. Everyone called her Mother Scale because of her trustworthy weights. Many a time a townsperson had insisted that a merchant use her scales when measuring out flour or sugar. Some of the townspeople even claimed she could read the future like a Dream Teller.

To the orphans, though, she was just their grandmother. She had sewn them cloth and cooked them meals for years. Twid and Him Too often did errands for her in return for peanuts, and if they were lucky, white honey.

Each grabbing one end of the pot, the two friends lifted. Iwala said, "Once we drop this water off, I'll tell you a story about Father Gebre."

"Tell me now."

"I can't risk you spilling this burning water on my feet. That's how funny th—"

A squeaky, high-pitched voice pursued them. "Wait for me, you hyena dung. You need someone to navigate for you or you'll spill the water."

Iwala said, "Twid, did you hear anything?"

Twid turned his head from left to right. "No. I didn't hear anyt...Actually. I do hear something." He bent his head low. "Yes. I think I hear a mouse."

Iwala squinted her face. "Mouse? I don't know. That sounds too big. I was thinking more like an ant. Or may..."

Him Too grunted, "Iwala — that's because there's been an ant colony living in your ear for years."

Iwala spoke to Twid. "No...it's not an ant. No, half an ant. No, an ant midget."

The friends laughed. As they passed Father Yemane's adobe to the right, Twid noticed two grim-faced strangers talking. Both wore swords, and one also had a bow slung over his shoulder. Twid quickened his pace.

"Iwala. Where are all these people coming from?"

Iwala adjusted the pot handle in her hand. "I don't know. Lemlem or Axum, maybe." She kicked a rock. "It's strange, not a one of them plays cards."

"*No one* wants to play cards with you," Him Too said. "Anyway, I asked Zeru about the strangers."

Iwala snorted. "Let me guess - he recited some Old Ones saying."

Him nodded. "He said that people in town are always saying they want more visitors so we can sell them goat milk and woven straw baskets. But now that visitors have come, we ask why they come."

Twid frowned. *When they said they wanted visitors, they weren't thinking mercenaries.* Forgetting the soldiers, Twid pointed with his stump. "Look Iwala. Here comes Him Too's betrothed."

A mangy-haired girl lumbered towards them. She towered a head taller than Twid. Little patches of hair dotted her pallid face, the individual hairs crawling in the wind like centipede legs over white clay. Scooping Him Too, the giantess tossed and caught him as if he were a baby. "My little Himmie walking again."

Laughing so hard that they did spill some water, Iwala and Twid watched their tiny friend squirm. Iwala couldn't restrain herself. "Geltam, even when *Himmie* was sick, all he did was talk about you. 'Geltam. Geltam. Bring me Geltam.' We would have lost him without you."

At that, Geltam squeezed the flailing Him Too to her bosom, muffling his groans. They walked a few paces before Him Too wormed out of her grasp and flipped to the ground. Twid found himself shoved from the pot handle, Him Too's short, stocky arms carrying the pot without strain.

"I promised Twid I would carry the pot for him. You know he's only got one arm, so it gets tired from working extra." Him Too shot his friends a look that could have withered a harvest.

As Geltam approached again, offering her hand to carry the pot for him, Him Too shook his head. "No. No. Zeru has insisted I do strenuous work to help me recover."

At the mention of Zeru, Geltam's face blanched and even the hairs on her face stopped crawling. Zeru had once chased Geltam with a broom across town when he found her holding Him Too. Zeru had screamed loud enough for the shopkeepers to hear: "You over-sized donkey! Get away from my son! He has no time for temptresses."

No one was shocked that Zeru chased her — it was common knowledge that Zeru forbade the youth in his care to participate in any courtship. The town had, however, puzzled for weeks about Geltam being called a temptress.

The three friends arrived at Mother Scale's adobe. The smell of burnt coffee wafted out as they opened the door.

Surrounded by measuring cups, weights, and scales, Mother Scale sat alone on a small stool. Her back hunched, she had the appearance of a wizened owl who had long ceased flying and hunting, and now spent both days and nights thinking.

"Mother Scale, we've bought you water."

Mother Scale's soft voice soothed like honey melted into morning tea. "Surely, my children, you will one day rise to heaven for this kind act."

The friends snuck quick smiles at each other. Every time they did something for Mother Scale, she assured them of their place with the Creator.

Twid had already turned to transfer the water into Mother Scale's wooden bucket when Him Too's screechy voice sliced the air. "Mother Scale, there is something I need to ask you."

Him Too lowered his voice. "Ever since my accident, I hear voices in my head. Screaming, furious voices. More furious than anyone, even than Zeru at his craziest. They always shout the same thing. 'Jigna! The Five Harmonies!'

"Mother Scale. We consider you our mother — that is why we bring you water even before we prepare our own. That is why I do not hesitate to ask you what no one else can tell us: What is a Jigna? What are The Five Harmonies?"

Twid nodded, the water forgotten. No one in town could tell them what the strange words meant. Twid had even asked Lab, who had traveled across the Three Lands. Lab, who had seen everything.

Lab's response still rang through his head: "Five Harmonies? Even my four-year-old daughter knows that there are only two Harmonies: Freedom and Dreams. And Jigna — strange word that one. Never heard of it but sounds like it's from ancient Giiz."

Lab was only able to tell Twid what everyone had been taught since childhood. There are two Harmonies: Freedom and Dreams. The Dream Kings, as indicated by their name, had dedicated themselves to helping everyone live with freedom and dreams.

Now, Twid and his friends stood before the person who many regarded as the most knowledgeable in Adwa. If she couldn't answer their questions, who would?

But Mother Scale gave no sign that she had heard Him Too. The moments passed, each moment more tense than the previous, as the friends waited for her response. In Twid's head, the voices frenzied to a crescendo. JIGNA. THE FIVE HARMONIES. JIGNA.

Mother Scale stared at them, the lines on her face frozen like a dried riverbed. Was she asleep? Was Mother Scale, true to her name, making some hidden calculation, some measurement, deciding what she would tell them, or whether she would tell them anything at all? She had never kept anything from them before, never hesitated.

Her bones creaked as she rose. As she hobbled towards them, she motioned with her staff for them to lean forward in the manner of someone receiving a blessing. The three friends bowed. In Ras, it was believed that the heartfelt blessings of the elderly always came true.

"Him Too, Twid, Iwala. May you live to see your children's children." Her voice magnified, towering, and the friends felt her words weigh on them like adobe-sized boulders. "May the sun never scorch you, nor the thorn pierce you. May your words be as ink, and your thoughts as edicts. May you always have sandals beneath your feet and shade above your head. May you have the brilliance of…"

The three friends stole glances at each other. They were used to receiving just one blessing, not five or six, and still the blessings rained on them. It was almost like she was trying to stave off their death; as if the words Jigna and Five Harmonies required some special protection.

Iwala felt Twid shuffle his feet and realized her own feet were shuffling too. Twid knew what Iwala was thinking. *How about blessing us with some honey or a mango?*

"…1000 people. May you be the giver and not the beggar. May the Creator himself guide you and protect you." Mother Scale lowered her cane like some seer of old lowering a staff after a prophetic utterance. Her eyes closed.

Him Too spoke again, "Though we had riches without end, we could not repay your blessings, Mother Scale. But what about The Five Harmonies? What about Jignas?"

Mother Scale did not open her eyes. She turned and creaked toward her stool. When she sat, she grabbed a half-woven yellow straw basket and wove.

Silence. It was as if Him Too had not spoken, as if they did not exist. The three friends stared at each other, unsure of what was happening.

After several uncomfortable moments, Twid grabbed the pot and dumped the water into two wooden buckets.

※ ※ ※

Twid walked home alone. Him Too wanted to avoid Geltam, so he and Iwala had gone to the well to get more water for boiling.

The friends had agreed on one thing: The words meant something to Mother Scale. They had seen it in her eyes. She knew something yet had chosen not to tell them.

As the evening breeze washed over him, Twid tried to relax. Maybe Iwala was right. Stop worrying about stupid voices. Everyone hears voices at some point in their life.

Twid shifted to avoid a giant wheelbarrow. Peering in, he saw raf, the new white grain from the Dream Kings. At first everyone had grumbled about raf, but then they realized that the grain was half as expensive as tef, the old grain, and tasted even better. Now almost everyone ate raf.

It was more than the new grain, though. The Dream Kings had created a Dream Wine that cured gout. They had provided farmers with new seeds that grew bigger, riper tomatoes faster. The Dream Kings had even created a new alert system, using birds, that warned villagers of attacks.

Twid nodded. Without the Dream Kings, the Ald Nald Orphanage wouldn't exist. Twid would have died as a boy, as would have Him Too and maybe even Iwala. And it wasn't just in Adwa. The Dream Kings had created Ald Nald orphanage houses throughout the Three La—

A scream cut the night air. The voice shrieked again. It was coming from Father Yemane's stables. Twid bolted inside. Not another stable accident! Just two weeks earlier, a horse had kicked a…

A short, boyish man stood deep in the stable. His face looked nice enough, but the eyes, there was something in the eyes. Twid stepped back. The boy-man, whatever he was, didn't look like he needed help. He just stared at Twid.

Something dropped behind Twid. Twid turned. Two large men faced him, dressed in all black, faces veiled. Their eyes gleamed in the near-night light. Twid glanced behind him. The boy-man had disappeared.

Twid's stomach flipped. His heart hammered. The shorter of the veiled men stepped forward. He whispered in a reasonable tone, as if he were an old friend.

"Boy. Where did you get that sword?"

Twid looked down. His hand gripped the wooden sword that Zeru had made him practice with for years. Every night, for the last eight years, Zeru had forced Twid and Him Too to practice with swords and staff.

"No. Not that one." The man pointed to the other sword Twid had; the sword from the tree.

Hadn't Iwala always said that the best lies were nine out of ten parts true? "I found it four weeks ago, hidden under some shrubs in The Adwa forest."

The questioner nodded to his companion who had a bow in hand. In one motion, the soldier notched and shot an arrow. The arrow nicked Twid's afro and thudded into the wall. Another arrow whizzed past his right ear.

Something slammed into Twid's back. It took him a moment to realize he had backed into the wall. Wood splinters sliced his hand.

This time, iron laced the questioner's voice. "Lie again and he won't miss."

The questioner smiled, lowering his voice, as if he were merely coaxing a reluctant donkey across a small puddle. "Listen, boy. There's no reason to quarrel. Just tell us the truth. Why have you been asking about Jignas? How did you and your little friend find The Ancient Tree of the Five?"

The questioner unsheathed a broadsword and pointed it at Twid. "Tell me. What is your concern with the Harmonies?"

Twid's stomach felt like he had eaten raw eggs. The hairs on his arms stood straight and his knees trembled.

It was insane. All of it. The invisible tree. The exploding wine barrel. Mother Scale's silence. These soldiers, going to all this trouble, asking him something he knew nothing about.

The voices raged. JIGNA! THE FIVE HARMONIES!

And they *had* gone to a great deal of trouble. To corner him like this, they had to have watched him, studied his routes. And they were going to kill him. If they wanted to talk, they would have just talked to him on the street. The Creator knew he had asked anyone who would listen about Jignas.

Twid squinted. Maybe he had even talked to them.

The leader pointed his sword at Twid's throat. "If you don't tell us, boy, we'll get it out of your little friend."

Twid didn't hear the threat. There was something about the way the man clutched the sword; his knuckles were white. When the realization struck Twid, he almost laughed aloud.

They were scared! They had an arrow pointed at his head and a sword at his throat. Yet they kept glancing around the stable, their eyes darting back and forth as if Twid hid an invisible army under the straw.

Who did they think he was?

✳ ✳ ✳

"Why would Mother Scale lie to us?" Him Too swung the pot as he walked.

"Actually, she didn't lie. She just didn't answer your questions," Iwala said. She spat. "Maybe she thinks we're too young."

Him Too nodded. Elders were always hiding things. Zeru for

example, had never told them where he was from, never told them of his own childhood. Even Twid had his secrets. They still didn't know how Twid lost his arm or how his parents died.

"Look, I'm the last person to advise caution, but if you want my opinion, stop asking about these Harmonies and Jignas," Iwala said. "Either people don't know the answers or they know but don't want to tell you. Either way it's trouble."

The evening breeze pushed Him Too's red hair over his eyes. Iwala was right. So far people had humored him because of his accident. But if he kept asking questions, he would only annoy the villagers. THE FIVE HARMONIES. JIGNA. The voices quaked again in his head.

A line of ants marched before them. Him Too bent and lifted one onto his palm. The ant crawled frantically. "I know this will sound crazy, Iwala, but after I awoke from the accident, I was sure of one thing. More sure than I've ever been about anything my whole life."

Him Too grabbed the ant between two fingers. "I was certain that I was no different than this ant. Everything I've done, all the times you, Twid and I played, ate together, everything all of us have ever experienced. We are no different than this ant.

"There's something out there, Iwala, that we don't know. Something important. I know there is. That's what the voices are screaming at me. 'Find out the truth. Find The Five Harmonies. Find the Jignas. Find them or you will spend the rest of your life crawling like ants.'"

Iwala's mouth fell ajar. Ants? That's what this whole thing was about. Ants? Maybe the townspeople were right. Maybe Twid and Him Too had gone mad. Him Too in particular sounded like he might dash off at any moment in search of The Five Harmonies.

A hunched shape approached the well. Iwala drew back. She gripped Him Too's arm hard. "You have to get the water alone." She pointed at Father Gebre. "I just played a trick on Father Gebre. He'll string me on his clothesline if he finds me."

Iwala turned and slipped away. "You get the water — I'll see you back at the adobe." Him Too nodded.

Iwala cut past several adobes. She never thought she'd see the day when Him Too and Twid were crazier than her. It just went to show that one could never predict life. Next thing you knew, Zeru would start apologizing and speaking softly.

Reaching up to her shoulder, she patted Kwee's foot. At least Kwee would not change. Iwala emerged back on the main road. She was steps away from the orphanage when she looked up and saw a shadow enter Father Yemane's stable. Where was Twid? Twid's favorite part of the day was evening; he wouldn't be inside the orphanage. Could he still be walking home? Two more shadows melted into Father Yemane's stable.

Iwala raced low among the adobes. Kwee's claws ripped into her shoulder. Iwala forced herself to stay calm. It was probably nothing. Just soldiers trying to sleep in the stable. Ran's inn was full, after all.

Why was she shaking?

❈ ❈ ❈

Twid saw a small movement behind the two men. He looked the questioner in the eye. It was his only chance.

"Look. I have nothing to hide. But I refuse to tell you anything unless your man lowers his arrow and you lower your sword. With a story this crazy, I won't risk you not believing me and firing."

After a long moment, the questioner motioned at his companion to lower his arrow. As they lowered their weapons, something soared through the air. Twid dove.

When Twid looked up, both the bowman and questioner snarled on the ground, daggers protruding from their legs. A young woman materialized from the shadows, and a small animal ran before her.

Iwala stepped closer, two more daggers in her hands. "What in Zeru's name is this?"

Twid shot his friend a look that was equal parts gratitude and bewilderment. They could talk later. He drew his sword and pointed it at the questioner who writhed on the ground. "I'm going to ask..."

The questioner spat on Twid's leg. "Fool. You'll..."

A sound whistled from above. Twid and Iwala dove. Rolling to his feet, Twid looked up to an opening above the loft, in the top corner of the stable. He had forgotten about the Scout-boy!

Scout-boy gave him a murderous look then leapt through a hole and disappeared. When Twid looked back to the room's center, he lowered his sword. Scout-boy had launched daggers through the throats of his own men.

# Four

Iwala dropped to her knees. "Quick, Twid. Guard the door." She removed the veil from the first man's face. It took her a moment to register what she saw. "Berhe the son of Teklu the son of Hagos!"

Twid glanced back as he heard Iwala curse her ancestors. "They're Nishan, Twid."

Twid swallowed his saliva. Nishan rarely left their deserts. What were they doing in Adwa?

Iwala continued searching both men's clothing, whistling as she found daggers, throwing stars, and steel darts. Iwala looked up at the loft. "They cornered you using a Merzee Trium. One man a scout, to track and study you. One man a questioner, to interrogate you. One man, an executioner, to finish you. It's a foolproof method. The scout leaves the battle scene while the other two question. In case of failure, the scout minimizes damage from a safe position and survives to assemble another Trium. The scout repeats the process until the target is eliminated."

Iwala yanked a braid so hard she winced. "Twid, I learned about Merzee Triums in Metka. Whoever hired the scout will kill the scout if he gives up. Could be tonight. Could be next month. But the scout will return. And next time, he won't be fooled."

Twid crumbled to the ground. Nishan assassins! Here in Adwa! Hunting him!

"Lightning take us, Twid! If Father Gebre hadn't jumped out on the way to the well; if I hadn't sent Him Too on alone; if I hadn't come back to talk to you...they would have had you!"

Kwee jumped onto Iwala's shoulder. Twid stumbled to his feet. The friends scanned the road and left the stables. Twid turned. "How about the dead bodies? We should have hid the dead bodies! The townspeople already think…"

Iwala grabbed her friend and shook him until his teeth rattled. "I don't know if you're in shock, Twid, but WAKE UP! WAKE UP! Who cares what the townspeople think? Who cares about ANYTHING? Listen to what you just said. 'Dead bodies!' If the scout was willing to kill his own men just so you couldn't question them, imagine what the scout will do to you?"

They continued talking as they crossed the street to the Ald Nald adobe.

Iwala said, "The tree. The voices you hear. These assassins. Hyenas take us, Twid! I believe you now. There's a reason Mother Scale didn't tell us anything. We have to get out of town." Iwala jerked her braid again. "Trust me, Twid. You and Him Too are like corn still in the husk. You haven't seen what I've seen. There are people out there who will slit your throat for a yam."

Twid nodded. Iwala had traveled throughout the Three Lands, had lived in Metka, the worst prison in the Three Lands, for over a year. A prison so vile, the very mention of it could scare adults, much less kids. In fact, the name Metka meant "You have died" in Giiz. And according to the stories, that was exactly what happened to half of Metka's prisoners each year.

Twid ran his stump along the sword from the tree. Although he hadn't been to Metka, Twid had seen evil. He'd had two arms long ago.

Twid massaged the sword again. The questioner had asked about the sword as if he knew it, as if the sword had special meaning. What did the questioner called the tree? The Ancient Tree of the Five?

"I'm talking to you, chicken brain. You can't stay here. Go in there and pack. The scout saw me too —I wouldn't stay for a Dream Carnival."

Twid rubbed his temples. "And leave Zeru a note? Think, Iwala. Think. We're in our own village, surrounded by friends and family we've known for years. If someone is out to get us, what's going to be safer: Adwa or some lonely wilderness trail? Even Father Gebre would die before letting someone harm us. Besides, how can we leave Zeru with just a note?"

Iwala grit her teeth. "It's your throat. Just don't call my name when the scout feeds you to hyenas. I'm leaving."

※ ※ ※

Later that night, as he dreamt, Twid heard a soft pulsating noise. It gained intensity. He sprang from his chair. Someone was pounding on the door.

Twid grabbed his sword and tiptoed forward. Scout-boy wouldn't fool him again. Peering through the hole, he saw Iwala's frantic face, hands motioning for him to open. The door was only halfway open when Iwala grabbed his tunic and slammed his face close. "They're here! Fifty soldiers. And they have torch sticks."

Twid went cold. Torch sticks. All it took was one piece of straw and the flames would spread from adobe to adobe. Adwa would burn.

Twid roused Him Too. Him Too had always complained that Iwala and Twid left him out. *You baboons. Just because I'm smaller and younger. I can take care of myself.*

No. Him Too would never forgive them if they left him. Besides, Scout-boy's questioner had threatened Him Too earlier.

"Leave the door open. They won't burn Adwa if they realize we've fled," Iwala said. Dragging the semi-unconscious Him Too, Twid followed Iwala. A lump rose in his throat. Crazy Zeru had cared for them for a decade. He would never understand, never know why they had fled. Twid could imagine his words: "I leave you for one night and you disappear. Of all people, you follow Iwala. Instructing you is like instructing a stone."

They raced up Adwa's hill. They had climbed every tree on this hill; had launched stones at the townspeople below; had raced goats and sheep, even after Twid had fallen and shattered his good arm.

Looking back, Twid saw movement near the Ald Nald House. The soldiers had arrived. With a final push, the friends crested the hill.

And stopped. A dozen archers stood before them with arrows notched. Behind the archers, spearmen stepped in perfect unison until they formed a semi-circle. The moonlight shone on their matching dark uniforms and polished boots.

A small shape stepped forward. Scout-boy. He smiled at them with genuine appreciation in his eyes, "Thanks for bringing the midget."

✸ ✸ ✸

Scout-boy walked close. In one quick motion, he smashed a staff into Twid's stomach and whipped the other end into Iwala's head. Twid doubled over and gasped. Iwala writhed on the ground. She felt dampness on her head.

"That's for my dead soldiers."

Iwala heard another crack and Him Too lay flat.

"That's for making me come to Adwa."

Scout-boy smashed Twid's thigh. "Get up or I'll kill you right here. Get up and carry the midget."

But Twid still convulsed on the ground, still gasped for air. Scout-boy smashed Twid's leg again and then again. Twid screamed. Forcing himself up, he lurched toward the unconscious Him Too. Twid's right leg trembled like a chair leg on the verge of breaking. Taking quick, short breaths, he lifted Him Too to his shoulder.

Using his staff, Scout-boy prodded him into the Adwa Forest. Twid fought to keep his balance. As the spinning in his head slowed, Twid realized they were walking straight towards the tree. He swallowed. He didn't have any illusions of escaping– the soldiers walked with weapons drawn. Nor did he believe that Scout-boy would let them go after a few questions. Not after the beating he had already given them. Not after killing his own soldiers in the stable.

No. Once they returned to the tree, Scout-boy would interrogate and then execute them. Glancing at Iwala, Twid grimaced. An egg-sized bump protruded from her forehead. Blood streamed.

Twid slipped; his leg gave out, and he fell on top of Him Too. Scout-boy called a halt and motioned for a man to approach Twid. The veiled man walked over and spoke in a soft, soothing voice. Another questioner.

"Boy. We have no quarrel with you. Tell us the truth and we'll forget about the stable."

Twid lifted his head. Who cared? It seemed like they already knew everything anyway. He stammered. "I have nothing to hide. If your men hadn't attacked me I would have told them. Four weeks ago we were running out of food at The Ald Nald Orphanage where I live. My brother and I went hunting in the Adwa Forest and came upon an invisible tree that we found through our slingshot. We went inside. We took this sword that I'm wearing and my friend took the black staff you see tucked in his tunic. Lightning struck the tree and the wreckage landed on my friend. He barely survived."

The questioner lowered his voice, speaking in a tone that could have convinced one to sleep on a bed of burning coals. "How did you find the tree? Why are you asking about Jignas?"

"Well, we saw this ram-sized red fox and we followed…"

He stopped. As soon as his questioner heard the words "red fox," venom had flashed in his eyes. Pure hatred. They were dead. There was something about the fox.

"Continue."

The questioner cuffed Twid on his head so hard he flipped over, landing on Him Too. Twid's eye swelled. Another soldier butted his leg with his spear and Twid cried out. Blood dripped down Twid's leg. Twid tried to talk but nothing came out.

Scout-boy shoved his face close. His hot breath scalded Twid's cheeks. "Don't worry, the head questioner will make you talk when we get back to the tree. And if that doesn't work, the Dirg will be here tomorrow. That's right, DIRG! I promise you– you'll tell the Dirg everything. You'll tell him how many times you milked your goat last month; how many times it rained last year; you'll tell him about the fox – you won't stop talking." He smashed his staff into Twid's leg again and motioned for Twid to pick Him Too up.

A Dirg! A Dirg! Numbness spread throughout Twid's body and even Iwala's face blanched. A Dirg! Who were these people? Were they emissaries of Idgistu, the mad overlord of the North?

Hundreds of years ago, during The Harmony Wars, the mad overlord Idgistu had created four Dirg Lords to lead his hordes. According to legends, he had created them with just one decree: *"Ye-matfat Zemacha."* Ancient Giiz for "Kill all living creatures, spare none."

And kill they had. The Dirg had used their supernatural strength to destroy hundreds of villages and murder hundreds of thousands of villagers. Just last year, a single Dirg had massacred five villages outside of Dream City. Neither children nor women, elderly nor bed-ridden were spared.

Adding to the terror, the Dirg looked like ordinary human beings—one could never be sure who a Dirg was. And after thousands of battles, only once had a Dirg been slain. Alula the Unconquerable, Ras' greatest hero, had slain the Dirg Talia during The Harmony Wars. The remaining three Dirg still hunted the Three Lands and even the Dream Kings couldn't kill them.

Twid trembled as they approached the rickety wooden bridge over The Selam River. The ancient bridge fit four men abreast. Twid looked down at The Selam's rapids, more than a hundred feet below. *Selam* meant peace in ancient Giiz, but Twid didn't feel any peace. Rocks jutted out along the banks, guiding the river south toward The Perilous Mountains. One hundred yards downstream, The Selam Falls thundered into one of the greatest waterfalls in the Three Lands.

Then there were the Hyeks. Always with Dirgs, the stories said, there were the Hyeks: Long-snouted, mutant hyenas that ran with ease on four legs but could fight on two. Hyek packs could devour lions, let alone humans.

Twid shifted Him Too to his right shoulder. Once they crossed the bridge they would reach the tree in a half-mile. They would die.

Looking at the waters below, Twid thought of the Old Ones saying, "The lame man marries the blind woman." Twid had always thought it a strange saying. Until now. Sometimes life offered few choices. Sometimes one had to choose anyway.

Iwala stepped on Twid's foot. She was rotating her eyeballs right and left. Twid nodded. They were thinking the same thing: Whatever the cost, they had to avoid the Dirg.

Firming his grip on Him Too's tunic, Twid took a deep breath. Pretending to trip, Twid launched himself towards the south end of the bridge. He saw Iwala wiggle past the soldier to her right. Iwala ducked an elbow and kicked a soldier's kneecap – the sound of bone crunching punctuated the water's gurgling. Iwala leapt over the north end of the bridge, falling almost one hundred feet to the rapids.

Scout-boy screamed and leapt toward Twid. But it was too late. Twid leapt over the bridge's south side, gripping Him Too like a mother protecting an infant.

Creator be with us! Creator be...

But then Twid felt a tugging and a jerking. He shrieked as he plunged down to the rapid waters below.

They had him! Scout-boy had grabbed him. They had Him Too.

# Five

They had Him Too. They had Him Too! The water rushed up to meet him. *Arms to your side. Feet together. Hope the water is deep enough. Hold your breath. Concentrate.*
They had Him Too. Him Too would awaken—if he awoke—and not realize what had happened to Twid and Iwala. The Dirg would have Him T...Him Too wouldn't even know a Dirg was coming!

The water smashed him and Twid almost blacked out. He tried to move his arms and legs but the water spun him like a pebble in a maelstrom. Darkness flooded and he couldn't tell which way was up. Something smashed his feet. Rocks sliced. The river bed. Lungs shrieking, Twid churned his weakening arms. Panic suffocated him. He flipped again. His arms stopped moving and he welcomed the darkness.

Then he saw light. Light. Light! Twid pumped his arms and legs until he couldn't pump. His head broke through. Water swirled everywhere. He coughed and gasped and his tears mixed with the churning water.

They had Him Too.

Twisting his head, he looked for Iwala. Iwala had jumped on the other side so she would be north. But the current was so strong that Twid could barely keep his head afloat, much less turn it.

A rumbling grew. It deepened into a stampede. The Selam Falls. There was no point trying to get over to the banks. Even if there was time, the rocks would smash him.

Something bumped his head. It was Him Too's wooden staff. Twid grabbed it. He felt something against his leg and realized he still had the sword from the tree. Water thundered.

Something slammed Twid's head like a donkey's hoof and he knew no more.

❉ ❉ ❉

Iwala knew her arm was broken as soon as she hit the river. Forcing herself to ignore the pain, she fought her way back up to the surface.

Quick. She had to think. What had the old man said? Think! She had gotten drunk once with a man from Nisha, who worked the Blind River. He claimed to have survived three waterfalls.

What was it that he had said? Try to jump forward when you plunge. Swim forward right away. Above all, do not let the waterfall trap you behind it.

Cursed current. It never seemed this powerful when she was looking at it from land. Now, she couldn't even turn her head to look for Him Too and Twid. Pain shot through her arm and she readied herself.

Well, if she survived, at least she'd have a great story. She'd have to find that old man again and tell him her own story of survival. Over a drink of course.

The waterfall thundered. She braced herself.

At the last moment, she propelled herself forward. *Stay straight this time fool, or you'll break your other arm.* She landed ahead of the fall, the water smacking her like a sledgehammer. *Swim forward. Swim forward. Don't get trapped. Ignore the pain.* She broke clear, swimming with her right hand.

The current swept her south.

She saw a small log. She had to get to it. She kicked with her legs and right arm and grabbed onto the log. Now she knew what Twid felt like with only one good arm.

She looked behind her again, trying to find him, but the waves continued to obscure her vision. Just ride it out. Get past the rocks.

After several miles, the current slowed and the rocks disappeared. She waited for the current to slow even more, and then kicked with her feet, mostly in the same direction of the current, to the west bank. Push. Kick. Push. Kick.

Twenty feet away from shore, she abandoned the log and swam forward. She stopped swimming as her feet hit dirt. She stood and stumbled another thirty feet, just in case the tide rose and dragged her back.

A thought struck her, and she searched all over her body. She collapsed. Where was Kwee?

❄❄ ❄❄ ❄❄

The pain stung everywhere, as if an entire colony of red ants had gotten under his clothes. Him Too felt a piercing sensation above his left eye. In the next moment, claws scraped his lower back, then, with every breath, a giant hand crushed his ribs until all he saw was red.

He was about to call for help, to Zeru, to Twid, to anyone, but then he remembered. Taking short breaths to reduce the pressure against his ribs, Him Too remembered. Their flight. Scout-boy. The soldiers.

Where were Iwala and Twid? Were they still alive? How long had he slept? Him Too peered into the darkness. Soldiers, shrouded under night's cover, surrounded him. He saw the weapons on the wall and realized that they had taken him back to the tree.

Who were these crazy people? What in Zeru's name had happened? Voices interrupted his thoughts and he closed his eyes.

A soft, young voice spoke. "Are you sure the plan will work? The runt and one-arm seemed to have a good reputation among the townspeople."

"Trust me. Remember what the Old Ones said, *'To know a man, know his friends.'* Their friend Iwala has committed more crimes than a Nishan smuggler. According to the townspeople, at age twelve, she assaulted seven guardsmen and almost killed two of them. She had no parents; her mother died at childbirth; and her father spent most of his time roaming from town to town getting drunk. She left home at fifteen and somehow got a job as a tax collector for the governor. Here's the best part: she lost all the governor's money gambling in N'Mote."

The other voice whistled.

"The governor sent her to Metka for a year. Metka! She was the youngest person ever sent. On top of that, apparently the other two have been acting strange, telling the townspeople about the voices in their heads. So the townspeople are already wondering about them. But I've left nothing to chance. I've paid the High Septon ten harvests gold to swear that he saw the three push the old man into the pit."

All air left Him Too's body and he forgot his physical pain. Scout-boy had told the townspeople that they had killed Zeru. Him Too choked back the tears. He knew what that meant! Zeru! The only father they had ever known!

"Didn't the thief also create some sort of rat epidemic?"

The first voice laughed. "Yes. That's why they forced Iwala out of Adwa when she was fifteen. The town had a rat infestation, and even the cats couldn't keep things under control. So the village elders issued an edict that for every ten dead rats anyone brought in, they would receive a birr. Well, the girl started bringing in a few rats here and there and the townspeople applauded her. Then she brought pillowcases bursting with dead rats. Then a wheelbarrow, and finally, at the end, she filled a horse-drawn cart with rotting rat meat piled so high that the grey stench covered every adobe in Adwa."

"The townspeople paid her, but were confounded not only that the girl could kill so many rats, but that the number of rats wasn't decreasing. She was homeless but they had someone follow her for several days, and she led them to an abandoned barn where she had been raising rats by the thousand."

As both men laughed, Him Too forced himself to concentrate, forced himself to forget, if only for a moment, what he had heard about Zeru. He had to escape. He had to find out what had happened to Iwala and Twid.

Then pain exploded in his side as something hard jabbed him. "Get up boy – we know you're awake."

# Six

Sitting in a cove, nestled under dark rocks, Iwala gazed past her fire, past the sand, to the Selam's knee-high waves. Few would call Iwala spiritual, but she had always found water soothing, the rhythmic, never-ending flows synonymous in her mind with some unknown power that granted order to an otherwise chaotic world.

Tonight, though, she could scarcely remember a time when she'd felt more anxious. After her crazy father, after Metka, after wandering the Three Lands, she had assumed she could overcome anything, and if not overcome it, at least face it without anxiety.

Twid coughed again, the sound ricocheting against the rocks like death knells. Two days Iwala had searched. Two days! She had found Twid, half-dead among the rocks, his body gashed from head to toe like a carcass picked apart by vultures.

Fortunately, her own arm was just bruised, not broken, and she had dragged Twid to the cove. They had no money, no blankets, no food. She looked at her friend's bruised face. If he slept outside again tonight, he would not survive.

Then there was Him Too. Twid had come to consciousness for brief moments, and despite his delirium, Iwala had gathered that Scout-boy had Him Too.

What a nightmare. If Iwala left Twid to help Him Too, Twid would die. If she didn't help Him Too, Him Too would probably die—if he wasn't dead already.

What could she do anyway? Him Too was surrounded by dozens of soldiers, and according to Scout-boy, a Dirg. A Dirg!

Lemlem was only a mile away, but the guards would never let Twid enter in his current condition. Yellow fever had killed tens of thousands in Lemlem two years past, and now, they let no sick outsider within their city limits. Besides, what if Scout-boy

had posted his guards at the gate? Two days was enough time to
make the trip down to Lemlem.

She asked herself again: Who were these people? If a Dirg was
involved that meant that Idgistu himself had taken an interest.
But what would Idgistu want with two boys on the other side of
the world?

Walking to the fire, she kicked sand over it. Her teeth ground
again, her helplessness only increasing her fury. She could see
no other way: Him Too would have to find a way to help himself. Kneeling next to Twid, she hoisted him onto her shoulder,
and rose. Her knees wobbled. How in the world was she going
to carry him?

Well, hadn't the Old Ones said, "The construction of an
adobe begins with a lone piece of straw." If they survived this,
she would never let Twid live it down. *A hippopotamus would have
been lighter. I carried you for three weeks while you slept, fighting
Hyeks, and Dirgs, and Idgistu himself. I even faced Zinna down in
single combat, and saved twenty kids from drowning, all the while,
carrying you on my back.*

*You probably weren't even asleep. Haven't the Old Ones said, "He
who feigns sleep cannot be awakened even by a rhinoceros?"*

*In fact, I'm sure you were feigning to get a free ride. That's what I
get for befriending a…*

Muttering, working herself up as she stumbled toward
Lemlem, Iwala almost forgot the pain in her arm and Twid's
crushing weight. After resting a dozen or so times, Iwala found
herself at the city wall. The wind hissed against the white stone
like a horsewhip.

Her friends in the Smuggler's Guild had once shown her a
little hole on the south wall across from a lone sycamore tree.
The hole had opened into a small stable. She could still hear her
friends' warnings: "Only use it in cases of emergency, Iwala. If
the hole is discovered because of you, the Smuggler's Guild will
have your head."

She had no choice. If only for a night, Twid needed to sleep in a stable. Straw wasn't a blanket, but it would keep him warm enough. And she could pilfer food and maybe even a blanket from a neighbor. Feeling with her hands, she tried to find the opening. If only she had Kwee with her. Kwee could find any opening.

An irregularity in the wall scraped against her hand. She pushed and a narrow section of the wall opened, just big enough for a body to crawl through. Iwala whistled a soft tune. Her spirits lifted. Who knew? If Twid got better quickly enough, maybe they could find Him Too. Iwala pushed Twid through then followed.

Before her eyes could adjust, Iwala heard feet rustling and a shriek. A flying body slammed her. A claw ripped her shoulder. Iwala screamed and tried to wrestle away. Straw stabbed her eyes. She twisted and drew a dagger.

But something held Iwala's arm back and she couldn't stab.

Her attacker was just a boy. Iwala's eyes watered and her dagger dropped from numb hands. She swayed like a scarecrow caught in a tornado.

He wasn't attacking her.

He was hugging.

He was Him Too.

※ ※ ※

Iwala crumbled. She called out, "Him Too. Are you haunting me, you crazy fool?"

Before Him Too could answer, Kwee leapt atop Iwala. As Iwala felt the familiar tugging on her braids, Iwala jumped Him Too. She bowled him over, yanking his shaggy red hair and small nose as he laughed and embraced her back. Forgetting her weariness, forgetting the soldiers and the Dirg, and Scout-boy and Twid's illness, Iwala felt that somehow, they might survive.

Him Too reached up and placed the stone back over the hole. He pointed at a small chunk of bread and cheese. "Eat in case we have to leave. There have been voices outside."

Him Too gasped as he took in Twid's lacerations. Iwala paused between a bite of bread. "Don't worry. We'll get him under some straw; we'll feed him some of this food. It might take a week but he'll recover."

Him Too touched Twid's face and nodded. It was more than he could say for Zeru. He still didn't know how he was going to break the news to his two friends. It would have been easier if he could have told them both at once.

Iwala and Zeru had always fought, not just the light banter that went on among the three friends, but real fights, where one of them would stay mad at the other for months. A mist came over his eyes as he remembered the dozens of times that Zeru had chased Iwala out of the Ald Nald House with a broom.

Yet beneath it all, everyone knew that the two of them cared for each other. As much as she complained about Zeru, Iwala considered him her real father, coming to see him first every time she returned from her wanderings. And as much as Zeru cursed Iwala, Zeru played cards with her more than anyone else.

Iwala rubbed Kwee's curved neck while she ate. "What happened? How in the Creator's name did you get here? I see you but I still can't believe it's you."

Him Too told his friend about waking up and the conversation he had overheard, describing with great relish the part where they referred to Iwala's record of wrongdoing.

Iwala laughed. "Seven soldiers? That's it? They have to get their rumors straight. I was attacked by no less than twenty guardsmen and overcame them with my bare hands. And the rats, they were already breeding in that barn. All I did was transport them."

Him Too laughed for several seconds then stopped. Reaching over his shoulder, he scratched his own back. He could feel his Adam's apple, bobbing and...

Iwala flicked a piece of straw at him. "Well, what happened next?"

Him Too said, "The soldiers said something, Iwala. Something about Zeru."

Iwala's body tensed. Each moment hung in the air, a tidal wave of unknown magnitude. Him Too forced himself to continue, knowing that waiting would only make it worse. Tears sprang to his eyes. "Iwala, Scout-boy said that they shoved Zeru into a pit and then told the townspeople that we killed him." Him Too's voice broke and Iwala almost didn't hear him. "They paid the High Septon to say he saw us do it!"

The tidal wave smashed and Iwala blacked out. Hunger forgotten, weariness forgotten, Iwala convulsed. Him Too joined her, the pain magnifying now that he had Iwala to mourn with him.

Iwala's smashed the straw with her head, her hands. Zeru! They had never thanked him, never told him they appreciated him. What would they have done without him? Where would they have gone?

How did he really die? Did Scout-boy murder him at the house? In the woods? Iwala wiped her eyes. It didn't matter how many soldiers Scout-boy had – Iwala would feed them all to snakes.

Him Too heard Iwala sputter, "Never thanked him. Never thanked him." Then, "Drink his own blood. I will feed Scout-boy his own blood."

After twenty or so minutes, Him Too continued, his voice still breaking. "When I heard that they had killed Zeru, I knew that they would not hesitate to kill me as well. But what could I do? I was tied to a gigantic wine barrel, surrounded by dozens of soldiers. I couldn't feign sleep anymore because one of them smashed my stomach and told me to awaken.

"Then Scout-boy worked himself into a fury. He was beside himself about losing the two of you, saying something about the Dirg never forgiving him, and that's when I lost all hope. A Dirg! He said a Dirg would be there within hours.

"Scout-boy whispered softly and asked about the fox, about

the Harmonies, and some strange questions about The Golden
Eagle and The Map of Legends."

Iwala browed. "What? The Golden Eagle? Map of Legends?
Those are just children's stories."

Him Too gave Iwala a stony look, "That's what Scout-boy
said."

Him Too paused, his hands circling before him. "This next
part is the part that I don't even believe myself. I already told
you about the voices in my head. The more Scout-boy questioned me, the more the voices escalated until I couldn't hear or
see anything. JIGNA! THE FIVE HARMONIES! JIGNA! THE FIVE
HARMONIES! The voices blocked out every other thought."

"Then the voices exploded and something surged inside
me like wildfire. My veins burned and suddenly, I could see
everything. Iwala, I flexed my arms and the ropes burst. My
body felt bigger; I towered over the soldiers. Their shocked faces
stretched taut like a goat hide drum. Before they could move,
I bent low and lifted the gigantic barrel — an oak barrel that
ten men couldn't lift. I hurled it at them and before it landed,
jumped from one wall to the next. I saw Kwee on a ledge and
grabbed her. I fled then, Iwala. I covered in an hour what would
normally take a day. Don't look at me like that, Iwala. How else
could I have escaped?"

Iwala's palms tingled. "No. No. I believe you. It's actually the
only thing that makes sense." She spat into the straw. "Why else
would someone send a Dirg? Why would Scout-boy and his soldiers come after you? Why would they care about two orphans
in Adwa? No. I have no doubt of it. You and Twid unlocked
some hidden power in that tree and someone is very scared."

Him Too nodded, "I felt it, Iwala. I just don't know what the
power is or how to use it. I can't even hear the voices anymore.
They come and go whenever they want."

"How did you find us here?" Iwala asked.

"Earlier, Scout-boy had screamed that you two would never
escape, that he had sent his soldiers to Lemlem," Him Too said.

"So I headed in this direction. And then the voices subsided, and I felt myself slow. I walked the rest of the way with Kwee, arriving this morning, and spent all today looking for you. When we walked past this place, Kwee insisted that we enter, screaming and raking me with her claws when I tried to leave. I thought maybe Kwee had gone crazy, too. But then, right when I was thinking of leaving again, you arrived."

# Seven

Stretching his arms from side to side, Twid tried to loosen the cramps along his right shoulder. Iwala had popped the shoulder back into place, but it still didn't move well. Not that he was complaining. He was lucky to be alive.

Hearing Him Too laugh, he looked over to his friends who were playing a game of cards. They were all lucky to be alive. Well, not all of them were alive. He thought back to one of Mother Scale's favorite sayings: "Life gives you nine, never ten."

Twid swallowed. Life might have given them nine portions of luck, but the one it had withheld hurt like ten. Zeru, their father, was dead, and those who murdered him still hunted them.

Pulling out the sword from the tree, he pondered their options. As he settled into the offensive Nishan stance of fighting, he marveled again that he hadn't lost the sword during the fall.

They couldn't go back to Adwa. Even if the townspeople somehow welcomed them back, Scout-boy would likely have soldiers stationed nearby. Staying in Lemlem was out of the question, too. Scout-boy had no doubt sent his soldiers looking for them.

In fact, Scout-boy and his soldiers were likely already in town. The three friends had stayed in the stable for a week, with only Iwala sneaking out to pilfer food at night.

Where could they go? Where could they find safety? Where could they find out about the strange voices in their heads or the tree? Why was the Dirg pursuing them?

They had asked Him Too to demonstrate his new powers, but Him Too could barely lift Twid off the stable ground. It was hard to believe he had hurled a wine barrel back in the tree. Twid slashed with the sword.

But if they wanted to discount Him Too's story, how else could he have escaped? No. The Harmonies had to have some

sort of secret power. Otherwise, why would Scout-boy and his
soldiers care so much about the questions Twid and Him Too
had asked? Why would a Dirg pursue them?

Twid jumped to the room's center and thrust upward with
the sword. The power couldn't have come from the staff or the
sword. Him Too had had neither with him.

Was it the strange voices? Twid called over. "Iwala. You can't
think of one place we can learn about the voices or how Him
Too escaped?"

"I already told you, our best bet is the monastery here in
town. We risk getting discovered by Scout-boy, but the monastery is known for having one of the largest libraries in all the
Three Lands."

Iwala placed a card with the gusto of an explorer planting a
flag on a newly conquered land. "It is said that if their archives
don't have a document, then it's not important."

Twid said, "But how will we get into the library? A great gathering of scholars we'd make. A midget, a one-armed boy, and a
woman with a monkey on her shoulder."

He sliced again with the sword. "Him Too, can you still hear
the voices in your head?"

Him Too looked up. "I've already told you twice today. Not as
loud as before, but I still hear them."

Twid nodded then spoke the words as if they were a poultice.
"Jigna. The Five Harmonies."

Iwala turned her head. As she heard Twid say The Five
Harmonies, a small tremor rushed through her. Why hadn't
she remembered before? The tremor grew, peaking in a cloud
of half-panic, half-excitement. She put down her cards. "I don't
know why I didn't remember this before. It's strange, almost
like it was erased from my mind until this moment, when you
spoke."

Twid lowered his sword. After the craziness of the last month,
Iwala could proclaim herself a cave rhinoceros and Twid would
consider it.

"When I was in Metka, I met almost every kind of evil person you can meet."

Twid and Him Too glanced at each other. In their time knowing Iwala, she had rarely mentioned her year in Metka, and never in great detail. That she had survived was enough — fewer than half who entered Metka walked out.

"Murderers. Rapists. And a few thieves like me. I survived only because I made people laugh, and because I could strum songs while the soldiers sang. During my last month at Metka, I had the task of delivering food to a few prisoners that were kept alone."

She paused, looking at the ground. "There was one prisoner in Metka, who was kept under heavier guard than anything I've ever seen. Even the dream bank in Dream City didn't have guards like this.

"He was a wrinkly old man—if it was possible to live five hundred years, he'd be a thousand. But more than 100 soldiers guarded his cell in layers, including three 8th Circle Defenders."

Twid whistled. Three 8th Circle Defenders to guard one old man!

"I always kept my head down when bringing his food, not wanting to draw attention from the Defenders or soldiers, or from him. But one day, I looked at him, and on a tattoo on his right arm, I read three words that didn't any make sense to me. I don't know why I didn't remember them until now."

Twid stared at her, imploring her to finish, but it was Him Too who completed her story, his eyes gleaming. "The Five Harmonies."

Iwala nodded. "He could be dead by now. He could have been exiled to the Cursed Lands. Who knows? Maybe they cut his tongue and he can't tell us anything."

The same thoughts ran through the friend's heads. But what if? What if he was still there? What if he was the only one who could shed light on The Five Harmonies? What if he could tell them who their pursuers were? What if he was being guarded because he knew something no else knew?

They sat, card game forgotten, taking in the enormity of Iwala's unspoken suggestion. It was suicide. Even if they survived The Perilous Mountains and reached Metka safely, they'd have to get past the outer guards. Even if they got inside Metka, they'd have to get past the guards outside the main prison area. Even if they got within the main prison area, they'd have to get past 100 soldiers and three 8th Circle Defenders and then convince the old man to talk to them. And then they'd have to fight their way back out.

Twid shook his head. "I don't see how we can do it. We don't even know if the old man can help us. Who knows, he could be crazy. We need to find someone else."

Him Too stood up and leaned on the small staff he had taken from the tree. "Like who? If Lab, who's traveled throughout the Three Lands has never heard of the Five Harmonies; if Iwala, who's collected taxes everywhere has never heard of them except on this man; if Mother Scale, our own grandmother, refused to tell us, what makes you think we'll just stumble onto someone who can?"

Him Too was right. Still. Searching for the Five Harmonies was one thing. Storming Metka was a whole other matter.

Iwala nodded. "How about this? Let's go to the monastery first, and if we find what we need there, we don't have to worry about Metka."

As they nodded, Iwala smiled. "Haven't the Old Ones said, 'Before you carry a donkey, ensure he cannot walk on his own?'"

※ ※ ※

The three friends stepped out of the stable and emerged onto a small dirt road. Fresh cow manure assaulted the morning air. Donkeys and sheep chewed on the sparse vegetation next to the road; a young boy carried a bundle of thin sticks; an old woman peered at them as she ground her wheat; next to her, a young girl wove straw baskets.

Twid stared at the homes. Even in these shanty parts, everyone had stone homes, not the mud-and-straw thatched adobes he was used to in Adwa.

Iwala caught him gawking and said, "We're at the footsteps of the Perilous Mountains. Merchants send young boys up with wheelbarrows to bring down six or seven large stones at a time. Everyone has a stone home."

Iwala pushed Him Too toward a pile of manure but Him Too jumped over it. Iwala continued, "I forget that country bumpkins like you and Him Too have never seen anything. I've got a surprise for you on the way to the monastery."

The friends continued walking through the street, talking among themselves.

Seeing an old man with Zeru's salt and pepper stubble, Twid started. But it wasn't Zeru. A sudden feeling of loss overwhelmed Twid; tears welled. He said to his friends. "Can you imagine what Old Zeru would say if he could see us now?"

Him Too lowered his voice and mimicked Zeru's wild gestures. "No one ever listens to me. Yes, no one respects an old ram who has lost his horns. But did I not prepare you for this? Did I not tell that you must climb today's hills to ensure you can scale tomorrow's unexpected mountains? Tell the truth. Did old Zeru not tell you all this before it happened?"

In spite of the pain, Twid smiled as he recalled. "Remember the time when the new magistrate questioned Zeru's record-keeping, asking Zeru to account for all the grain sent in from the Dream Kings?"

Him Too laughed. "Zeru packed his bags and marched all six of us brothers and sisters down to the magistrate's house. When the magistrate opened the door, Zeru looked him in the eye and said, 'Since you can do a better job raising these kids, I'm going to leave them to you. I'm off to Axum.'"

The poor magistrate chased down the street after Zeru, beg-

ging forgiveness. But Zeru refused to return from Axum until
the magistrate issued a public apology explaining in detail why
Zeru was a great overseer for the Ald Nald House and why the
magistrate was wrong.

That was Zeru for you, though. There could be a raging fire
burning the house down. Zeru wouldn't care. He'd keep talking
to you until there was absolutely no doubt that you were wrong
and he was right and not only that, until you understood ALL the
ways that you were wrong, and ALL the ways that Zeru was right.

Iwala led them around a corner.

Before them stood a magnificent marble home that could
have housed fifty guests. A dozen pillars adorned the front,
leading up to a sparkling gold dome. Lush gardens filled with
flowers of every hue surrounded the home, intermixing with
fountains inlaid with ornate carvings and towering statues.
Gardeners and other servants attended to the property under the
dutiful gaze of armed guards.

A fly buzzed inside Twid's gaping mouth but Twid didn't
even notice. "What is this place, Iwala? I didn't know the Dream
Kings owned a regional home in Lemlem."

Iwala smiled. "Now you know why I never forget to enter my
lots for the Dream Lottery. This is it. This is a Dream Mansion.
According to the stories, the person who lives here used to be a
beggar."

Twid walked closer to the iron gates. In the past five years,
the Dream Kings had built ten majestic homes throughout the
Three Lands called Dream Mansions. In a lottery that cost citi-
zens nothing to enter, the Dream Kings gave away all ten mansions for free. Twid had forgotten that they had built a Dream
Mansion in Lemlem.

He shook his head as the friends continued walking. You
had to hand it to the Dream Kings. They had redefined the possibilities for every man and woman in the Three Lands, offered
everyone new, unimaginable dreams. The Dream Mansions had
seemed a bit extravagant at first, but that was the Dream Kings

for you: Anyone and everyone deserved to have the best that life offered. With some luck, even an orphan like Twid could live in a Dream Mansion.

As they continued walking, Twid smiled again as he thought of Zeru. He had never lived in a mansion, but old Zeru had often acted like a Dream King.

Stepping around an abandoned wheelbarrow, Twid said, "I'm still thinking about old Zeru. Remember when the witch doctor fell on hard times after drowning Lete's cat?"

Iwala remembered. No one had gone to see the witch doctor for months, and the witch doctor had run out of money. So she had set aside one Saturday as a free day, when no villager would have to pay, thinking she could see ten or twenty villagers and restore her business.

Zeru had awoken at five in the morning, taken the six brothers and sisters to her house, and had her see each one of them. She finished offering the remedies by early morning.

But then, she made a colossal mistake. She asked Zeru if he had anything wrong with his body. Him Too laughed. "First, Zeru told her how the entire left half of his body had stopped working decades ago. Everything from his left eye to his left lip, to his left arm, left leg, left stomach, left liver, left lung, left ribcage, left foot, and of course, the entire left half of his mouth with its missing teeth. And for each body part, he wanted a separate remedy.

"It was mid-afternoon by the time the witch doctor finished answering all his questions and outside her window, the witch doctor could see a long line of villagers waiting in the blistering sun. But old Zeru was just getting started. He asked her about a rash on his leg that burned like a thousand bee stings. Then a pulled muscle in his back that pounded faster than a newborn's heart. Then a morning dizziness that trampled his head like a stampede of oxen. And of course, did she know how to relieve the volcanic eruptions in his gums and the uneven swelling in his left eye?"

Iwala and Twid laughed, their bodies shaking. "She didn't finish with Zeru until eleven that night and the villagers who had waited in line vowed to never visit the witch doctor again."

Him Too shook his head. He thought back to a saying the Old Ones had: "Sweetness passed you by before you called it sweet." Zeru, their crazy father, had passed them by.

"If he were alive, old Zeru would probably be cursing our names to the other brothers and sisters. I can see him now, head arched back as if he were addressing the Dream Kings themselves, imploring our brothers and sisters to not be like Him Too the Impulsive or Twid the Disrespectful who just go off in the middle of the night."

Iwala laughed. Him Too continued, a twinkle in his eye. "Then I can see Zeru saying, 'But it's not their fault. That's what happens when you befriend Iwala the Irresponsible.'" Iwala punched Him Too's arm and smiled. Iwala the Irresponsible. It had a nice ring to it.

The friends were so engrossed in their stories that they did not pay close heed to their surroundings. The smaller street had merged into a larger one and a loud commotion intensified, growing until it sounded like a stampede. The three friends shifted their heads. Could it be the soldiers? What in the Creator's name could be that loud?

As they merged into an even larger street, they lowered their guard. It was a Dream King parade. Drums, watas, and krar guitars blasted as thousands of people stood on the street, waved from balconies, and even tossed flowers from the roofs.

Fathers carried toddlers on their heads. Children hung from tree branches. Soldiers wearing Dream Kings blue uniforms marched, legs striding in perfect rhythm with the goat-hide drums.

On a dais carried by twelve solders sat a tall man, waving his hands back and forth: The emissary of the Dream Kings. A large banner proclaimed the constant credo that the Dream Kings espoused: "Freedom for all People. Dreams for all People."

The masses shouted, "Freedom! Dreams! Freedom! Dreams!"

Twid couldn't blame the crowd. The Dream Kings had discovered new medicines to help people live longer; they had
provided cheaper foods; they had fought off Idgistu's armies in
the north and built the Dream Wall to the west.

Twid joined his friends in shouting. "Freedom and Dreams!
Freedom and Dreams to all! Freedom to all! Dreams to all!
Long live the Dream Kings!"

The dais stopped at the center of the square and the Dream
Emissary stood. His large head jutted from his too-small body
like a rose from its stem. The crowd quieted.

"Lemlem. City of Dreams, City of Freedom, City Exalted
above the Perilous, I greet thee in the name of the Dream
Kings."

The crowd's deafening roar shook the plaza anew and this
time the emissary had to wave his hand for several minutes
before they quieted.

"I stand before you, dear ones, at a rare moment in our land's
history. A moment unimaginable to those who came before us,
yet a moment we can extend forever."

"You know better than I, dear friends, that for thousands of
years, men lived here in the Three Lands as brutes, governed by
a simple yet unforgiving creed: That the mighty should rule over
the weak and the strong over the feeble."

"During those lost millennia, few could foresee, few could
imagine, few could DREAM of a new age, an age where the
sword would lower not before a mightier sword, but rather,
before an ideal."

"For is that not what our Harmonies are? Is that not the
foundation of our happiness, that we have submitted ourselves
to ideals, and not just ideals but truths, and not just truths, but
the most noble, powerful truths: That each of you deserve to live
with freedom, that each of you deserve to pursue your dreams."

The crowd listened with bated breath as the emissary extolled
the virtues of the Harmonies. Twid nodded. They were lucky to

live in this age.

"And so, my brothers and sisters, as I stand before you…" The emissary dropped to a knee. "Nay, as I kneel before you, I ask you to continue your preeminent support not just of the governor here in Lemlem, or the Dream Kings in Dream City, but of Dreams and Freedom themselves and the bright new millennia we can bequeath our children."

As the emissary finished, the crowd's earlier roar seemed but a murmur in comparison. Twid joined them, "Freedom and Dreams! Freedom and Dreams!"

But then, as Twid pumped his hand, his eyes somehow met those of the emissary.

The emissary's eyes froze then widened as he surveyed Twid's companions. After a long moment, the emissary shouted at one of the soldiers below and pointed toward Twid.

Twid didn't wait to see what would happen next. Yanking Him Too's shirt with his good hand while yelling at Iwala, he ran back the way they had come.

"Run, you fools! That emissary is after us."

Had the whole stinking world gone raving mad? The same Dream Kings who had supported the Ald Nald House now pursuing them? Then he remembered. Maybe the emissary had heard that a group of three had killed Zeru—a recipient of Dream King aid! The news and their descriptions had no doubt reached him.

Iwala screamed at them to follow her as she ran into a bar called The Three Wrists. Twid kept low as they bolted through the common room.

As soon as they were out the back door, Iwala made a hard right into an almost invisible cove; it looked like a shaded area for baking bread. They held their breaths, not daring to move. Twid tried to quiet his heart. It pounded louder than horse hooves in full gallop. Sure enough, a dozen or so soldiers wearing Dream King insignia stormed out the back, fanning out along the street.

Iwala ground her teeth, cursing their luck. They had almost made it to the monastery. Why had they stopped to cheer? What was the Old Ones saying? "Don't change your cloth until you have finished your work."

She saw Twid gazing up at a small sign above the backdoor to the tavern: The Three Wrists. The small script under the sign read, "Founded by Wena, the three-wristed woman." Twid almost grunted. This woman had three arms, and Twid had just one?

Iwala nodded, answering Twid's unspoken question. She whispered, "She's famous in Lemlem. Lost her hand in an accident, and when the witch doctor treated her, the witch doctor separated her wrist in two, so she can hold some things in between."

They waited a few long minutes. Then Him Too lifted his head and scanned the street. "At the risk of sounding as hotheaded as Iwala, I say we still proceed to the monastery."

Twid nodded. The strange incident with the emissary had only reinforced their need for answers. "If we don't learn what in bloody heavens is going on, we will continue running without knowing why." He looked at Iwala. "Can you get us to the monastery with the soldiers hunting for us?"

Iwala said. "Oh. So now, when the situation is impossible, and there are soldiers looking for us everywhere, and we're stuck in a cooking hovel, you want me to come up with a new plan. That's funny. Aren't you the same ones who just called me Iwala the Irresponsible?"

Him Too gave her a sharp elbow.

Iwala winced. "Okay! Okay."

Bending closer, she lowered her voice.

# Eight

The sunset hit the top of the perfectly symmetrical building, giving the ancient bronze walls a divine glow. Wrapped in light evening cloaks, townspeople entered and exited the building at a constant clip. Few noticed the runt, woman, and lanky young man who slid from an adjacent building and entered.

As the three friends walked in, they heard monks chanting in ancient Giiz. The monks' combined voices echoed in the stone building with magnified power, giving the impression that the Creator had added his own deep voice to the chanting.

Gold and silver adorned the wide corridor, ushering them into a larger room lined with altars where hooded monks stood over kneeling parishioners. Iwala rushed to an altar and prostrated herself. She wailed and slammed her hands onto the cold stone floor.

So much for not drawing attention to ourselves, thought Twid.

A darkly cloaked, bearded monk approached Iwala. "Sister. Fear not. The Creator himself feels your pain."

Iwala tore at her hair, actually managing to extract a few strands, her wailing a sharp dissonance to the melodic chanting in the background. "Father. I have sinned. I have sinned. I have sinned." Twid started as he saw her place a handful of gold pieces in the offering plate. Where had she gotten that gold?

At the giving of the offering, the stocky monk placed his hand upon her head and chanted on her behalf, his whole body shaking with the effort, his hood almost falling off his head. Iwala's sobbing subsided, but didn't stop.

"What is it, my daughter?"

"Father, I have sinned! Before my sister died, I swore that I would teach her two children here the essence of the Harmonies. 'SWEAR,' SHE BEGGED ME. 'SWEAR!' AND I SWORE!"

Iwala sobbed again. "But I fell into drunkenness and wickedness." She let out a shriek. "I left them to the street father, and
now they have become pickpockets."

As she let out another shriek, Twid looked down, trying to
hide a smile. *At least the part about wickedness and drunkenness is
true.*

"Daughter. The Harmonies are simple and true. Freedom and
Dreams. Live with Freedom and Dream mightily, and you shall
live the blessed life."

"Father. I have heard that all my life and it's done me no
good. No. No. I have traveled here all the way from Seraye that
I might read and understand the essence of the Harmonies. I
must read the great Harmony Books you have here. I must read
the words that they might burn in my mind forever. BURN.
BURN. BURN."

She wailed anew, slamming her head into the ground. The
priest jumped back as a little blood soiled the marble floor.
Bystanders stared. Iwala reached back and placed a much bigger
handful of gold pieces into the offering.

The priest gazed up to the heavens as if consulting the Creator
himself. He looked down and nodded. "Has the Book of
Harmony not decreed, 'Come all ye who thirst for Harmony, for
ye shall drink from the River of Life. Prostate thyself, for wisdom
ever welcomes a broken heart?'"

Iwala wailed again, continuing to wail as the monk led them
through a corridor, then another corridor. They descended for
a few minutes until they arrived at a chamber guarded by two
soldiers. The soldiers nodded at the priest as he led them by.

They entered a room that could have held a wedding for ten
thousand guests. Huge bookshelves lined every wall, easily measuring thirty feet high. The priest pointed to a small section of
books and scrolls. "This is our collection on the Harmonies."

He handed her a red book with a single dot on top, and then
a line running across the bottom of the cover. "One of ten cop-
ies of the Book of Harmony in the Three Lands. Read, daughter,

and learn the truth."

Him Too crowded around Iwala, looking over her shoulder as she turned the pages. Twid stood to the side as if he didn't care.

Iwala wailed. "See, Father. He cares not." Her body shook. "Check your pockets, father, he's a thief." She started sobbing again, but Him Too patted her shoulders and she settled down.

The bewildered priest approached Twid. "Mock not the Harmonies, my son. Choose Freedom and Dreams that you might live."

Twid frowned like he wanted to spit on the Book of Harmony. "The Harmonies are for maids and fools." A thought crossed his mind. "I want to read about warriors. Show me some books about great warriors."

Youth. Ever focused on swords and warriors. The priest led Twid to another section, pulling out several books. "If you can read, here are some battle histories."

But Twid had already forgotten the priest. He was looking up at four paintings that depicted the Prince Defenders, the greatest warriors in the land.

Every seven years, the Dream Kings held a tournament to select a new Prince Defender. Anyone in the land could enter. Tens of thousands competed, seeking the riches, nobility, and fame that came with being a Prince Defender. But only 1024 passed the preliminary round to enter the tournament. From there, there were ten rounds of fighting until one winner remained: A Prince Defender.

Twid studied the portraits of the winners.

Delgam. A giant, the strongest. His long blond hair flowed past his chiseled face to rest on massive shoulders. The stories said Delgam had used a log as his weapon for part of his tournament, and simply hurled it at his hapless opponents, crushing them to death.

Kahn. So explosive, he could kill with his smallest finger. So quick, it was said that opponents didn't see Kahn's spear, they felt it. Twid took a step back in spite of himself. Dark hair

gleaming, eyes bent in concentration, Kahn looked like he
might explode from the portrait and attack.

Tah. The smallest, but most aggressive. She fought with two
swords in her hands, and two blades attached to her feet. Most
opponents had fallen before the opening bell had stopped
chiming. Her pale skin contrasted with her black hair, the pall
creating an aura of death.

And Inj. The maniac, the most ruthless. Clothed from head
to toe in black, he had killed more people than the other three
defenders combined. Some said he forced his own soldiers to
duel to the death.

Of course, Zinna, the traitor, the first Prince Defender, was
not pictured.

Twid shuddered at the thought of meeting any of them in
battle. Sitting on the wooden bench, he flipped through the
books. He heard the priest lecturing Him Too. "Young one.
Here is a passage, written by Solon the Wise himself: 'Good acts
performed in youth blossom into a lifetime of harvests. Dreams
beget dreams and freedom…'"

Blocking out the priest, Twid skimmed through the first book.
Find it. Find it. Find it. Nothing. He picked up another book,
and skimmed through it. Battles dating back a thousand years,
explaining how the Three Kingdoms were united by Menelik.
Accounts of how Idgistu invaded the Three Lands, ending the
Age of Harmony and starting The Harmony Wars. Of countless
hordes lead by Dirg Lords that slaughtered entire generations of
children. Entire nations, wiped from the land.

Twid kept skimming, taking in the familiar stories of the
original Dream Kings who had pushed Idgistu back into his
mountains and saved the Three Lands. Of Zinna, the Betrayer of
Dreams, who had joined the Seekers.

The priest rose and called out, "We must depart—I must lead
evening prayers."

Twid picked up another book and skimmed through it. The
priest called out again, growing irritated and muttering about

insolent youth. Twid read several paragraphs before the priest closed the book.

"Your aunt is right, boy. You must learn obedience."

They followed the priest up the corridors. As they climbed, Twid scanned his friend's eyes but he could not tell if they had found anything. He had to ask.

When they got back to the main room, the priest raised his hand to give them a final blessing. Twid stepped forward. "Father, a question for you from the books you showed me. I saw mention in one book of The Five Jignas of Adwa? I lived in Adwa for much of my life but never heard of them. Who were they?"

The priest straightened. Coldness radiated from his body, as if Twid had asked him to drink human blood. "Assassins. Murderers. Warriors with skills beyond imagining and evil beyond measuring. The chief allies of Idgistu during the Harmony Wars."

He looked at them one last time, his blessing forgotten. "They are the opposite of the Harmonies. I advise you—forget you ever saw the word Jigna and go back to Adwa or Seraye or wherever you are from." Gathering his dark robe close, he gave them an angry look and stormed off.

The friends exited the monastery and walked to the side, melding into the building's shadows. As they walked away, Iwala pulled out a bag that jingled. It had hundreds of gold coins. Twid gave his friend a disbelieving look. "Tell me you didn't get those from where I think you got them."

Iwala laughed. "If there really are Five Harmonies, I'm sure the third one is called Wisdom: Make sure you eat every day." Leaving them cursing her name, Iwala walked across the road, to an old woman selling peanuts and mangos.

She walked back to her friends, food in hand. "Did you see how much gold was in that place? They won't miss this from the offering plate, I assure you. Besides, if the Creator was here, who do you think he would want to have the gold: a priest who

eats more than five donkeys or the old woman I just bought this
mango from?"

Twid shook his head, but didn't reject the mango. Iwala had
a way of making thievery sound like charity. The friends walked
back to the stable, taking care to use back roads.

Iwala looked at Him Too. "I don't know about you, but I
didn't find anything new in the books. They just talked about
Freedom and Dreams. No Five Harmonies anywhere."

Him too nodded. "I didn't see anything either. Twid, why'd
you ask about the Jignas?"

"In the book I was reading, there were brief mentions of the
Five Jignas of Adwa. Him Too, there were five cots in that tree,
weren't there?"

Him Too nodded, everyone thinking the same thing. What if
the voices in their heads were from the Five Jignas? What if the
Five Jignas were assassins, emissaries of Idgistu, the greatest evil
the world had ever known? In searching for the Five Harmonies,
were they nothing more than the pawns of Idgistu himself, resurrecting an evil the world had barely contained in the past?

Iwala said, "I don't know. There was something strange
about that Harmony section. Monks have been writing about
the Harmonies for a millennia, but the Harmonies had just a
few shelves. Him Too, didn't the books seem a little too new to
you?"

Him Too cracked a peanut shell. "I looked at the titles of all
the books in our section. Most of the titles were written in the
common tongue, yet Giiz is the ancient language."

"It's almost as if someone eliminated all the old books and
put just enough books about the Harmonies in the library to
make the section big enough to be believable," Iwala said.

Her hands grew sticky as she finished the fruit closest to
the seed. "You know what else was strange? I thought that
surely in the Book of Harmony, somewhere it would describe
why or how the Harmonies worked. What they did. Why they
mattered."

She tossed the seed into some bushes. "Don't get me wrong. I liked the emissary's speech and I'm as much for dreams and freedom as anyone else. I just thought there would be something more, something that could explain how Him Too escaped from the tree."

Glancing about to ensure no one saw them, they entered the stable. Then stopped.

Four soldiers wearing Dream King garb surrounded them. Another soldier emerged from behind the door and kicked it closed.

Blood hammered in Twid's head. His eyes tightened. Twid unsheathed the sword he had taken from the tree and stood back to back with his friends. Bending his knees, he steadied himself on the uneven, straw-littered ground.

For eight years, crazy Zeru had trained them in the evenings. Twid with the sword, Him Too with the staff, and Iwala, when she was around, with daggers and short swords. They had asked Zeru where he learned to fight, but old Zeru had never told them.

Still, despite the training, Twid had never killed anyone in his life, never squared off against anyone other than Zeru, Iwala or Him Too. He had always wondered: In a real fight, would having one arm disadvantage him too much? Would he be able to kill another human being? Twid held his stump close.

The soldiers charged. Iwala kicked straw into one of their faces and launched a dagger while the soldier grasped.

Twid parried a soldier's blow and then feinting right, stabbed low and left, into a soldier's leg. The soldier screamed, and brought up his sword again, but he was too late. Twid thrust the blade through the soldier's neck, wincing as he felt the sword slicing.

*Why did you attack us? I didn't want to kill you.* Twid shifted. The soldiers seemed to focus on Him Too. Twid met a tall soldier's blade, and settled into the defensive Rasan style. No need to hurry now. There were only two soldiers standing. Making small feints and parries, Twid waited for the soldier to make a mistake. Then a dagger appeared in the soldier's throat and the soldier fell, turning the straw red.

Twid lowered his sword. The fight was over. Three of Iwala's daggers had pierced three different throats. Another soldier had choked to death, his windpipe destroyed by Him Too's staff. Twid had killed one.

Hand on his knee, Twid retched.

While Iwala retrieved her daggers, Kwee jumped from the rafters, landing on Iwala's shoulder. Gathering their meager provisions, the three friends pushed the stone out and climbed through the wall, into the cold wind.

They had to find out what was going on.

Metka.

# Nine

Iwala's face tightened as sharp pains sliced her knees. The Perilous Mountains, so named for their steep inclines and declines, would have been better named The Perilous Cliffs. She had a staff in each arm to soften the impact of each step on her knees. After two days of holding the staffs, her arms ached.

Him Too and Twid had thought going down would be easier than going up. Looking behind her, Iwala smiled. Him Too's face strained as he leaned on his short staff and Twid struggled to steady himself with his good arm.

Iwala shuddered as they reached the base of the valley. Once they walked past the canyon, they would see Metka.

Him Too and Twid had asked her repeatedly what her plan was. She had stalled, hoping she could find a better one. But she hadn't come up with anything else, and now they had no choice. If they didn't like her plan, they'd have to turn back. She motioned for them to sit by a brush.

"I've considered every way of seeing the old man. We can't sneak in; the gates are always shut and armed guards surround the entire complex. We can't force our way in. Even if we somehow fought past the perimeter guards, there are over one hundred guards watching the old man, not to mention the three 8th Circle Defenders.

"If I had the right tools, I could maybe forge a letter with the Dream King seal, instructing the commander to let us interview the old man. But I don't have the proper paper, or the proper coloring, and they probably wouldn't believe that the Dream Kings would ask *me* to interview anyone, let alone the old man."

Now came the tough part. She alternated, looking each of them in the eye, gauging their reactions as she shared her plan. If they were lucky, they'd get turned away at the gate. If they got in, they'd have to do heinous, unspeakable things. If they were discovered, they would suffer even worse. But the plan had enough truth in it. It was so ridiculous, so painful that it *might* work. Twid and Him Too nodded. They could see no other way.

Lost in their own thoughts, they stood. As they rounded the canyon, Iwala motioned for Him Too and Twid to proceed. Let them see it first.

Him Too passed. Twid followed, scratch marks decorating his stump. He had fallen earlier and reached out with his stump to preserve his balance.

As he rounded the canyon, Twid almost tripped over Him Too who stood frozen. He followed Him Too's gaze upward. A massive fortress made of black stone sat upon a barren, gravel hill. The castle's spires twisted up like dark spears stabbing the sun. Soldiers lined the castle's walls, and a perimeter guard patrolled the exterior.

Twid whistled. "Have the Old Ones not said, 'Let he who tempts death with warnings on his ears be buried with his eyes wide open?'"

Iwala came around the curve but didn't look up. Better to keep her eyes down until she had to. Once inside, she'd have to notice every look, every gesture, every detail. If they were caught, they'd be imprisoned for the rest of their short lives. There were three 8th Circle Defenders waiting up there. *Three!* Even if Twid could handle one, he could never handle all three.

Every seven years, in the Prince Defender Games, 1024 warriors fought for the right to be the Prince Defender. To become the Prince Defender, you had to win ten straight battles. If you won just one battle, you became a First Circle Defender; if you won two, you became a 2nd Circle Defender, and so on. To become an 8th Circle defender, you had to win eight battles and be among the final four warriors in the entire competition. After five Prince Defender Games, only ten 8th Circle Defenders existed in the entire land, and three of them were guarding the old man.

What kind of knowledge could he have that the Dream Kings

would guard him so? If he was so dangerous, why not just kill him and get it over with? Even more troubling, what if the old man refused to talk? In the dozens of times she had brought him food, he had never moved from his place in the corner. He had never spoken even one word. She bit her lip. What if he wasn't even alive anymore? True, the food was gone most times she came back, but what if the rats were eating it?

She shivered as she looked up at the dark castle, memories of beatings and horrific chores overwhelming her. A group of five soldiers wearing full body armor approached them.

"Freedom and Dreams to you in the name of the Dream Kings," she called out.

The head soldier looked at her as if seeing a four-headed rooster. No one who left Metka ever came back willingly.

"Freedom and Dreams to you in the name of the Dream Kings," she called out again.

"Freedom and Dreams to you," he responded. "What business do you have in Metka?"

"I come on a mission from the governor of Adwa. These two young men have caused unrest in the province and he has asked me to bring them here for one day, to show them what awaits should their insolence persist."

The soldier stamped his spear. "Metka is no warning school for provincial rabble."

She approached the soldier and lowered her voice. "I tried to tell the governor that myself, good captain. Truth be told, these two would already be at Metka if they weren't relatives of the governor's wife." Iwala paused and leaned closer, "The governor is offering a reward."

The soldier hesitated at the mention of a reward, "I'll have to check with the commander."

They waited, four guards watching them.

A few minutes later, they heard a deep bellow from the other side of the gate. "Can you still play the wata?"

Smiling, Iwala whistled a few melodies then yelled out, "Like the son of Tikul, himself!" Several moments passed, and then they heard levers screeching and the gates grated open. Iwala gathered her breath before following the soldiers. Should she be happy or sad that they got in? When they stepped through, she found the commander waiting for them. He looked the same. Wide-faced, with a torso as commanding as Metka itself, and black, spiky hair that shot out like a porcupine's.

"Back so soon. We must be getting soft around here." His whole body shook as he laughed. Iwala craned her head and looked past the commander. In a large courtyard, two prisoners hung by their arms. Blood dripped from their bare backs. In the other corner, a prisoner screamed. He had a sack over his head and he sat over a boiling pot. The blinding peppers. It was perhaps the cruelest punishment at Metka. The guards boiled the hottest jalapeno peppers, then put a sack over a prisoner's face and had the prisoner breath in the scalding air. Some prisoners went blind; all emerged with their face scarred.

Iwala swallowed. "Commander, you know how unruly this next generation is." Older folk always seemed to believe that the current generation was a thousand times worse than their own generation and just a moment away from destroying everything previous generations had fought to create.

"Yes. Yes. Well, as long as you can still play the wata like the son of Tikul, we'll have you. Obviously, you'll have to put your weapons aside."

She nodded. Twid handed them his two swords, and Him Too gave them his bow and arrow but kept the staff from the tree. His knees still hurt.

Iwala reached into her bag, then into her tunic, then into her boots, pulling out dagger after dagger until she had twelve daggers before her.

Even Twid and Him Too stared. The commander hesitated then laughed. *He is so much friendlier when you aren't an inmate. Or is it the reward?*

She approached the commander and lowered her voice.

"Commander. The governor has tried everything; threats, whippings, even food deprivation. Nothing has worked. He has promised you 1000 birr if the boys reform after visiting Metka."

The commander's eyes lit with the intensity of a beacon light. 1000 birr would double his annual salary. Nodding, he appraised Him Too and Twid, "I'll show them Metka within Metka within Metka. Trust me, they won't last an hour."

Now came the moment of truth.

"These boys consider cleaning the work of women. Who has the filthiest, foulest cell in this prison? A cell filled with waste and excrement. A cell that has never been cleaned. Have them clean it. Tell them if they return, it will be their job to clean all the cells each day."

The commander lumbered past Iwala until he towered over Him Too and Twid. "So you think cleaning is for women?" He grunted. "Fools. Everyone's a woman in Metka except for me."

He led them through a corridor, to a dark room where two prisoners worked in a kitchen. The aroma of meat rose from two gigantic cauldrons. Twid and Him Too looked at each other; it didn't smell bad.

The commander grabbed a tin bowl and filled it with the stew. He motioned for Him Too and Twid to eat, placing two wooden spoons before them. Twid grabbed a spoon and scooped up some meat, but Iwala grabbed his arm.

Iwala took the spoon out of Twid's hand and placed it in the soup. She circled until she found meat and pulled it up. A rat's head. She dug some more, pulling out a cockroach and several beetles. The two friends pushed the stew away, faces crinkled in disgust. The commander nodded. "If you come here, lads, you'll be begging for rat stew in less than a week. I promise you that."

Twid spat. How had Iwala managed it?

The commander led them out through another corridor. An avalanche of rot and decay overwhelmed their noses, growing stronger as they walked. Him Too and Twid put their hands over their noses, shutting their nostrils, but the smell permeated

every particle of air. Twid bent against a slimy wall and wretch-
ed. They reached the stench's source, a row of fifty cells. Each
cell could reasonably hold four men, but held fifteen instead.
Men slept atop each other on dirt floors teeming with rats, ants
and cockroaches. Many of the men had sores on their skins; all
had red, bloated eyes.

The warder pointed as if he were showcasing a priceless
painting, "These are actually the cleanest quarters in the prison,
where those with good behavior stay."

"Let me show you where you'll be cleaning until dawn tomorrow." He looked at Iwala. "You do want them cleaning through
the night, right?" Iwala nodded.

The warder took them to a row of twenty cells where thirty
prisoners filled cells designed for four. Every prisoner had
pus-filled infections and most resembled corpses. The smell of
rotting flesh mixed with the smell of excrement. Even the rats
stayed away.

The commander called out to a soldier, "Get several rags and
some water. Then empty out these cells and have these boys
clean them. If they rest or stop, whip them with camel-hair,
barbed whips. They've already refused our hospitality; offer
them no water or food."

He laughed. "They can, of course, drink the water they use to
clean."

Iwala wanted to scream. They would never get to the cell they
had hoped for now. It would take the entire twenty-four hours
to clean just these cells. She tried to give her friends an apolo-
getic look, but they couldn't stop staring at the hideous cells.
Iwala closed her eyes. They were never going to forgive her for
this. She was never going to forgive herself.

And the old man. She could try to visit the old man in secret,
but the old man had over one hundred guards watching him.
There was no point in even trying.

The commander motioned for her to leave them and walked
her back to the main hall where the soldiers and guards ate.

The commander let out a whistle. It was his lucky day. Not only was he going to double his salary, he was also going to hear the wata. "Eat, then regal us."

Iwala nodded. There was no point in starving herself. Besides, how many prisoners at Metka ever ate with the guards? She grabbed a side of mutton and bread. Working at top speed, Twid and Him Too would finish maybe seven cells. Once they realized the task was impossible, they'd probably pace themselves and finish three. More than ten was impossible.

She picked up Metka's wata. It still amazed her that rubbing two bows strung with goat intestine could produce such piercing music. She tuned the large bow first, then the smaller bow. As she walked to the stage, the guards cheered.

She held the larger bow stationary on her lap, and held the little bow in her right hand. She took a few preliminary swipes with the smaller bow, quieting the crowd.

She thought of Twid and Him Too as she sang:

> *Thought she was kind,*
> *That she had a sound mind,*
> *Thought she was wise,*
> *That she wasn't full of lies.*

The soldiers burst out and sang the familiar chorus.

> *Fool, didn't you know you can't trust a woman?*
> *Fool, didn't you know you can't trust a woman?*
>
> *Thought you could trust her,*
> *You could give her your life,*
> *Thought you could trust her,*
> *Just because she's your wife.*
>
> *Fool, didn't you know you can't trust a woman?*
> *Fool, didn't you know you can't trust a woman?*
>
> *Thought you could trust her,*
> *That your love endures,*

*Thought you could trust her,*
*That your kids were yours.*

*Fool, didn't you know you can't trust a woman?*
*Fool, didn't you know you can't trust a woman?*

*Now that you're ruined,*
*Don't try to blame her,*
*Now that you're broke,*
*Don't try to shame her.*

*Fool, didn't you know you can't trust a woman?*
*Fool, didn't you know you can't trust a woman?*

They sang the chorus again several times, the men waving their tankards and laughing. She sang more songs, songs of Tayle the Lucky Goat Herder, and Fisoom the Hungry Guest. She sang all day, taking several breaks to eat and talk with soldiers. At nightfall, the commander thanked her and showed her to a room with a small cot.

As she tried to fall asleep, the song's chorus echoed in her head: "Fool, didn't you know you can't trust a woman?"

⁂ ⁂ ⁂

A scratching and hissing woke her. "Down Kwee. Off me."

Bloody monkey! But Kwee refused to relent, yanking her braids. Scratching her face. What was wrong with the crazy monkey? Was Metka driving her mad, too?"

Kwee leapt to the door then leapt back at Iwala, claws digging into Iwala's feet. *She wants me to follow her.* Iwala pulled on her sandals. Maybe Twid and Him Too had an emergency. Stubborn Him Too probably refused to clean and the guards beat him and he fought back and more guards beat him. Twid had likely tried to help and then…

She crept from wall to wall even though the likelihood of running into soldiers was slim. Metka was so immune to entry from without and escape from within that the commander didn't even post guards at night in most sections of the prison. Even if they escaped, most prisoners were so famished that they would never survive the mountains.

She looked at the path again. Where in bloody hell was Kwee going? Iwala didn't even know this corridor existed.

*Kwee, if this is some stupid chase, or you just want me to grab some banana you cannot reach yourself, so help me the Creator.*

As the corridor widened, Kwee slowed. Iwala tiptoed past, shaking for some reason unknown to herself. *Why are you shaking? Even if the guards find you, you can tell them that your monkey went crazy and led you here.*

The corridor dead-ended in some strange type of cell with two rows of prison bars, each row with its own lock. She peered into the darkness; there was a shape lying on the ground.

If this was some random prisoner, she'd have Kwee's head. As if reading her thoughts, Kwee jumped on her shoulder, then on the lock.

Iwala pulled out a needle and inserted it into the cold lock. Pulling out another narrow metal piece, she jiggled the two together, her hands shaking. The lock popped and the door creaked open.

As she fumbled with the next lock, Iwala's body convulsed, and a chill ran down her spine. *It can't be. I can't be seeing what I'm seeing. It's impossible. Kwee you crazy monkey.*

The second lock opened. On her shoulder, Kwee's claws scraped again, filling the air with the scent of blood.

Heart racing, Iwala walked to the sleeping figure. Kneeling down, she waited a long moment, then reached out with trembling hands and shook the prisoner's thin shoulder like some ancient prophet resurrecting the dead.

"Wake up, Zeru. It's me, Iwala."

# Ten

**D**irt, grime, and waste covered Twid's arms. He finished cleaning the top of the bars with a rag then rinsed the rag in a bucket. He looked at the dark water. A few more hours and it would look drinkable.

Zeru had always insisted. Start with the highest points in a room and clean downward from there. If you cleaned the floor first, when you cleaned the walls, more dirt would fall on the floors. Then you'd have to clean the floors again.

So he and Him Too had split up the cleaning. Twid would clean the top half of each wall and cell, then move on and clean the top half of the next cell. Him Too had the nastier job. He had to come behind and clean the bottom half of each cell, including the floors. But because of his height, Him Too could more easily clean the lower parts.

The time was up and they still had three cells to go. Twid ground his teeth, resisting the urge to kick the wall. To come so close, to win passage inside Metka, and yet to fall short of their goal.

He couldn't blame Iwala. They had known the risks they were taking. There was a chance that the commander wouldn't choose the old man's cell, even if it was the dirtiest cell in the entire complex. Even if it had never been cleaned, except for the ants and vermin that ate or transported waste from the room.

They heard the loud laugher of the commander behind them. "My bet is that they cleaned six cells."

He emerged from the corridor with Iwala. Iwala and the commander stood shocked as they saw seventeen cells cleaned. The commander wandered in and out of each finished cell. Iwala heard him mutter. "Gonna spoil my prisoners."

He came to where Twid and Him Too still cleaned. "So, boys, learned your lesson, did you. Won't be coming back here anytime soon?"

Twid continued to clean. Him Too approached the commander, his back straight, head held high like a king addressing a commoner. "This was great sport. I will tell the governor you have a nice summer house here."

The commander's jaw almost plunged into the bucket of excrement-filled water. Iwala stepped back, unsure she had heard right. *What are you trying to do, fools? Forget the old man. Forget your game of pride. Him Too you stubborn fool. Help me get Zeru out of here.*

Him Too continued. "See, the truth is that you can't break us or control us. You've shown us your worst cells. You've deprived us of water and food. But you cannot control us. We're stronger than Metka."

Iwala looked at Him Too as if seeing him for the first time. So that was it. After a long moment, Iwala lifted her hands in frustration. "Commander, do you see why the governor has problems with them? They are stiff-necked, haughty, unapologetic, proud. They will never submit."

She stuck out her hand. "Thank you for trying. I will tell the governor that even mighty Metka could not humble these two."

The rolls on the commander's face vanished; his face took on a chiseled, stony look. What would happen if people heard that a one-armed boy and a midget had bested Metka? What if word got back to the Dream Kings? He would be the laughingstock of the Three Lands.

He shook his head. Youth. So stubborn. So prideful. He had seen the tall one trying to stand straight. Another half hour and he would collapse, begging for mercy. Begging for water. Begging for rat stew.

He turned to Iwala. "Give me just two more hours with them."

*He has no choice but to take us to the old man's cell now. But if we stay any longer, and the sun keeps rising, it will be even more impossible to sneak Zeru out in broad daylight.*

Iwala had contemplated every possible way of getting Zeru

out of Metka. What if she started a fire and forced the commander to evacuate the prisoners? Could they sneak Zeru out in the mayhem? What if she created chaos by unlocking the prison doors? Could she somehow drug all the soldiers? Could she hide Zeru in a wheelbarrow?

None of the plans made sense. If she started a fire, the commander would force the prisoners to fight the flames, even if they died. Even if she unlocked the doors for the prisoners, most of them wouldn't move. She had no drugs or poisons with her. Zeru would never fit in a wheelbarrow and why would they give her a wheelbarrow anyway?

She couldn't think of any way to get Zeru out, so they might as well try to see the old man. She shrugged her shoulders. "I have to be fair, commander. We told the boys one day."

Seeing the commander's scowl, she said, "I'll give you one more cell. That's it. Pick your dirtiest, foulest cell, and have the boys clean it. While they clean it, I will sing a final round of songs for you and your soldiers. I have a new one I made up that you'll enjoy."

She looked at her friends. "Yes. I have a new song about a ram who lost his horns, only to get them back again in the most unexpected place."

Twid's brow furrowed. A hornless ram? Zeru had always called himself an old ram who had lost his horns. What was Iwala saying?

The commander paced the cell. Eyes crinkled, he frowned at the gleaming cell floor. He looked up and nodded. "Follow me," he said. Twid tried to ask Iwala about the ram but soldiers surrounded them the entire time.

The commander led them through long corridors and twisted passageways, sapping their energy as much as he could. They descended lower and lower until they came to a large group of soldiers surrounding a walled-off cell. The commander talked to them briefly and then let them pass. Iwala looked for the 8th Circle Defenders but didn't see any.

They entered the cell through a thick stone door. A small window in the corner allowed some of the external corridor's torchlight in, but beyond that, darkness reigned.

Twid's heart sank. There was no one inside. That is, unless you counted the mice, the roaches, the ants, and other vermin. If his stomach had anything left, he would have retched.

Two soldiers appeared with six buckets and several rags. Walking to the nearest wall, the commander smiled. The fools probably thought they could finish this last cell in an hour. He reached into the wall and scrubbed with a rag. The grime didn't move. "You might have to scrub a little bit harder to clean these walls. I do expect them spotless, though, as well as the floors."

Twid closed his eyes, wanting to scream. They had lost the gamble, again. They had cleaned the earlier cells for nothing. And now this one room alone would take twenty-four hours.

Before Twid could protest, Him Too said, "We thank you, good Master."

The commander laughed and headed for the door. They'd see how thankful they were in an hour. He paused before stepping out and pointed in the farthest, darkest corner. "Ignore him. He never moves."

Twid closed his eyes, not needing to look to know who lay in the corner. He bit his tongue to keep from smiling.

The commander closed the door behind him and left, following Iwala out.

Twid and Him scurried to opposite walls and searched the corners. No sign of the 8th Circle Defenders. The friends looked up to ensure no one hid in the ceiling.

Twid took a deep breath and approached the old man. White wisps of hair clung to a wrinkly yellow head. Thin cobwebs stretched across eyelids.

Twid squinted. Was the old man even alive? Moving closer, Twid looked through the old man's tattered cloth for the tattoo. Even in the dark, the words gleamed, radiating from the old man's right arm like hyena eyes on a moonless night. *The Five*

*Harmonies.* Next to the words, a bird soared.

Twid waved his hands at Him Too and pointed to the tattoo. Him Too nodded, eyes shining. Twid knelt close and called out. "Father."

No movement. He touched the old man's bony shoulder. "Father, wake up."

Twid watched the old man's still chest. "Father. Can you hear me? We would speak with you of the Harmonies."

Still no movement. Despair mounted in Twid's heart. After everything they had been through. The Perilous Mountains, the filthy cells, the risk of being discovered.

Twid bent low, even closer towards the old man's chest, straining his ears for any sign of breathing. He turned his head back to Him Too. "I don't think he's ali..."

An icy hand froze Twid's wrist. Bones creaked and eyelids opened like a butterfly's wings flapping for the first time, revealing yellow eyes that gleamed like firebugs. Rats hissed and insects rushed from tattered clothing. The old man's beard remained flat, frozen by time, even as he pushed himself to one elbow. He coughed with the strength of a baby, then spoke, his voice fighting past scattered teeth like bits of gravel kicked into a crumbling wall.

"Have I not suffered enough? Are they now sending fools to mock old Mogus?"

Twid tried to move his arm. *Mother of Zeru—he's strong. And his breath, it makes Metka seem a rose.* Twid said, "Father Mogus. We mock nothing. We've come far to see you, to learn from you. The Dream Kings have taught us the first two Harmonies. Live with freedom and become your dreams. But now, voices in our head speak of Five Harmonies. Of Jignas. We've asked everyone. Father, we've searched the monasteries. No one can tell us.

"Please. Answer us. Why does your tattoo say Five Harmonies? What are the Third, Fourth and Fifth Harmonies?"

The old man tightened his grip — Twid thought he meant to take the arm.

His steely whisper slashed. "Is it not written: 'Ask not for a shearer if you own no sheep? Ask not for a kettle if you have no water?'"

Mogus glared at Twid with the intensity of a Nishan Sun. "You march in here like Alula himself and you demand the Five Harmonies." Mogus's crinkled eyes sharpened. "But did you not learn what the Old Ones taught: 'Little knowledge is worse than no knowledge.'"

Twid tried to turn his head but Mogus's iron gaze bound him like steel shackles. "Think the Harmonies can save you, boy? Think the Harmonies can save any of you?" He snorted. "Fools. The Harmonies failed those one thousand times your betters."

Eyes drifting, Mogus whispered, "The Harmonies failed the likes of Minja the Majestic and Tirhas the Light, The Golden Eagle. And here you stand, boy." Mogus scowled. "Like the fools of old, you speak of freedom, yet you know nothing of freedom's price. Like the seeing blind, you glimpse freedom, but you lack the courage to embrace it. Don't try to hide, boy. I can see your heart."

What was this crazy old man talking about? Twid tried again to wrench his arm free but old Mogus gripped him like a lion's jaws. This wasn't going the way Twid had imagined.

Him Too walked closer. The old man stared at Him Too, curiosity flickering in his eyes.

"Begone. Leave me now. Ask not for the Fifth Harmony when ye know not the First."

Him Too extended his small staff until he almost touched the old man. The old man stared at the staff as if he knew it. On the ground, Him Too drew a point. "The power of the First Harmony is like a point. Just the beginning."

He extended the point until it became a line. "The power of the Second Harmony expands into a line, with infinite points." Him Too expanded the line into a square. "The power of the Third Harmony is unto a square, with infinite lines."

Him Too stepped back. "Father…"

They heard a click above them, and three shadows dropped. A sharp voice called out, "Funny. I thought you were here to clean, not teach shapes."

As the three shadows materialized, Twid's stomach spun like live eels. The three 8th Circle Defenders. They had dropped through a hidden trap door. And each held a sword in attack stance.

So this was how it would end. Him Too and Twid had known the risks when they started, known that they could be killed. But Twid had never thought it would actually happen.

If he had a sword, and was facing only one defender, maybe he would have a small chance. But against three, with no weapons, and little energy left after cleaning without rest or sustenance.

The tallest of the Defenders raised his sword. "Tell us who sent you. Was it Zinna? Did she really think we'd let you in here, unguarded."

"Tell us or we'll just torture your other friend and get it out of her."

Him Too and Twid stared, unable to answer. Behind them, they heard a noise. Teetering, the old man crawled forward until he faced the defenders.

"Stand back, old man."

Mogus fell. Reaching over, he grabbed Him Too's staff and leaned on it.

Mogus pointed the staff at the nearest defender, just a sword's length away. "Ye would attack an old man and two children. All hail the freedom and dreams of the Dream Kings."

Mogus twisted the bottom of the staff. Twid heard a sharp sound; a long blade emerged from the tip of Him Too's staff. Twid would never forget what he saw next.

Mogus lunged at the three Defenders with the staff turned spear. Before the Defenders could act, one was dead, blade through his throat. The other two defenders fell back, stunned. Then they attacked, one from behind, one from the front.

But the old man darted between them like a hummingbird

evading elephants. Mogus countered each attack and somehow managed to press both Defenders. Leaping up, he kicked one Defender in the throat and stabbed his chest. But as Mogus landed, the other Defender stabbed Mogus's back. Mogus fell. As the final Defender approached to finish him, Mogus hurled the staff's blade into the Defender's throat.

Twid and Him Too rushed to Mogus. His face strained, he whispered, "Trust not in the Harmonies. But if trust you must, seek the Source of Harmony in Himlee. Find your answers there you shall."

Mogus let out a faint cough. His chest raised and fell like a butterfly's final fluttering and did not move again.

Him Too and Twid stared at each other. It was maddening. One second the old man had ridiculed them, the next he had saved them. He had told them to seek the Harmonies yet had warned that the Harmonies would betray them.

Not knowing what to say, the two friends dragged the Three Defenders to the darkest corner, where Mogus first lay. They then lifted Mogus and positioned him in front of the three bodies. They stood at the door and surveyed the corner. If someone looked hard, they could see the bodies, but given how dark the corner was, and that the old man never moved, it might work. It had to work, at least for a few hours.

They banged on the door until soldiers came. Now was the moment of truth. If the soldiers knew that the Defenders had gone inside, it was over. The soldiers opened the door.

Twid bawled, real tears streaming down his cheeks. "We give up. We give up. We submit. Get us out of here. Please. Take us up. We can't clean this cell. We'll be here for weeks."

The soldier laughed. This was what happened to those who challenged Metka. He led them up. Him Too and Twid still sniffled. They smelled of excrement.

The soldier led them to the common room where Iwala was playing her wata. Twid screamed. "Iwala. We submit. Get us out of here."

Him Too stumbled to the commander, "We can't spend another moment in this cesshole. You win, commander. Metka wins."

The commander slapped his hands together and smiled. "Couldn't maintain your bravado anymore, aye. Once you saw how long that cell would take, you gave up."

Iwala approached the commander. "I will compose a new song of how Metka humbled Ras' proudest and most insolent."

Wrinkling her nose, she looked the two boys over. "My only request, commander: Please bathe them and lend them some new clothing. I cannot travel with such filth."

Twid and Him Too gritted their teeth at the delay. *Forget the bath fool! If they find those bodies, we're all dead!*

But the commander had already motioned and two soldiers left to prepare basins. Him Too and Twid bathed in an adjacent room.

When they came out, they saw the commander leading a small donkey. Iwala was emptying out some gold pieces. "So there's five hundred birr for your training of the boys. You will get the other five hundred from the governor in one half year if the boys are still repentant."

"Now here is a hundred more birr for the small donkey to carry the large bag of supplies I took from your store rooms."

The commander motioned for his two soldiers to lift the bag up, but Iwala waved her hands. "No. I plan on punishing these two all the way home." She motioned for Him Too and Twid to lift the sack of supplies onto the donkey.

"Commander, soldiers, I have one more thing to show you." She walked a few feet away; the soldiers and commander followed her.

As Twid and Him Too walked to the bag, both thought back to Iwala's comment about the hornless ram. *This cannot be. You crazy woman. This cannot be.* Him Too lifted from the bottom while Twid lifted from the top, using his good arm for gripping and his bad arm for support. *Oh my Creator!* He almost forgot the old man and the defenders.

The gate grated open. The commander escorted them out with Him Too leading the donkey down. A soldier held out several bowls of steaming stew. Him Too and Twid snatched the bowls. As the stew slithered down their throats, the greasy liquid felt like raw eggs but tasted hot and salty like oversmoked venison. The friends handed the bowls back and looked at each other. The commander was right.

Rat wasn't so bad after all.

# Eleven

One could have mistaken the cave for the maw of some gigantic creature. Man-sized stalactites jutted from the ceiling like gigantic fangs, emitting an emerald bluish color. Jagged rocks poked in and out of the ground.

In the middle, before a small fire, the three friends hunched over Zeru's body. His once salt-and-pepper stubble was now mostly salt. He had lost two more teeth on the right side of his mouth. Burn marks lined his arms.

The journey down the Perilous Mountains had almost killed them all. Twid had developed a fever, and Him Too suffered from dehydration.

But they had had no time to rest, no choice. A few hours, maybe a half day, and the prison would miss Zeru. Even if Metka's guards somehow failed to miss Zeru, the smell of the rotting bodies would overwhelm the already heinous stench in the old man's cells. The three Defenders would be discovered, and the hunt would begin.

They had started down the Perilous Mountains as if heading east, back toward Lemlem, Adwa, and the governor. But as soon as they had passed from sight, they had doubled back, and headed west toward Nisha.

Whatever they fed Zeru, he had vomited. Whatever he drank, he had retched. Worst of all, he had regained consciousness only for short spells, babbling incoherently while they tried to feed him.

Once it had started to rain, Twid had convinced them that they needed to hide out for a few days, to avoid pursuers and to give Zeru a chance to recover. After everything, how could they let Zeru die now?

That had been two days ago.

Twid looked at his friends. "I'm telling you, he has tikh-tikhkha. If we don't get him some *hiwot* root, he will die."

Iwala replied. "And I told you for the fifth time: the only place we can get the root is in Lemlem. You won't find it on this mountain; they have to bring it in from Wirba."

That was where the conversation had broken down. They had decided that Him Too absolutely couldn't go back to Lemlem.

Him Too had complained at first. "Just because I'm small doesn't mean I can't keep up with you two buffoons." But in the end, he had agreed that he would draw the most attention due to his size and red hair.

But neither Iwala nor Twid would let the other go.

"Twid, they're going to be looking for a one-armed young man – how many of those do you think there are in Lemlem?"

"I don't care, Iwala. I'm going. I will get the root and return."

"Listen. No one blames you for what happened to Zeru. And if you get sent to Metka, I can't rescue you this time. You'll be stuck forever," Iwala countered.

"What am I talking about? Forget being sent to Metka. They will kill you if they find you in Lemlem. They will torture you, kill you. Trust me. The last month has been rough, but you still haven't seen everything I've seen. Zeru himself would tell you if he was well. You and Him Too are still like newborn lambs."

Taking in Twid's scowl, Iwala raised her hand. "No one is saying you wouldn't know a wolf from your mother. All I'm saying is that there are more than wolves out there. Let me handle it. I will slide in and out."

Twid waved her off. "They will be looking for you, too. And don't worry about how much I've seen. I've seen more than you know." Twid stood and grabbed his pack. "By my mother, Nigiste, I'm going. Take care of Zeru."

Him Too and Iwala stopped and even the unconscious Zeru seemed to shift on the ground. In all the years they had known him, Twid had never brought up his mother's name, never even indicated he knew her name. Never had he spoken of his life before the orphanage, never had he shared how he had lost his arm, or what had happened to him and his family.

Iwala's eyes tightened. There was something else. Making sure Twid did not see him, Him Too arched his eyes at Iwala. *Let him go. You can't stop him. There's something he's not telling us.*

※ ※ ※

Wearing a long cloak that covered his arm, hand and stump, Twid walked east until he found the main road. He joined the steady caravan of people traveling to Lemlem's Friday market.

A woman walked with a wooden bucket full of tef grain. She carried an umbrella to protect the baby on her back from the scorching sun. A farmer and his two boys rumbled past on a cart stacked high with corn and tomatoes. A herder drove a dozen sheep.

Twid doubted that Lemlem's guards could spot him amidst so many people. Still, as he approached the gates, Twid slipped his left arm even further under the cloak, just in case the gate-keepers were on the lookout for a one-armed man.

Forcing himself to look straight ahead, Twid walked through the gates.

Twid had entered Lemlem using the opposite gate from last time, but he thought he could remember. He kept his eyes open, reading the signs for every eatery and tavern they passed.

Iwala had thought Twid mad. And maybe he was mad. But the old man had challenged him. He could still hear the words ringing in his ears: "Like the fools of old, you speak of freedom, yet you know nothing of freedom's pain."

Well, if Twid didn't know, he was about to find out.

As he walked, Twid took in Lemlem's sights. A fruit merchant waved his hands, offering passersby tomatoes the size of mangos. A street apothecary proclaimed a root that could cure sadness itself. A veiled Dream Teller sat atop a stool, a line of people waiting to hear how they could live with Freedom and Dreams.

Twid kept walking. The Dream Kings lived and breathed freedom; freedom to everyone, all the time; to have anything, to do anything, to be anything. But the old man had mocked him. The words rang in his head: "Like the seeing blind, you glimpse freedom, but you lack the courage to embrace it."

Twid adjusted his pack. They had risked their lives to talk with the old man. They had cleaned filth, waste, excrement, and even eaten rat to talk to him. How could they then ignore what he had said?

Stepping into an apothecary, he found the *hiwot* root and purchased it using a bag of coins Iwala had tossed at him.

What would Zeru say when he awoke? Would he thank them? Twid laughed aloud. Small chance. *"Can you thank a thief for returning your goats? If it wasn't for you fools, I wouldn't be in this mess. I'm just surprised that you managed to rescue me."*

No, there would be no great thanks from Old Zeru.

Twid stopped. A cart swerved to avoid him and a man cursed. But Twid ignored the man. He had found it. The Three Wrists. As he approached, he noticed the well-maintained exterior walls and the lively music emanating.

He paused under the wooden sign. He didn't have to enter. He could walk back; Iwala and Him Too would leap for joy at seeing him return so quickly with the *hiwot* root.

*"You glimpse freedom, but you lack the courage to embrace it."* The old man's words rang in Twid's ears. He walked inside.

Huge barrels of ale dominated the center of the room. Tables kept guard around the perimeter, crowding every inch of wall space. The low hum of conversation combined with the crackling of the fire to create a welcoming buzz.

Twid chose a table in the darkest corner, away from the other guests. A red-haired waitress bounced over and he ordered honey ale. He drank four tankards. As he ordered the fifth tankard, he asked the waitress. "So, does the owner really have three wrists?"

The girl laughed. "Of course she does. How else could we call it The Three Wrists?"

Twid tried to laugh along with her. "She's not here, is she? I'd like to ask her a question." He threw a coin on the table for the girl. The girl snatched the coin. Twid almost hoped the owner was not there.

Moments later, a tall, thin woman wearing a stained apron brought him his drink. She carried the drink in her left arm. Twid looked at her right arm to see if she had a stump or some sort of third wrist.

"I think you're looking for this." She put her left arm before his face. He stared. She had no hand. He looked closer and jumped. It was true. Her left arm started at the elbow like any other arm. About two-thirds of the way down, the arm separated into two narrow shafts, like a two-pronged pitchfork. She nestled the tankard's handle between the two shafts. The shafts both ended right before her hand would have started.

"Maybe the best thing that ever happened to me. People come from all over to see it and eat and drink in my tavern."

Iwala had spoken the truth. "What can you do with the shafts?"

"It's not the same as a hand if that's what you're thinking. But I can still lift things and carry things if I get the right position." She enunciated her point by lifting the tankard again with her two shafts.

He had to ask her one more question. Just one more. Twid pulled his arm out of his tunic. When she saw the stump at the end of his arm, she sat down. They talked for several minutes. Then she grabbed the now-empty tankard and returned to work.

The ale burned in Twid's stomach and Twid felt his head dizzy. He drank another tankard. He was going to need all the alcohol he could get. *Like the fools of old, you speak of freedom, yet you know nothing of freedom's pain.*

His whole life, he'd made small excuses about his stump. Not to others, but to himself, in his own head. If he didn't have the stump, he would have been a better fighter. He could have done his chores faster. He could have been stronger, faster. Better.

Somehow, the old man had known. Read his mind and challenged him. What was freedom, if not the freedom to create new possibilities? What was freedom, if not the freedom to choose? Even actions that hurt, that devastated. JIGNA. THE FIVE HARMONIES. JIGNA. The voices in his head raged like rabid dogs in a cage.

Twid threw several coins on the table and rose. He walked out without looking back. A half-mile down on the left, the woman had told him.

"Your forearm has two thin bones that run next to each other," she had said. Twid felt his arm as he walked, trying to feel the two bones.

"When I lost my hand, the doctor cut down the middle of my arm, and separated my arm into two. Then he burned the wounds so I wouldn't bleed to death. Thanks to him, I can use my arm at least a little bit now."

If Iwala and Him Too were here, they would never let him do it. The risks were too great. That's why he had come alone. He saw the small, dimly-lit blue home, just as the woman had said. He knocked. An elderly man answered.

※ ※ ※

Him Too and Iwala finished packing their meager supplies. It was the fourth day. Twid had made them promise to not come after him until the fifth, but he could be dead by now. And Zeru still lay in the grip of death. They had to do something.

As they stepped out of the cave, they heard a noise. They paused and stepped back into the darkness. A phantom materialized. It wobbled left and right like a sapling caught in a windstorm. The warm scent of blood cut the cave's static air.

The phantom tossed a small pouch. Then it lifted its other arm. The friends stepped back.

Bandaged shafts protruded like a two-pronged pitchfork.

# Twelve

The week after they left the cave, the companions traveled only at night, heading west out of the Perilous Mountains. Once they made it past the surrounding hills and into the neighboring flatlands, they walked by day.

True to form, Zeru hemmed and hawed at first, cursing them a dozen different ways when he regained consciousness. "What do you mean we can't go back to Adwa? You fools! I knew you'd ruin me in the end."

It was good to have old Zeru back.

Him Too still couldn't believe everything that had happened. Crazy Twid cutting up his arm. The old man killing three 8th Circle Defenders. Finding Zeru in Metka. *What is the world coming to? I never thought I'd see a time when Iwala was the most clearheaded one.*

Him Too reached to his brow and wiped sweat from his eyes. His skin had already turned olive. Another three weeks in the sun and he would be as dark as Twid.

Zeru was telling the three of them another story. "So none of you have heard the story of Ato Wir's lackwit son?

"A hundred and fifty years ago, Ato Wir governed the northern land of Wirba. A vicious man, he used to roast his enemies alive in the public square."

The friends nodded. Everyone had heard of Wir the Scorcher.

"Wir hired a special instructor to teach his son numbers and letters. The instructor worked with the son night and day for two years but couldn't make any progress. After two years, Wir sent a messenger to the instructor, asking him to report on the progress that his son had made."

Zeru waved his hands. "The instructor tossed and turned in his bed the entire night. If he told Wir that his son was a dimwit, Wir would roast him alive; if he told Wir that he hadn't instructed the boy well enough, Wir would roast him alive.

"The next day, the poor instructor knelt at Wir's palace, shaking. Wir sat on his iron throne. The instructor tried to explain. 'Ato Wir. I don't know how to say this, but your son may not have inherited your intelligence. I have not been able to make progress.'

"At this, Wir shook with rage and flames crackled in his eyes. The poor instructor hurried on, his voice quivering. 'If you would only bring the boy before us, I could show you what I mean.'"

As the friends walked, they saw tall trees ahead. They were almost to The Hungry Forest! Once they entered, it'd be impossible for the soldiers to find them.

Zeru continued. "King Wir summoned his son and had him stand before the two of them. The instructor turned to the boy and said, 'Son, your father, King Wir, is in another room, somewhere in the palace; find him and come tell us where he is.'

"The son left immediately and searched and searched and searched. He returned about four hours later, exhausted, and announced to the instructor and King Wir. 'I have searched all the other rooms and couldn't find the king,' he moaned.

"Before the instructor could say anything, the father, King Wir leapt from his throne and struck his son. 'You son of a woman! Go search the rest of the palace. Do not come back until you have found him!'"

The three friends roared with laughter. They might be good herders, but the Wirbas weren't known for their intelligence.

As they entered the old forest, Iwala added one of Zeru's favorite sayings. "Have not the Old Ones said: 'Lacking wisdom is worse than lacking eyesight?'"

Zeru nodded. "Yes, indeed. Don't you have any stories, girl? Surely you learned something other than thievery on your wanderings."

Iwala pushed a branch away from her face. "How about Him Too? I miss the old Him Too stories that didn't make sense, or tried to be funny but weren't."

Him Too poked Iwala's leg with his staff. "Well, I do have a story, come to think of it. Since we're in the Hungry Forest, let me tell you a story about a hungry traveler."

"Is this story about us?" Twid asked, as his stomach rumbled.

"Maybe it is," said Him Too.

"A weary traveler arrived at a town and he inquired about where he could find lodging. The townspeople told him, 'There are two places you can go. The first place, you'll receive no food, you'll have to sleep on the floor, and you'll have no company. The second place, you'll eat a sumptuous feast, sleep on the finest bedding, and enjoy great dinner conversation. The only problem with the second place is that the father will beat you from head to toe in the morning with a massive cudgel.'"

"I'd stay at the second house and sneak out early morning," said Iwala.

Him Too continued. "Of course you would. But our poor traveler happened to be honest. Anyway, our traveler thought it over and finally decided that he was too hungry. He'd have to accept the beating. So he went to the second house and knocked on the door. Just like the townspeople had said, he was welcomed with great gusto. He enjoyed a three-course meal with honey wine, and he ate seconds and even thirds. After dinner, he laughed and told stories with the family for hours. When it was time to go to bed, he crawled into goose-feather blankets and slept like a child. As he awoke, he told himself, 'I don't care what happens now! It was worth it.'"

"He crept out of bed and had breakfast with the family. After breakfast, he sat in his chair, waiting for the father to beat him. But the father did nothing. So he rose to leave. On the way out, he inquired of the father. 'Father, I've never enjoyed such hospitality as this. Thank you. My only question is, aren't you going to beat me before I leave?'"

"The father went to the corner and grabbed an enormous club. He waved it at the traveler and said, 'This club is for those who when asked to eat, pretend they're not hungry; who when asked to talk, ask questions about my daughter; who when asked to go to bed, keep us up all night.'

"The father smiled at him and said, 'But you? We asked you to eat and you ate; we asked you to tell stories with us and you told stories; we asked you to go to bed and you did so immediately. For what would we beat you?'"

Iwala smiled and slapped Him Too on the back. "So you're saying that you would have gotten beat but neither Twid nor I would have?"

The companions laughed. But then Him Too stopped walking. He motioned for them to quiet. Hearts pounding, they strained their ears, making out a faint voice. They crept forward, tip-toeing over leaves, taking care not to snap branches. The light breeze carried the tantalizing smell of meat roasting. Iwala winked. Maybe they could feast like the traveler from Him Too's story.

As they stepped closer they heard a melodious voice. Twid preened his ears.

"If you cut a man's leg off then give him a crutch, can you claim to have helped him walk? If you steal his home and then let him lodge in the stables, can you be called generous? Brothers, we risk being the dog that barked after the thief left. Sisters, 'tis time to open both our eyes and ears, or we will bury not just ourselves but truth itself."

The companions stepped behind a scraggly shrub and peered through its branches. About fifty people, mostly men, stood in rapt attention. Each carried multiple weapons. A deer roasted above crackling flames. The friends crept closer until they saw the speaker.

Her midnight skin glowed like black oil in the noon sun. Her bald head and bald eyebrows accentuated her bold cheekbones, giving her a sculpted look. Clad from top to bottom in forest green, she enunciated her points with explosive gestures that somehow maintained the grace of a viper.

A wild glint appeared in Twid's eyes. Raw, unbidden images exploded in his head; fire and smoke burned. He found himself unable to breath. It was her!

Iwala leaned forward. But then something bowled Iwala over, into the clearing. Iwala was about to curse when she saw Twid exploding forward. Twid jumped to the stage before anyone could stop him. He slammed his sword into the ground before the dark-skinned woman and motioned, demanding that she lift it.

Then Twid pulled his other sword, the one from the tree and attacked the woman. Iwala, Zeru, and Him Too watched, frozen with the helpless shock of a family seeing their home burn. Kwee howled and dug her claws into Iwala's shoulder.

Right before Twid's blade reached her, the woman shifted her stance and avoided it. Twid swung again. Zeru leapt forward. But several men in the audience pounced on him and kept him from the stage. Iwala couldn't understand why no one in the audience leapt to help the woman.

She continued as if neither Twid nor Zeru existed. "Brothers, Sisters. The enemy poisons our minds. Brother attacks sister. Sister attacks sister. And yet, our common enemy prospers."

Twid swung again at the woman's head. Again, she side-stepped him. He fell again. This time the woman placed her foot on him, trapping him against the ground.

"Stranger, why do you attack me?"

Twid leapt up and attacked the woman again. Again, the woman sidestepped him as if he were a fluttering leaf. The crowd laughed.

Twid spat at the woman. "Twelve years ago, you and a group of soldiers dressed like you attacked my family." Tears coursed down his face. "You murdered my mother and my sister. You cut off my left hand." He held up his bandaged arm.

Him Too dropped his staff. Iwala covered her mouth, goose bumps rising along her arms. Zeru stopped struggling.

The woman stepped back. She looked at the crowd. "Do you see why the enemy is impossible to defeat? Betrayals within betrayals, lies within lies."

She turned to Twid. "Boy. This I swear to you by my father Abraha The Bold, who was the son of Zedengel The Fierce, who was the son of Woldegiorgis The Kind, known among men as the Lion's Lion, and the Eagle's Eagle. This I, Zinna, First Defender swear by everything I hold true. I never harmed you or your family."

Twid's sword dropped from numb hands. There was no point.

She was Zinna. The First Prince Defender. Zinna. So skilled at defense she needed no offense. Zinna. The Betrayer of Dreams.

He was dead.

# Thirteen

The scent of burning deer wafted over the clearing. But no one moved to turn the deer. No one moved to do anything. A tall man boomed from the front, "We believe you Zinna. But we want to hear the boy's story."

Iwala and Him Too shuffled forward until they stood next to Zeru. Iwala heard Zeru mutter something about never hiding with children.

Twid steadied his quivering mouth. "I'm nothing compared to a Prince Defender. She can kill me if she likes. But I'll still call her a liar. It was her. I remember her skin, her face. I'll never forget."

He breathed deeply. "My family lived in a small village called Hidmo outside Adwa. I lived there with my mother and sister. We were simple farmers. We meant no one harm."

"One night our dog barked louder than usual. We heard a muted sound and then nothing. My mother told me to stay inside but I ran outside. I disobeyed. My mother and sister followed me."

Twid stopped. He had never given it voice, never said it aloud. He felt a giant stone over his mouth. It would have been easier to spit out a mountain. He tried again but couldn't push the words out. He tried again, his mind shrieking as the words escaped.

"I saw a mass of soldiers dressed exactly like you." He pointed at Zinna. "You cut my mother's head right off her neck. You slaughtered everyone in my village. Your soldier chopped my arm and left me to bleed to death."

He looked at her again. "You can kill me. You can chop my other arm off if you like. But I won't let you lie in front of these people. I saw you do it." He spat at the ground before her and then braced himself for her attack.

Zinna closed her eyes, reopening them after what seemed like an hour. The crowd shifted. A few wiped tears.

Iwala exhaled. It finally made sense …why Twid was so deferential to authority, always trying to please Zeru, always trying to please the village elders. In Twid's eyes, his mother and sister had died because he had disobeyed his mother.

Zinna spoke, "Boy. As all can see, you attacked me and I could have easily killed you, had I so desired. Listen then, and learn the truth."

She turned to the crowd. "As all of you know, I come from northern Ras, from the village of Massawa. I entered the Prince Defender Games at age fourteen, and to this day am the youngest to ever win the games. I served the Dream Kings faithfully for years and helped train and develop Delgam and Tah after the second and third Prince Defender Games."

"As a Prince Defender, it was my duty to ensure that Freedom and Dreams ruled the Three Lands and to serve and protect the Dream Kings, who as you know are Nin of Nisha, Ran of Ras, and Wirla of Wirba. We had many enemies, of which the Seekers were chief."

At this, several in the crowd grunted, a few stamping the ground with their staffs. A short man turned the deer.

"For fifteen years, I served the Dream Kings faithfully and was admired throughout the land. But my life changed one morning when I overheard King Wirla of Wirba talking with a group of his leading bureaucrats. They spoke in a secret chamber that I happened upon only because I was exploring a nearby corridor and could see them through a crack in the wall. I was about to call out but some sixth sense prevented me, perhaps the instinct for defense for which I am reputed.

"What I heard next shocked me. The men were discussing a crop that they had discovered and were developing. A white grain that would destroy men's stomachs, even as they craved it. The only desire that King Wirla and the men had was to profit from the crop."

Iwala put a hand to her mouth. *Raf.* Zinna was talking about the Dream Kings' new grain!

Zinna continued. "Horrified, I went immediately to Ran, the Dream King from my homeland of Ras, and told him of what I had heard and seen. He listened to me with a grave face; asking many questions, completely bewildered and dismayed. He asked me to speak to no one for my own safety and to hasten to the throne room at dusk, where we would confront Wirla.

"Heartened by his words, I arrived at the throne room at dusk. I saw all three Dream Kings there, as well as Tah, Delgam, and the honor guard of two hundred soldiers.

"Ran bade me approach the throne room, and I advanced and bowed before the three kings, certain that I would be asked to testify against Wirla. But when I raised my head, I saw a hundred arrows pointing at me. Delgam had his hammer positioned to smite me, and Tah had her swords drawn. I looked upon Ran's eyes and saw that I had been betrayed.

"Ran spoke then and said, 'At dawn today, Zinna counseled me, speaking of the glory of Ras, of Menelik the Mighty and Alula the Unconquerable, of how we could restore the glory of Ras. Zinna vowed to eliminate Wirla and Nin and make me the sole Dream King. I told Zinna to meet me here tonight to discuss further. The traitor has returned here, so brazen she would discuss treason in the throne room.'

"I could say or do nothing. I might have taken Tah or Delgam alone, but never together and never with one hundred soldiers pointing their arrows at my head. I was doomed.

"Not wanting to shed my blood in the throne room, they led me out, to behead me in the Hall of Traitors. Weaponless, head down, I marched, surrounded by the guards and Tah. Delgam had an unshakable grip around my throat. With just a squeeze, he could have crushed my windpipe.

"But they forgot what the Old Ones taught, 'Beware the hyena that limps, for he shall rush upon thee like a lion.' Having no choice, I showed no resistance, letting them believe I was defeated. When we entered the corridor leading to The Hall of Traitors I knew I had to act or forfeit my life. I let my body fall limp, until Delgam had to bear the entire burden of my weight on his fingers. I knew even he, with his great strength, would have to shift his arm to realign his grip and in that moment, I reached up and snapped his thumb, breaking it.

"The close quarters aided me. Soldiers stabbed soldiers; Tah stabbed Delgam's leg. I snatched two daggers from the soldiers nearest me and hurled them at the two torches illuminating the passageways. In the darkness and chaos that followed, I climbed up against the corridor wall until I was near the ceiling. I crept back the way we had come. Passing the last soldier, I smote him upon his head and quickly donned his garb. I raced up the corridor and thought I had escaped, but at the end, I found twenty soldiers waiting with their arrows pointed at me. Behind me I heard Delgam's crashing footsteps. All was lost.

"But have not the Old Ones said, 'The desperate man marries a woman with ten children and then raises the offspring of other men?' In my desperation, I leapt into the option that was no option. The Tunnel of Doom was located next to the corridor and I leapt in. Everyone who had entered had become blind, and most were maimed. No one had ever escaped. But I leapt in.

"Immediately, I was consumed by the most hideous smell and felt a burning liquid scald my skin. I closed my eyes to protect them and finally I landed on the other side, where the tunnel emptied, almost breaking my legs. I remembered that when it rained a pool of water gathered not far from the other side of the tunnel. With my eyes still closed, I felt my way to the water, knowing the others would be upon me in moments. I bathed myself as quickly as I could.

"Finally, not knowing if I would go blind, I opened my eyes. When I looked at my skin, it had turned midnight black as you can see and my hair had fallen out, never to return. I left the pool and escaped the palace through secret passageways that my years of service had revealed. The Old Ones have said, 'The enemy of the lion is the friend of the antelope.' So I searched out the Seekers.

"The Dream Kings were incensed when they heard that I had joined the Seekers and was spreading stories of dissension about the Dream Kings. To defame me, and to counter the truth, they dyed Tah's body black, shaved her head, and sent her around the countryside with a group of soldiers dressed in green, killing and maiming all they found."

Zinna turned back to Twid. "Friend. I say to you again. 'Twas not me, but the Dream Kings who killed your family and maimed your arm. If vengeance is what you seek, I advise you to find Tah, though if you do, I fear she will kill you easily.

"Besides." Zinna raised her staff. Whipping it with incredible fury, she stopped just an eyelash short of his nose. "Everyone knows that Zinna kills with the staff, not the sword."

The crowd tensed. Twid closed his eyes, sure of his doom.

A woman from the crowd called out. "The tinker told me that a one-armed boy, a midget, and a woman infiltrated Metka, murdered an old man, and fled. 'Tis you, isn't it?"

The crowd appraised the four companions again and several others in the crowd called out. "He killed an old man, and now he attacked a woman, unprovoked."

Zeru raised his hands and implored, "Wait, friends. Remember what the Old Ones said, "That which you do in haste can take a lifetime to…"

But the crowd's mutterings drowned Zeru out. A throng of men surrounded Him Too, Zeru and Iwala, shoving them back and forth. Iwala ducked under a fist.

Pushing Zinna's staff from his face, Twid took a deep breath and shouted with all his strength. "'TIS TRUE! WE WERE IN THE ROOM WHEN THE OLD MAN DIED." The crowd paused, and Twid lowered his voice. "But we did not kill him."

If Zinna hadn't just finished telling her own wild story, if Twid would have had more time to think, Twid might have

lied. But Twid took in the angry eyes and before he knew it, the
words rushed from him. He told them of the fox and the tree, of
Him Too's near death, and the voices they both heard. He told
them of how they had fled, of the library in Lemlem and their
trip to Metka, of rescuing Zeru, of the filth and grime they had
cleaned, of the old man's supernatural fighting skills and his
strange words.

As he spoke, the crowd's eyes oscillated between disbelief and
wonder. Zinna's eyes narrowed.

Twid pulled up the sleeve covering his bandaged arm. It was
time. The old healer had told him four weeks would be enough.

"We went to Mogus to learn the Third, Fourth, and Fifth
Harmonies, but he mocked our understanding of the first."
Twid continued speaking as he undid the bandages, telling
them of his trip back to Lemlem, to the Three Wrists, and finally
to the healer. "What is freedom? Is it, the happy, inspiring feeling that comes from the belief that we are 'free?' Is freedom the
option to choose from an increasing selection of wares? 'Not
so,' Mogus said. 'Freedom is a terrifying double-edge sword.
Freedom is infinite possibilities, if we have the courage to create
them.'"

Twid reached into his pack and pulled out a wooden carving,
designed to fit smoothly over the two prongs on his left arm. "I
was free to look at my arm as a weakness. I was also free to cut
my arm, and to forge it into a powerful weapon, however painful the process."

Twid slipped the carving over his two prongs, and then
slipped a strap over his shoulder to secure the appendage in
place. He twisted the left prong. A half-foot blade sprung out.
He twisted the right prong. A leather cord sprang out. It unrolled into a whip.

Twid turned to the woman in the crowd who had accused
him. "Yes. The old man is dead. But his question is alive."
He shifted into attack stance, wielding sword, dagger and whip.
"Are we free?"

Looking at Twid as if seeing him for the first time, Zinna broke the silence. "Truly the Old Ones have wisdom, for have they not said, 'Not everyone who smiles is a friend, nor everyone who frowns an enemy?'"

Iwala's brow furrowed. Zinna had more old sayings than Zeru and Mother Scale combined.

"Boy, what do you know of the Seekers other than that we murdered your family?" Zinna asked.

Twid shifted. "Only what all in the Three Lands know. That you're murderers. That you've always hated the Dream Kings and the Three Lands. That you don't believe in any Harmonies."

Zinna nodded. "The Dream Kings have done their job well. What they didn't tell you is the reason they hate us. Do you think they hate us because we oppose 'freedom' and 'dreams'?"

Twid didn't answer. Zinna continued. "Two hundred years ago, the Great Harmony Wars ravaged the Three Lands. During those wars, the chief defenders of the Three Lands were Jignas — master warriors who used the power of the Five Harmonies, yes five, in ways unimaginable to any of us. Yet somehow, even the Jignas were betrayed, and decimated, until only a few remained. But those who remained were the greatest of the Jignas. Tirhas the Golden Eagle, creator of the Map of Legends, was their leader, and they did dwell in the tree you discovered."

"Somehow — some say by betrayal — even the Five Jignas of Adwa were destroyed. Those who called themselves the Dream Kings ushered in a new era, teaching two Harmonies instead of five, blaming the war on the Jignas and the latter Harmonies. The Dream Kings squelched all opposition through terror; they massacred children, women, anyone. They even wiped out an entire people, the red-haired folk known as the Twelve Villages." Zinna glanced at Him Too.

"But the Old Ones taught, 'Even the finest sieve cannot strain truth.'" Zinna stamped her staff. Her voice lowered to a whisper. "Yes. The Old Ones taught, 'The rod of truth might bend it but it will never break.'"

"And so it was that the most unlikely of heroes, the thief named Hibu the Sly, did sneak past the Dream Guard, to the legendary Mirror of Life and beheld many things past and many things to come and yet one thing above all: A prophecy that the Harmonies would return, that the Jignas would return, that the Golden Eagle herself would return and restore a new age of Harmony to the Three Lands.

JIGNA. THE FIVE HARMONIES. JIGNA. The voices boomed in Him Too's head.

"After he emerged from the Mirror, Hibu fled to the deserts of Nisha, and with a few followers, he organized the Seekers. Though Hibu has long since died, he left us the prophetic lines he read on the Great Mirror, and now all who join us are initiated with them." Zinna expanded her hands, as if she could summon Hibu and The Golden Eagle herself. The crowd joined her as she chanted:

> Lost and forgotten, the Harmonies will falter,
> Sacrificed in secret upon power's altar.
>
> Freedom will smite freedom, schemes hide schemes,
> Deceit harbor deceit, dreams halt dreams.
>
> Invisible not extinct, silenced not dead,
> The Harmonies yet await in heart and head.
>
> The red fox will point, the Eagle soar
> The Seekers restore the Jigna lore.

JIGNA. The words exploded in Twid's heads. JIGNA. THE FIVE HARMONIES. JIGNA.

Zinna stamped her staff. "Boy, the fox has pointed. Join us. It's time to find the Golden Eagle."

# Fourteen

The four companions sat near the stage as the crowd dissipated; some walking to the deer, others congregating in small groups.

Back near the stage, Him Too broke the silence, "So we're supposed to believe that all the Ald Nald Houses the Dream Kings have built, the grain the Dream Kings have given away, the Dream Mansions, the Prince Defender Games—that EVERYTHING is a lie?"

Iwala picked through Kwee's dark hair until she caught a louse between her thumbnails. Iwala snapped her thumbs and the louse crunched. "Even when we were attacked at the stables by the Dream King soldiers, I thought it was just a misunderstanding. Just an accident."

Iwala shook her head. "But now Zinna is saying it wasn't. Good is bad and bad is good. The Dream Kings are evil, the Seekers good."

Iwala found another louse but instead of crunching it, flicked it in the air. She looked at Twid. Twid looked the most stunned of the four, and why not. He had always been the most trusting of the group, the most likely to respect authority. And now, he had learned that the same Dream Kings who had provided him with an orphanage had murdered his family.

Zeru frowned at Iwala. "You yourself have said that the best lies are nine out of ten parts truth. And now you talk like a simpleton." He closed his eyes. "No one is all good or all bad. Not me. Not you. Not Zinna. Not the Dream Kings. And every story can be told a hundred ways."

Him Too asked, "Are you saying that Zinna is lying?"

But before Zeru could answer, Zinna appeared. Accentuated by her black skin, the whites in her eyes glowed. She stood next to them then sat in one fluid motion, a lioness descending.

"Where do you go next?"

Zeru said, "We follow Mogus's counsel from Metka. We go to Himlee, the Source of Harmony."

"Do you know where Himlee lies?" Zinna asked. They shook their heads. "Himlee is ancient Giiz for the innermost palace of the Dream Kings, in Dream City. A place so protected that even I as a Prince Defender beheld it only thrice."

Zinna gripped her staff so tight her black knuckles turned white. "I promise you. As surely as a rabbit retreats to her hole, retreat to your death you will if you seek Himlee."

She paused, weighing her words. "But have the Old Ones not said, 'Two is like one, and one is like none?' Not by accident have we met and perhaps we are meant to aid each other."

Zinna looked at Twid. "Boy, try me once more. You may use the whip and blade on your left hand." Twid started. What? She had already proven her vast superiority to him.

Zinna stood and motioned for him to join her. She was serious. That got Zeru going. "Get up boy, before I stretch your ears. I don't care if she's Idgistu himself. No son of mine will back down from a challenge."

Twid rose. He knew what Zeru's next words would be. "And earlier. Have you forgotten everything I taught you all these years? You trampled basic rules of combat, fighting in anger instead of with your head." Zeru shook his head. "Sometimes I wonder why I even bother."

Zinna looked at Zeru as if seeing him for the first time. She spoke to him.

"Rarely does Zinna the daughter of Abraha forget a countenance. Yet place you I cannot, even as my heart tells me I know you." She paused, the furrows in her brow deepening. "Tell me. Does my heart deceive me?"

Zeru spoke. "I cannot speak for your heart, only for my own. And I say to you, Zinna, daughter of Abraha, never would my eyes forget a warrior so skilled. You and I..."

Twid ignored them, focusing instead on stretching. Maybe

Zeru should just fight Zinna. *Remember your head Twid. Don't forget what I taught you, Twid. Why should I bother, Twid?* It was all easy to say when you didn't have to face a Prince Defender. Why did Zinna want to fight him again anyway?

At least there weren't as many people around to watch him get thrashed. After releasing the blade in his left hand, Twid drew the sword from the tree. No point using the whip; he'd never practiced with it.

His only hope was to somehow get lucky in the first minute. The longer they dueled, the more certain his defeat. Facing Zinna across a flat section of grass, he leapt into the aggressive Nishan fighting style, attacking her with low and high swings, intermittently slicing at her with his smaller blade, inching his way forward, trying to gain advantageous positioning. Zinna blocked each attack with simple, minimal movements of her staff.

He faked. He feinted. He pretended to slip and he attacked her from the ground. They fought for five minutes, then ten minutes. Sweat drenched his body. Nothing worked. He shifted to the defensive Rasan style. Her staff whirled so fast he saw three staffs. He felt a light tap on his shoulder. On his foot. On his head. On his neck.

Why were they doing this?

After several more minutes, he realized she was just testing him, trying to gauge his development. He attacked without restraint. Low, high, he tried to draw her off balance. He aimed at her toes. He feigned in, then out; left, then right. Nothing worked. Or even came close to working. The longer he fought, the more he realized how superior she was.

Then he felt her staff under his ankles and he went flying. Zinna stepped on him, pinning him as she had earlier in the day. "Would you do anything to learn the truth? Would you do anything to reach Himlee and the Source of Harmony?"

Panting, Twid looked at his companions but they just stared back, still in awe at Zinna's display. All the stories were true. She was invincible.

Zinna lifted her leg and helped him up. "Like Metka, there is only one way to gain entrance to Hilmee: to be invited. But there is only one way to be invited."

"Every seven years, the Dream Kings hold the Prince Defender Games. The Games start with tens of thousands of warriors. Of those, only 1024 warriors pass the preliminaries. After eight rounds of elimination, just four warriors remain."

Zinna's eyes bore into him. "To honor the final four combatants, the Dream Kings stop the games and invite the four warriors to rest in their innermost palace, in Himlee, for three days before the finals commence and they crown a new Prince Defender."

"The Prince Defender Games are fourteen months from now. I don't know if you can win. But with a year of training, perhaps you can reach the final two rounds. If you reach the finals, during the feasting, once you are inside Himlee, that will be your best chance to find the Source of Harmony."

She stamped her staff. "But know this: You could lose in the opening round, you could be injured, you could be killed; you could be discovered, you could be beheaded in the Hall of Traitors."

Twid shook his head. She was crazy. She had destroyed him for the last hour. Shown him how inferior he was to a Prince Defender. And now she wanted him to fight in the games, in front of the very people who were searching for him.

He stammered, his words running together. "Look. I want to enter Himlee. I want to know what the voices in my head are saying, before I go mad. But I can't even lay a blow on you. And besides, the Dream Kings know what I look like. How many one-arm boys are there?"

Zinna nodded, the afternoon sun gleaming on her forehead. "The Old Ones have taught, 'If a neighbor comes knocking at your door at midnight, you shall feed him not because you want to, but because of his boldness.' In the same way, boldness shall be your disguise."

Zeru grunted. "Foolishness. Have the Old Ones not also said: 'He who enters death with warning on his ears shall be buried with his eyes open?'"

Zinna nodded. "Yes, Old One, you are not without wisdom. But nor am I without forethought." She looked at Twid. "Come with your companions and train with me in the battlegrounds near the Cursed Lands. We will live in a village with a dark-skinned people called Barias. You will learn their language and customs. When the games come, we will blacken your skin using an ointment and you will enter from their region."

Zinna reached out with her staff and touched the fuzz on Twid's face. "We shall pour *zeyti* oil upon your face; your beard shall grow; we shall shave your head. Your foes will not know you with the blade and whip over your left hand. We can disguise your companions, too, that they may support you however they can."

Twid stared, unable to speak. She was insane.

Zeru asked, "And what do you seek from us in return?"

Zinna lowered her voice, *"The red fox will point, the Eagle lead."*

That again. Him Too spoke. "You think we can help you because the fox pointed to us?"

Zinna answered. "Yes. Hibu saw that Tirhas, The Golden Eagle, will rise again from the Cursed Lands."

The three companions stared at her like she had ten heads. She grew crazier by the minute. She expected them to enter the Cursed Lands to search after some mythical warrior.

Zeru retorted, "Zinna. You best of all should know that it is impossible to enter the Cursed Lands. The Dream Kings built the Dream Wall hundreds of years ago and none have ventured past."

Twid nodded. Two hundred years ago, during the Harmony Wars, monsters and marauders had emerged from the western territories of the Three Lands. To protect the three lands, the Dream Kings had built a gigantic, insurmountable wall, guarded day and night. For centuries, no one had gone beyond the walls to the Cursed Lands. Not even Prince Defenders.

Zinna balanced herself on her heels. "Know this: even as we speak, the Dream Kings search for the Golden Eagle. They sense she will come soon and they focus all their might on killing her. The Seekers will do anything to keep her alive."

She looked at Iwala. "You infiltrated Lemlem's library. You entered Metka. You will help us find a way into the Cursed Lands. Once the rainy season ends in Baria, we will have six months to search for the entrance. On our way to Baria, and while we search for the entrance, I will train the young warrior. When the Prince Defender Games start, I swear by my father's grave that I will personally escort the three of you back, though I cannot enter Dream City, for all know me and I shall be killed on sight."

She rose. "I depart on the hour. I leave you now to seek counsel with your companions." She walked away.

Even before Zinna had gone out of earshot, Iwala spoke. "Twid, this whole thing is foolishness. I have friends in N'Mote, where the Dream Kings would never find us."

Him Too nodded. "I agree, Twid. Courage is admirable, but remember what the Old Ones taught: 'The coward comes home safely to his mother.'"

Twid looked at Zeru, who sat motionless. Finally, Zeru said, "You will be the one in the hornet's nest. So I cannot make this choice for you." Twid shook his head. That was a first. Zeru *not* telling someone what to do.

Twid looked at Him Too and Iwala again. "Him Too, Iwala. Tell the truth. I can see it in your eyes. You think we should help Zinna, but you'd never forgive yourselves if you advised me to enter the Games and I came to harm."

Him Too sat still for several moments. He closed and then reopened his eyes. "After I awoke from the tree, I felt like my whole life had been a waste, like I had been sleeping on beds full of leeches sucking the life out of me. Instead of bread, I and everyone around me had been eating pig manure. I felt like a giant pickpocket had his fists in my heart stealing everything that mattered."

"Something happened in that tree, Twid. It *was* the Five Jignas of Adwa in that barrel and I can still feel their thoughts jumbled up in my head. They're screaming, 'IT'S A LIE.' There are Five Harmonies. Not two. Five. And they matter. Not a little bit, they matter more than anything. Find them. Find the Five Harmonies unless you want to spend the rest of your life eating pig manure, sleeping on a bed of leeches, with pickpockets robbing your soul."

Iwala followed, "Twid, do you remember what happened when you said the word 'fox' to Scout-boy's questioner?"

Twid nodded. "Yes. Death flashed in his eyes."

"The fox meant something. Now we know what it meant." Iwala raised her hands over her head. "You know me. I'm not one to tell anyone what to do. But my whole life, I've always jumped from one adventure to another. Metka. Getting kicked out of someone's house. Stealing. Lying. It's all the same to me."

Twid nodded, translating his friend's words. Nothing worse than boredom; nothing worse than insignificance.

What could be a greater adventure than sneaking into the Cursed Lands and fighting in the Prince Defender Games? What could be a greater adventure than training with the First Prince Defender and sneaking into Himlee?

Suddenly, Zeru called across the clearing to Zinna.

Him Too, Twid and Iwala looked at each other, each thinking the same thing. *Crazy Zeru said Twid could make the decision. Is he going to make it now?*

As soon as Zinna got within earshot, Him Too spoke first, hoping to prevent Zeru from making the decision for all of them. "Zinna, we haven't made up our minds yet, Zeru just wanted to…"

Lightning flashing in Zeru's eyes, and Him Too cut himself short. Zeru began, speaking in a hushed, soft tone, "Twid, Him Too, Iwala. You are my children, and despite my sometimes harsh tones and ways with you, you know no one is closer to me."

Sudden sweat covered Twid's palms. He quelled an impulse to stand up and flee into the trees.

"I invite you, Zinna, to also hear these words. Words no one has ever heard. For I, too, believe that we met not by chance."

Zeru looked down, not knowing how to say what he had to say. "You will not believe what I tell you, but you must believe.

"About two hundred years ago, I awoke with my mind empty. I knew not my name. I knew not where I came from. I knew not my family. Nothing." Zeru sighed, eyes filled with sorrow. "I knew nothing."

Ignoring the disbelief in their eyes, Zeru continued. "By what force I am kept alive, I know not. But I awoke deep in the deserts of Nisha and found that I had enemies — men who pursued me relentlessly — for what reason, I knew not. But I also found myself adept at hiding and grew one with the land, dwelling deep within the lush lands of Wirba, until my enemies forgot me.

"Try as I might, I could remember naught of my background. I only felt in my heart that I had been robbed, that something deep and beautiful had been stolen forever. Throughout the Three Lands I traveled. Searching. Trying to find something that could tell me who I was and what I had lost. I worked every job you can imagine. Farmer. Soldier. Instructor. I was the instructor in the story I told you about Wir the Scorcher. I knew him. I knew Wir. I knew his son.

"After decades of wandering, I arrived at Adwa. And I knew. As the mother bird knows her nest, I knew. Adwa was home. So I settled in Adwa and opened the Ald Nald House, partnering with the Dream Kings to care for orphans. As the decades passed, I did on some nights consider leaving Adwa. But I knew that if I left, I would never find myself."

Zeru looked at Twid and Him Too. "And then, you, my children, found that tree. And I knew. I knew that tree was important. I knew that tree was the reason I had come to Adwa.

I didn't know what Jigna meant, didn't know what The Five Harmonies meant, but I counseled you to keep the sword and the staff.

"Now, after hearing Zinna's story, my heart wavers not." Zeru looked at Zinna. "Again, I say to you: Not by chance have we met. And while I would counsel my children to avoid a path so perilous, I know it is our path."

Zeru narrowed his eyes. "We will help you find your Golden Eagle. We will enter Himlee. We will help you restore the Harmonies."

Twid's heart raced and chills overwhelmed his body. Not because Zeru's story was too crazy, but because Twid had always known. He had always known that crazy Zeru was more than he appeared.

How else could an old man from Adwa speak Giiz so fluently, raise orphans with such drive and purpose, know so many Old Ones sayings?

Not knowing what else to do or say, Twid bent to one knee, his friends and Zeru joining him. Twid sprung the blade from his left hand. Iwala drew a dagger. Him Too twisted his staff and the blade emerged. Zeru put forth his walking staff. Each brought their weapons together and touched the bottom of Zinna's staff.

Lifting his head, Twid stared into Zinna's dark, impervious eyes. "Lead the way."

# PART II
## The Thirteenth Village

*"Hope is not the light at the end of the tunnel
but the light when there is no light."*

Alula the Unconquerable

# Fifteen

I wala scowled at the rain. They had been in Baria for six months now, and it had rained every hour of every day. Who ever heard of a rainy season at the desert's edge?

Twid was obsessed with his training, spending every moment with Zinna in the large hut several rows down. Him Too was lost in his own world reflecting on the tree, the Harmonies, and Jignas. Kwee had disappeared the last month. No one in the dratted town drank, and the few who gambled had stopped gambling with her after the first week.

If that weren't enough, with the dratted, never-ending rain, one couldn't go exploring outside without turning into a walking mud ball.

Iwala cursed as she walked to the gigantic training hut. Pushing the door open, she walked to the side, finding a seat next to Him Too.

"They working on balance again?"

Him Too nodded. Zinna had refused Twid any weapons the first month, insisting that Twid first master keeping his balance. "Balance is like your windpipe," Zinna had said. "Lose it, and you lose everything."

Iwala had to hand it to Zinna. She trained Twid eight hours every day, only giving him one break. Balance. Hand-to-hand combat. Staff. Sword. She left out nothing and had insisted on the training even during the two months it had taken them to reach Baria. In fact, on the journey to Baria, Zinna had required that Twid not ride his horse, but stand straight on its back for at least two hours each day. By the second month, Twid rarely fell off. That first month though…

Iwala pointed at Zeru, who stood watching the training. Every once in a while, Zeru would interject with some point, "Lower your sword, Twid," or "Don't kick up so much dust when you jump, Twid."

After a particularly flagrant violation, such as uneven breathing, Zeru would scratch his head in frustration and ask, "Really, Twid. Who are you going to say trained you in Adwa all those years?"

That was Zeru for you. You had the greatest warrior in the Three Lands teaching Twid, and Zeru still didn't care. Nobody could tell old Zeru anything.

A devious smile on her face, Iwala tapped Him Too's foot, then called out to Zeru, "Zeru, you can't give it all to Twid. Your other kids need your wisdom too."

As Zeru hobbled over, Him Too laughed. Few things made Zeru happier than sharing his "wisdom."

Zeru grunted. "Even a fool can become wise if he asks." Him Too moved his chair back.

Iwala said, "Well, Zeru, here is my question: Twid told us that he heard a voice in his head, telling him that the First Harmony was 'Freedom: You choose your actions.' But my question is: what does the first harmony harmonize with?"

"Harmonize with? It just is; it's the first harmony."

"No. When I'm playing my wata and someone is playing a krar with me, harmony means two or more different pitches coming together. Harmony can also mean agreeme…"

"Fool. I don't need you to tell me what harmony means. I was harmonizing before your grandmother was born."

"But harmonizing with what? What were you harmonizing with? What do *the Harmonies* harmonize with? Shouldn't it be, 'Freedom: You and your actions come together,' or 'Freedom: Your actions connect with your freedom?' Shouldn't something connect, come together, *harmonize*?"

Zeru shook his head. "See, that's the problem with today's youth. No imagination, no ability to use figures of speech. Did the Old Ones not say, 'Lacking wisdom is worse than lacking sight?'"

Iwala shook her head. "That saying doesn't make sense, Zeru.

Who cares how wise you are if you can't see where you're walking? I'd rather be a fool who can see."

Zeru put his hands on his forehead and bent low in the chair, staring at the ground as if only those dead and buried could understand Iwala's lunacy.

"Must I explain everything to you?" Zeru asked. "Have you not heard the story of the blind man who walked at night with a lantern? He was walking through the woods when he happened upon a neighbor. The neighbor laughed and said, 'Blind fool. Both noon and midnight are the same to you and yet here you are wasting this light.'"

Zeru stood. "And the blind man replied, 'Both light and dark are indeed the same to me. But I carry this lantern for clumsy dimwits like you who would otherwise run me over.'"

Zeru pointed at Iwala's head. "I say to you Iwala, you are the seeing blind. Repent from your words and seek wisdom before it is too late. Doubt not the Old Ones."

Iwala winked at Him Too who by this point had left his chair and retreated to the other side of the adobe. "Him Too, have you noticed that whenever an older person has run out of arguments, they just quote some Old Ones saying, followed by an ancient story, and expect us to nod our heads? My question is this: Why should we care what some Old Ones said? I mean, who are these bloody Old Ones anyway?" She looked at Him Too. "Have you ever met one of these Old Ones?"

Him Too shook his head. "Leave me out of this."

Zeru reached for Iwala's ear, but Iwala was already stepping back.

"Who are the Old Ones?" Zeru exclaimed. "After all these years, who are the Old Ones? Woe unto me that one of my own kids would ask me who The Old Ones are."

Iwala stepped back. "So you're saying you don't even know who the Old Ones are?"

Then, the chase around the room was on, and even Twid and Zinna stopped to watch, joining Him Too and Iwala in laughing.

# Sixteen

Iwala gathered her things. Sure, Zinna had told them to not go exploring during the rainy season. Sure, Zinna had warned of the mudslides. But that was Zinna. A Prince Defender who was legendary for her defense. Legendary for her caution.

But hadn't the Old Ones said, "One cannot retrieve honey without getting stung?"

Yes. Six months was long enough and Iwala didn't care if the rainy season had lasted longer than usual. Zinna had brought her to find a way into the Cursed Lands and that was what she was going to do. Let Twid train all day and Him Too and Zeru watch. Let Zinna wait until the Creator sent a perfect day.

Iwala would have the entire Cursed Lands mapped out while they waited. She wouldn't even leave a note. Let them wonder. What was it that Him Too had called her in Lemlem? Iwala the Irresponsible? It still had a nice ring to it.

As Iwala whistled a tune about a farmer and his talking pig, Kwee dropped from the rafters, landing on her shoulder. Good old Kwee. She always knew when to show up.

It was still dark when she tiptoed out of her adobe. Within minutes, the rain had soaked her to her skin. She walked west. Zinna had said the Cursed Lands were about an hour's walk.

It didn't matter that she didn't have a plan. She would figure something out. Lightning flashed above her and thunder reverberated. Everyone was so afraid of storms, but she liked the elements; they were uncontrollable, spontaneous.

As the faint light of dawn emerged, she saw the outlines of a massive structure. It blocked out the sky like a tidal wave. It grew bigger as she walked, a cosmic giant about to squash her. Iwala looked down as a sense of panic overwhelmed her. What was going on?

"It's unsettling, isn't it?"

Iwala jumped. It was Him Too.

"Don't tell me this is your first time seeing the wall?"

Iwala shook her head. Little Him Too. Always full of surprises.

As they approached the wall, Iwala felt Kwee digging into her shoulder. Before them lay a patch of massive thorn trees, with thorns the length of spears. As thin as needles and as densely packed as a porcupine's hide, the spears pointed in every possible direction, making further approach impossible.

Iwala pulled out a dagger and sliced the edge of one thorn. The needle hit the ground and disappeared. Iwala heard a rustling then she jumped back. The needle was sprouting. Within seconds a new thorn tree sprung up where the needle had fallen.

Zeru's name! Why even have a wall? The Dream Kings had an ever-expanding thorn forest that was impossible to penetrate. She looked up. The thorn trees rose a hundred feet along the wall, far too high for anyone to scale.

Looking higher, she saw the wall retreat into a shelf. Staring down at them from the shelf were wolf-canines the size of horses. Even if someone got past the thorn-trees and scaled the walls, the canines waited.

Up even higher, above the canines, she saw another indentation in the wall. She could barely make out small movements. Soldiers, probably archers, who served as a last defense against infiltration.

No wonder Zinna and the Seekers hadn't penetrated the Dream Wall. Even Metka was nothing compared to this.

Iwala heard a shifting behind her and turned around.

Him Too was looking out, facing the direction they had come.

Iwala blinked to make sure she saw right.

Standing before Him Too, so thin Iwala almost missed her, was a girl of about seven years old. Rain splattered the young child's muddy body as her frightened eyes darted left and right.

Twid groaned as he felt something dig into his side. He retreated further into his bed, trying to ignore the sensation. But he felt the object dig again. When he opened his eyes, Zinna towered over him, her staff at her side.

"Rise. Against my counsel, your companions have ventured to the Cursed Lands."

She motioned to the wall, where Twid's weapons hung. "Bring your weapons."

Avoiding Zinna's scowl, Twid strapped on both swords and slipped the appendage over his stump. He should have predicted this. No one could coop up Iwala.

The rain greeted them as they stepped out. It was actually a nice break from being stuck in the hut all day.

Twid walked toward Zeru's hut, but Zinna interrupted him. "Let the old man sleep. He might get sick in the rain."

As they walked west, Twid said nothing. Even after eight months of training with Zinna, he still felt awkward. What did one talk about with someone like Zinna? She was a Prince Defender with more Old Ones sayings than a library.

He kept his eyes on the ground before them, looking for tracks even as he knew that no tracks had survived the downpour. It gave him something to do.

They walked for what seemed like a day when he felt Zinna's staff on his stomach, stopping him. Looking up, he gasped. The world had ended. One couldn't even see the sky beyond the Wall, let alone imagine breaching it. He craned his head back, looking as high as he could, but he saw no end. It had to be at least one hundred feet thick to support that kind of height, Twid thought. He wondered how far down the foundation went.

As they approached he saw massive thorn trees guarding the wall's base. Zinna turned them south, looking for any sign of their companions. Finding none, they doubled back and headed north, but the rain had washed everything out. There were no tracks.

Lightning flashed, punctuated by crashes of thunder, and the rain intensified, restricting their vision to no more than several feet.

Zinna scowled. "Fools. We cannot track them, and 'tis imprudent to stand here waiting for a mudslide. We must retreat."

※ ※ ※

How had the girl gotten there? Zinna had said their village was the only one for miles. Him Too put on his most reassuring smile. Maybe she was lost. Maybe she needed help getting back home.

He motioned for Iwala to stay still. They didn't want to scare her. Just stay still. Let her know they wouldn't do anything.

Like a deer poised to bound, the girl shifted her gaze between Iwala and Him Too, settling on Him Too. Thunder boomed. Lightning outlined the girl's red hair.

Then the girl turned and walked away.

Him Too motioned to Iwala. *Do not move Iwala. She's testing us. Seeing if we'll rush her. Don't move.*

The young girl stopped and looked behind her. Seeing that they hadn't moved, she turned and looked at them again. She was transfixed, thought Him Too. What had captured her attention?

The young girl walked toward them, pausing as she came closer. Seconds passed into minutes. She stood before Him Too, and he looked in her eyes. They were normal eyes. A little scared, maybe. But normal. He followed her gaze. She was looking at his staff.

The girl touched the bottom of Him Too's staff. She traced the wood as she made her way up, feeling the indentations and carvings.

Him Too saw excitement in her eyes.

Pointing at him, she said, "Minja!" Minja? Him Too had heard that word somewhere before...Again, she said, "Minja." Him Too looked at Iwala but she shook her head.

The girl turned and walked away from them.

After ten feet, she stopped and looked over her shoulder.

He heard Iwala's voice behind him. "She wants us to follow her."

To where, thought Him Too. Maybe they should just go back home. For all they knew, she was some type of emissary from Scout-boy or his soldiers. Win their trust through a little girl, then trap them.

He stepped forward, Iwala behind him. They followed the girl for several minutes, back along the path they had taken to the wall. The girl stopped before an adobe-sized rock. After scanning all around, she pressed near the rock's base with her foot. A thin doorway lurched open and the girl descended into the darkness.

"Him Too. Stay back. If I don't come out in an hour, go get Zinna and Twid."

Iwala followed the girl into the hole.

*Sure, and miss all the fun.* Him Too stepped into the rock after Iwala and winced as the stone door thudded shut.

� ✠ ✠

Zinna thwacked Twid on his forearm with her staff. "Concentrate, boy."

How could he concentrate, Twid thought? His friends had been gone for more than a day. Searching for them was impossible. The rain had intensified into a violent storm, what the villagers called the last murmurings of the rainy season.

He blocked another attack with his wooden sword, and lashed out with the whip in his left hand. In eight months of training, he had yet to land a blow on Zinna.

Twid could understand Iwala doing something rash. But Him Too? And Zeru? Zeru was gone when they returned, and he still hadn't come back. Zeru, who always advocated caution and responsibility.

Something was wrong. Something terrible had happened.

"Concentrate. Think of nothing else." Zinna jumped and thwacked him on his other forearm. "If they're not back by to-night; wall or no wall; rain or no rain, we have no choice."

No choice of what, Twid thought as he parried. Hadn't the first Harmony taught that one always had a choice? That one didn't always choose the choices one had, but one always had a choice.

Zinna continued, reading his mind. "Yes. We find a way to follow them into the Cursed Lands."

# Seventeen

Him Too followed Iwala and the girl down the narrow corridor. He hadn't been surprised when Iwala descended into the doorway.

Him Too still didn't know why *he* had come though. What would happen if they were both trapped in the tunnels? How would Zinna and Twid find them?

He cursed. He usually showed more restraint than this. But there was something about the girl. Nodding to himself, he looked ahead to the torch in her hand. Yes. He was sure of it. She knew the staff. The staff meant something to her.

He coughed. He could almost taste the craggy, limestone walls sliding down his throat. Stumbling, he looked down and saw thin, serpentine plants crisscrossing the uneven ground.

The girl turned and motioned for them to stop. Her torch light cast a red hue on the walls, reminding Him Too of the tree in the Adwa Forests. He felt a sudden impulse to bolt back up the corridor.

Then the girl turned and walked away. As he watched her torch light flicker then disappear, he realized that he was sweating from head to toe.

After several moments, Iwala said, "I'd heard rumors of an underground people but I'd never actually met anyone who'd been in the corridors."

A rat-sized animal crawled over Him Too's foot. Hoping it wasn't a snake, he tried to keep his body still. Then a larger animal jumped onto his foot and Him Too darted back before realizing it was Kwee. He heard a hiss, a light scuffle, and the sound of something scurrying down the corridor.

Feeling Kwee's familiar claws on his shoulder, Him Too exhaled. He whispered back to Iwala, "I hope that's not because no one who comes in ever comes out."

Iwala didn't answer. That thought had crossed her mind.

They heard the sound of people approaching. As the torch-light drove out the darkness, six short, stocky men materialized, staffs in their hands. Their faces wore no smiles. One of them, a red-bearded man, spoke in a dialect they could barely under-stand. Holding the torch near Him Too's face, he stared at Him Too, finally grunting, "Show your *Merkoos*."

*Merkoos?* What was the man talking about? Then Him Too remembered. *Merkoos* was the ancient Giiz for staff. He held it out. Redbeard took the staff. Like a master carpenter examining a finished carving, his hands explored every crevice and indenta-tion. He brought the staff so close to the torch, Him Too feared the staff would burn. Unlike the young girl, Redbeard's eyes betrayed no expression.

Redbeard appraised them for a long moment, focusing on Him Too. Him Too had the uneasy sensation that the man was weighing their lives.

"Follow."

They followed him below. Three of the six men fell in behind them. They traveled for only a short time before they came to a chamber large enough to fit forty adobes. Dozens of corridors split off from the chamber and people milled about. To the left, Him Too could see the girl. Almost everyone had red hair.

The red-bearded man barked a command and the girl fell in line with him. Ten men joined the front guard, and ten others joined the rear. They walked through a corridor to the right, marching in perfect formation. Though the guards were short in stature, their legs were still longer than Him Too's and he found himself running to keep up. Minutes stretched into hours.

They came to a gigantic chamber. Twenty of the first cham-bers could have fit in this one. Through the dim torchlight, Him Too saw hundreds of corridors splitting off in every direction. If they ever got separated from these people, they would never find their way out.

The red-bearded man entered a gigantic square home in the

center of the chamber. The young girl and the staff went with
him.

Redbeard returned and motioned for Him Too to enter. When
Iwala tried to follow, one of the guards thrust a staff before her.

Iwala grimaced. It was the oldest trick in the book. Question
them separately and see if they tell the same story. *Tell the truth.*
She thought. *Tell the truth, or we're both dead.*

⁂ ⁂ ⁂

After Redbeard closed the door behind them, darkness filled
the small entryway. Him Too felt Redbeard's hands guiding him
through another doorway, then pushing him to the ground.

Him Too sat, eyes straining, but he couldn't see anything. He
wondered if his captors had developed some sort of night vision
from living in the tunnels. Maybe they were looking at him right
now, seeing every expression. He kept his face calm.

No one spoke. Finally, Him Too heard a soft, authoritative
voice, "Young one. Where did you get this *merkoos*?"

He thought about lying, but decided against it. These people
knew much more about the staff than he did. And if they questioned Iwala separately…

He told them everything. How his mother had abandoned
him. The orphanage. His friendship with Twid. The fox. The
tree. The staff. The barrel. The voices in his head. Metka. Zinna.
Why they were in Baria. The Cursed Lands. Everything.

No one spoke after he finished. *I should have left some things
out,* Him Too thought. *The story is too crazy.*

The voice spoke again. *"Berhan."* The ancient Giiz for light,
Him Too thought. In the next moment, torches illuminated the
vast room.

Him Too looked around, his eyes adjusting. As he took the
room in, chills overwhelmed his body, leaving him clammy
from head to toe. Oblivious to his captors, he stumbled to the
nearest wall.

It was madness. All of it. The Tree. The Harmonies. And now these walls.

Behind him, he heard the door open, and a moment later, Iwala's gasp.

They were in a museum dedicated to a warrior. Magnificent color murals of the warrior's exploits covered every inch of the walls and ceiling. The warrior attacking a giant, wielding the staff from the tree. The warrior vanquishing a gigantic bear. The warrior soaring through the air, bounding from tree to tree. The warrior leading a battalion of soldiers. The warrior attacking six giants at once.

He always had a red fox next to him; always had the staff in his hand; always attacked giants. But he wasn't fighting giants. The warrior was a midget. The warrior was Him Too.

※ ※ ※

It was *impossible!* Crazy! Unable to keep his footing, Him Too crumbled to the ground. A chair scraped, and an ancient man stepped forward, his speckled beard dragging along the floor. His eyes gleaming, he called the young girl over, running his hand through her red hair. He spoke with the voice Him Too had heard earlier.

"Have the Old Ones not taught, 'The young shall lead the old?' Listen now, to my own story, then. A story you will not find in any Dream King library.

"Hundreds of years ago, long before I, Tefono, was born, long before the cursed wall was built, long before the Dream Kings reigned, our people lived aboveground in what was known as the Twelve Villages. Music flourished, art flourished, peace flourished and the Harmonies were taught to all from birth.

"In that time of sweetness, who could have known that the Great Harmony Wars had already begun? Who could have foreseen that entire civilizations would be wiped out, entire cultures destroyed?

"Yes. Who could have known that Harmony Masters of all backgrounds would vanish? Master artists gone, master blacksmiths destroyed, master teachers kidnapped. The Harmonies, lost and forgotten."

Tefono pointed to a painting of the warrior soaring through the air. "Of all the warriors, the greatest were Jignas, Harmony Masters of the highest order. Not like the pathetic warriors of today, Jignas could soar through the air, be in one city one moment and another city the next.

"Yet even the Jignas dwindled, defeated by some unknown enemy, until only a few remained. Then Tirhas, greatest of the Jignas, called four other Jignas to join her to defend each other and the Three Lands. The five lived together in an enchanted tree in the Adwa forest and became known as the Five Jignas of Adwa."

The voices quaked in Him Too's head. JIGNA. THE FIVE HARMONIES. JIGNA.

"One of the five was our leader, Minja the Majestic."

Him Too looked at the paintings of Minja the Majestic with the red fox. At least that made sense now. The fox from the tree was Minja's fox. It had somehow stayed alive all these years until they saw it in the forest. It must have thought Him Too was Minja and led them to the tree.

"Minja had long foreseen that the enemy would attack our people, to draw Minja out and weaken the five. So Minja developed this secret underground retreat as a final sanctuary.

"But the enemy came with no warning, like a mudslide during the dry season." As Tefono paused, Iwala sensed the misery and sorrow in the room, in the eyes and shoulders of their captors.

"Of 500,000 people in the Twelve Villages, only two hundred escaped to these tunnels. The rest were wiped out."

Him Too and Iwala stopped breathing. *Five hundred thousand!* "Our people fled, questioning everything. Had the Jignas failed us? Had Minja failed us? In their grief and shock, the remaining survivors withdrew into more than the tunnels; they withdrew into themselves, focusing only on survival."

Tefono paused and looked at them.

"Now, we are all that are left: the Thirteenth Village. We've lived here for hundreds of years, struggling, growing, struggling. Much we have forgotten, and almost nothing of the Harmonies is remembered."

Tefono pointed at Him Too. "Now, beyond all hope, after centuries of misery, you have returned, led to us by a child. Minja has returned."

Eyes glinting, Tefono shook Minja's staff and proclaimed to all in the room, "Ready the feast hall, for Minja has returned!"

Then he pointed at Him Too: "Today we feast. Tomorrow, you, Minja, the Jigna's Jigna, will counsel us and lead us back to freedom."

# Eighteen

The soldier had been climbing for almost an hour, but he hardly noticed the steps beneath him. Great reward awaited him. Gold beyond imagining. Birr beyond counting. Anything he desired.

Yes. The Prince Defender tolerated no failure. Failure meant death. But everyone also knew that the Great Prince was fair. He had told them from the beginning: *"I am a mirror. Bring me failure and I will fail you. Bring me victory and I will heighten your victory."* And he had proven true. No one could doubt the Prince's generosity to those who aided him.

The soldier bounded up the last step and rushed through, ignoring the guards standing before the gate. Pausing, he looked down from the wall, surveying the ground below. Yes. The Prince would find his information priceless.

The soldier rushed to the grand hall and knocked on the gigantic door. Two soldiers opened the door.

"State your business, scout. The Prince is busy."

He kept his back straight. "I must speak with The Prince on a matter of the highest urgency."

The soldiers frowned. "If you disturb him for naught, you know the consequences."

The soldier waved his hands. "The Prince will not be disappointed."

He passed by the soldiers. They were fools. Nothing more than door ornaments. No. It was scouts like him, serving on the frontlines, risking their lives each day, who mattered.

He heard the Prince before he saw him. He stomach flipped as he bowed.

The Prince's voice bellowed, "Rise young one, and state your business."

The soldier stood and looked up at the Prince. He didn't even

come up to the prince's elbows. And the prince's calves were
thicker than his own midsection.

"Prince Delgam. Earlier today, I was patrolling on the south-
ern flank during the intense rain." The soldier paused, making
sure the Prince understood he had been patrolling during heavy,
dangerous rain.

"Amidst the storm, I saw a midget and a woman standing
before the thorn forest. I remembered the alert you put out from
the Dream Kings, for a one-arm boy, a midget, and a woman, so
I followed the two."

He had the Prince's attention. "Majesty. I saw a strange sight.
A young girl came and touched the midget's staff and they followed her for a mile, to a large rock. But it was no ordinary rock.
It was an entrance to an underground passage. The girl led them
below."

Delgam felt his skin crawl. Could it be? It was rumored that
remnants of The Twelve Villages still survived in an underground lair.

He nodded. Yes. The soldier's information was priceless
indeed. And it made sense. The midget boy returning to Minja's
homeland, Minja's staff in hand.

"Well done, scout. Rest now. Tomorrow, a battalion will follow you to the entrance and we shall storm the corridors. If we
find them below, your reward will exceed your contribution."

Delgam walked to a large cactus plant that stood in the
corner. The Dream Kings would finally recognize his worth. All
these years, they had held him responsible for Zinna, asking
how he could let her escape when his hand was around her
throat. Reaching out, Delgam grabbed a cactus branch, ignoring
the thorns as they tore through his hands.

They had assigned him to the worst duties, to the cursed
wall for the last decade. He hadn't even attended the last Prince
Defender Games! Worst of all, they had favored Tah, and later
Kahn and Inj. That would all change this week. By tomorrow,
he would have one thousand soldiers in that tunnel. He would

kill the midget and the miserable girl. He would present the midget's head to the Dream Kings himself.

He turned his head. The soldier was still there. "Yes, scout."

The soldier smiled. "Great Defender. I suspected from their fearful and tentative stances that the midget and woman hadn't known the girl so I asked myself, 'From where did the midget and the woman come?'"

Delgam leaned forward. Blood dripped as he gripped the cactus harder. He could feel it. The soldier's earlier news was only a precursor for the real news.

"Majesty, I circled the area until I came to the land of Baria. I hid in the shadows there for hours and observed the people. And on the fourth hour, I saw him. I saw the one-armed boy."

The soldier continued. "She's there, Majesty. The Betrayer of Dreams is with him. If you act quickly, she's yours."

# Nineteen

Zeru awoke, not knowing quite how long he had slept. The adobe's well-made door allowed no light to enter. *What light is available in this God-forsaken rainy season anyway?*

Stretching his arms, he walked to the large adobe. He had to give Zinna her due. He'd always considered himself a taskmaster, but Zinna had pushed harder than he had ever imagined possible. Running every day for hours, stretching every other moment, sparring for eight hours, she had even taught the boy to ride the horse standing up! Twid wasn't ready yet, but give him six more months and Twid would have as good a chance as anyone.

Zeru knelt and scratched his left foot. His left side was acting up again. Like always, the twitching started in his left big toe and worked its way up until even his left cheekbone ached.

He stood again. It was more than Twid's fighting abilities, though, more than his training. Something made the boy different and Zeru, after all these years, still couldn't put his finger on it. The other two were easier to categorize. Iwala the rascal; Him Too the overachiever, always striving to catch up to his older siblings.

But Twid? What was his defining quality? He was responsible? That didn't seem right. Calling him responsible wasn't enough. Zeru had known many responsible youth; youth who would do as directed; youth who respected authority.

Maybe it was an awareness, a prescient understanding that life could be cruel, vicious even, and yet a realization that one *could* fight to make life beautiful, even if that beauty only lasted for a moment. Not just for oneself but for others. Most youth didn't develop that sense until they had kids of their own. Some never developed it.

*Seeing your mother beheaded, your sister killed. Tell me that won't change a boy. Tell me that won't teach him what life can be like.*

Entering the adobe, he found it empty. Walking to Twid's adobe, he found it empty as well, Twid's weapons missing. Without walking into Him Too and Iwala's rooms, he knew they were gone, too.

What happened? Why hadn't they waked him? *Iwala probably snuck out and the others pursued her. I knew that fool would bring us trouble.*

Thunder crashed above. He walked across the muddy road to one of their neighbors and asked if they had seen any of his companions.

Twid and Zinna were seen leaving together but no signs of the other two. That confirmed it. Iwala must have convinced Him Too to go exploring with her, and they hadn't told the others because Zinna would never let them go.

Zeru kicked the rain. He should have watched Iwala closer, should have known she would get restless.

Well, there was nothing to be done by sitting around and waiting. Even with Zinna to aid them, his companions might need him. Gathering his things, he disappeared into the rain.

❊ ❊ ❊

"Anger is like wind," Zinna said. "And your enemy a sailor who uses wind to his advantage."

Twid tried to keep his frustrations checked, to look for a weakness. He knew he wouldn't find one. He never did. He did a wind-up motion with his whip, as if he was going to strike at her left foot, but then a moment later, thrust his wooden sword at Zinna's right leg. Zinna hopped over his sword, seeming to hang in the air for seconds. Before she landed, she grazed his side with her staff.

They fought for hours until evening approached. Twid tried to concentrate on his training but his mind kept wandering to his friends. What was taking so long? He was especially worried about Zeru. At least Him Too and Iwala were together.

"In one way your friend's disappearance is a blessing. For in the Games, you will have to concentrate on self-defense, even as distractions cloud your mind."

To illustrate her point, Zinna, smacked him hard on his left thigh. *How did Zinna always seem to read his mind?*

It was time. For the last four months Twid had practiced with his whip every night. He could now pick up the ends of a chair and flip the chair, and last week he had used the whip to grab a cup by its handle.

He had been careful during the fighting sessions to not show Zinna his progress with the whip. It probably still wouldn't work. She was Zinna.

He wound up with his whip again, preparing the same feint, and then attacked Zinna with his sword. She hung in the air again and again he felt her staff graze his side. But then his whip was out, curling; he grabbed her left foot and yanked.

Zinna went flying, landing on her stomach. Twid stopped, not believing what he had done, laughing in spite of himself, raised his hand in victory, all the while backing up.

Who knew what she'd do now.

He looked down. Why wasn't she getting up? Why wasn't her head moving? Was this a trick? Could she be hurt? Zinna couldn't be hurt.

He walked over to her, but before he could speak she raised a finger over her mouth, silencing him. She had her ear to the ground.

"The ground shakes, boy. Someone's coming." She paused, eyes closed for a moment. "A whole lot of someones."

Faster than he'd ever seen her move, she leapt to the main beam in the middle of the adobe and scurried up. When she reached the ceiling, she pulled out a knife and she hacked the straw, creating a heap on the ground. Moments later, a mound of dirt piled beneath her. Her head disappeared as she crawled onto the roof.

A long minute later, she reappeared.

"Gather yourself, boy. Delgam is here." She wiped some straw off her tunic. "And he's brought a thousand soldiers."

# Twenty

**D**elgam stood outside the adobe, his heart pounding. Zinna had been his friend once, his mentor, his sister. What had happened to her?

Why did she betray the Dream Kings? The Dream Kings had given her everything anyone could want: limitless gold, fame beyond comparison, rare influence. Yet she had betrayed them and betrayed everything the Dream Kings had fought for.

He motioned his two captains forward. Each was an 8th Circle Defender and each had twelve soldiers with him. There was no way that Zinna and the boy could defeat them all. And if Zinna somehow did, a thousand soldiers awaited around the perimeter.

Delgam nodded and the soldiers kicked the door open. They peered in from the outside. The room appeared empty. Delgam smiled. It was just like Zinna. She was probably waiting above or just to the side of the door.

Delgam motioned and two soldiers took a running start and shot inside the adobe. He waited for an attack of some sort, but didn't hear one.

He stepped back. She was waiting for him to enter. An arrow to his throat, a knife in his back. As long as she killed him, she probably figured she could play some mind game on the rest of his soldiers and escape.

He directed all the other soldiers to enter and motioned for them to search under the tables and beneath the cots. She was in there. They had watched the adobe for hours. There was no way she could have left. He watched the soldiers from outside.

Too late, he felt a blade on his back. Then he heard a snapping sound and a whip grabbed the door handle, slamming it shut. A young man ran to the door and placed a wooden beam across, trapping the soldiers inside. And then he heard a voice he hadn't heard in decades.

"It's good to see you again, Delgam."

He turned, keeping his hands over his head. He almost jumped back. He had heard about her hair and skin but he had never stopped visualizing the old Zinna.

"My friend here and I are going to walk to your soldiers, Delgam, and you're going to lead us past them, to our three friends. I'm not going to explain which three friends I'm talking about. I'm sure you can explain their disappearance."

"You always were my favorite, Delgam." She twisted her sword into his side, drawing blood. "Don't do anything stupid."

### ❈ ❈ ❈

The melodies of the krar mixed with steady poundings of goat-hide drums as hundreds of villagers danced in the middle of the Great Hall, the large room Him Too and Iwala had seen on the way to the old man Tefono.

Villagers waved palm leaves, chanting, "The Majestic has returned, the Majestic has returned." Soldiers held swords up high, shaking them as they danced. Laughter, clapping, and the sounds of feet shuffling echoed with the music, and the Thirteenth Village celebrated as it had not done in hundreds of years.

A deep-throated, stocky man sang on the stage:

> *Mothers and daughters, have you not heard?*
> *Fathers and sons, have you not heard?*
> *Lions and tigers, have you not heard?*
> *Eagles and sparrows, have you not heard?*
> *Miiiiiiiiiiiiiiiiinja has returned!*
>
> *Forgotten sun, have you not heard?*
> *Forgotten stars, have you not heard?*
> *Forgotten trees, have you not heard?*
> *Forgotten flowers, have you not heard?*
> *Miiiiiiiiiiiiiiiiinja has returned!*

*Yes, ants and spiders, have you not heard?*
*Oh creatures of the oceans, have you not…*

The only unhappy person in the chamber, it seemed, was Him Too. *Have these people lost their minds? Do they actually think I can restore their kingdom? All these years underground must have addled their brains.*

He wanted to scream, "I'm not Minja, you bloody fools! I'm sorry I look like him but I'm not him!"

Then there was Iwala. Instead of explaining to the people that Him Too was not Minja, she had joined the musicians and was playing the wata with them. Iwala had simply said, "They're not going to believe you anyway so you might as well enjoy yourself."

Him Too had tried to ask the villagers who their enemy was, who they wanted him to defeat. Was it the Dream Kings? Idgistu? A Dirg? Who?

But all they would say was that he would restore their kingdom, and defeat "The Enemy," sometimes referring to the enemy in the plural, as "The Evildoers."

If Minja, who was a real Jigna, couldn't defeat the "Evildoers," then what in bloody hell made them think he could? But before he knew it, Redbeard had lifted him to his shoulder, brandishing him like a talisman. Then, different men clamored for him, and he felt himself passed from shoulder to shoulder. *Blood and ashes, your kingdom hasn't been restored yet. Where did you get the palm leaves anyway? You're an underground people.*

❈ ❈ ❈

After several hours of dancing and music making, the villagers pulled tables out, piled with meat, rice, and all sorts of spirits.

Him Too and Iwala found themselves at a table with Tefono, Redbeard, and the young girl who had found them. Him Too sat lost in thought, still trying to figure out how he was going to

explain to the Thirteenth Village that their celebration was for
naught; that he was not Minja returned, had no plans to restore
their kingdom, and that he was already preoccupied trying to
help Twid enter the Source of Harmony.

Thinking of Twid, Him Too grimaced. Their companions
would be delirious with worry by now. They needed to get back.

Servers brought them honey wine and goat meat. Iwala was
asking Redbeard if they had ever tried to explore west in the tunnels, to The Cursed Lands. Forgetting his troubles for a moment,
Him Too tried to hear Redbeard's response.

Redbeard pointed to a corridor that was sealed off with wood.
Apparently the corridor led to a passageway west. Many of their
men had tried the corridor, tried to explore west, but none
had returned, giving it the name: The Corridor of Death. Some
young men had tried to sneak through and others ventured
forth by accident, so the Village Council had walled it off.

Him Too grunted. Even underground, the way to the Cursed
Lands was barred.

Tefono interrupted Redbeard. Speaking from the stage, he
waved Him Too's staff in the air and addressed his people.
"Long centuries have our people suffered. Long have we lived in
misery, in pain, lamenting what we lost while fearing what we
might yet lose. Speaking of our unity, our great leader, Minja the
Majestic, once said:

> Not some for none, or none for some,
> Not two for six, or ten for three.
> But twelve for one, and one for twelve.

"But the enemy broke our unity and destroyed us. We lost
hope, and entered a darkness so blinding, that we couldn't even
wish for light, for we had forgotten that light existed. Forgetting
hope, we became the saddest of people, seeking not to find happiness, but only to reduce our misery.

"And yet hope against hope, led to us by a child, our greatest hero, our greatest warrior has returned, lighting a candle whose existence we had forgotten."

Caught up in the old man's words, overwhelmed by the sense of sadness that the people must have felt while also trying to understand their new joy, Him Too forgot his fears for a moment, forgot that he was not Minja. *Even if I can't restore their kingdom, at least they have felt hope for a day. At least they have feasted and celebrated like a free, hopeful people.*

Looking around, he saw tears in the villagers' eyes. But even as he noticed their tears, he looked next to him to Iwala and saw Kwee agitated, scratching Iwala's shoulder. Iwala was so caught up, with tears in her own eyes, that she ignored Kwee.

He reached over to calm Kwee, but she only hissed and scratched his finger. *Something is wrong. Kwee always knows when something is wrong.*

And then, out of the corner of his eyes, deep in one of the corridors, he saw an arm pull back. Leaping, he dove to the stage, but it was too late. An arrow screamed through the air, piercing the old man's throat. Pandemonium erupted as the room filled with soldiers wielding swords, axes, and spears. Few men in the Thirteenth Village had their weapons with them.

Him Too grabbed the staff from under Tefono, trying to avoid the old man's glazed look. Springing the blade, he found himself surrounded by soldiers. The voices in his head were silent. *Where are you when I need you, you useless Jignas?*

He tried with all his power to leap up as he had in the tree, but all he did was hop to avoid a soldier's sword. Looking out, he saw that many of the stunned villagers weren't even fighting as the soldiers butchered them.

Iwala stood next to him. The little girl that had found them quivered behind them. *They will not have you. I swear they will not have you.*

Then something struck his head and he knew no more.

✳ ✳ ✳

Even as she fought, Iwala saw hundreds more soldiers streaming into the great chamber, fanning out in disciplined formations, blocking each of the corridors.

She had to think! A few moments more and everyone would be dead. She almost tripped over something, and realized it was Him Too. She didn't have time to check his body. She dodged another soldier's thrust and sliced his leg.

*Think. Think! You won't escape this through might.* More soldiers flooded the chamber.

Then she remembered Zinna's story of escape from the Dream Kings. Reaching into her belt, she launched three daggers in rapid succession at the nearest torches, aiming for the pedestals holding them up. She ducked another soldier's thrust, and launched two more daggers.

The torches crashed and several wooden tables caught on fire. Iwala launched three more daggers, throwing her side of the great hall into chaos.

She ducked another soldier's attack and stabbed his side. As the chaos intensified, she launched three final daggers. Lifting Him Too's body to her shoulder, she dragged the sobbing young girl with her other hand.

They wove among the scattered bodies and soldiers, until she reached the Corridor of Death. Another soldier jumped at them and Iwala fired a dagger in his throat. She couldn't have more than two daggers left.

Across the hall, a commander must have seen what she planned, and he screamed at his soldiers. But it was too late. Adrenaline flowing through her, Iwala shoved her dagger into the crevice between the walled off wood and the corridor wall and shoved with all her might, praying that her dagger would not break.

A section of the wood broke, just big enough for her to push Him Too and the young girl through. Iwala darted after them. An arrow whistled past her face.

Peering out into darkness, Iwala reached down and grabbed

a small rope from her belt. She tied the young girl's hand to her own and Him Too's hand to the young girl's. Iwala felt Him Too's pulse. He still lived.

The girl cried out in fear as axes slammed into the wooden wall behind them. Whistling for Kwee to lead the way, Iwala stumbled down the corridor.

What a nightmare. The Thirteenth Village had thought them saviors, but they had become executioners. Minja had failed them not once, but twice. Tefono was dead; Redbeard, dead. They were all dead, except for this little girl, and who knew how long Iwala could keep her alive. Behind them, the soldiers pursued; before them, an unknown danger that no one had ever survived: the Corridor of Death.

She heard footsteps rushing behind them. She whistled for Kwee and Kwee hopped on her shoulder. Pulling the rope holding the young girl, she flattened all of them against an indentation in the corridor, praying that they wouldn't be seen.

As the footsteps approached, Kwee jumped off her shoulder. *No Kwee!* Kwee bounded down the corridor, creating a clamor as she launched stones from wall to wall. Hearing the noise ahead, dozens of soldiers rushed passed the three companions, confident that their prey lay just ahead.

After the soldiers rushed past, Iwala lifted Him Too to her shoulder and followed, keeping a firm grip on the girl's hand. *I carried Twid before and now I'm carrying Him Too. My monkey is more useful in a pinch than these fools.*

If they followed closely enough, maybe they could watch as the soldiers sprang whatever trap or awakened whatever enemy lay ahead. Iwala wasn't too worried about the soldiers catching Kwee, but she was concerned that the unknown enemy might surprise Kwee. Quickening her pace, she rubbed the young girl's hair, trying to comfort her.

She slowed as they saw torchlight ahead, stopping just short of some larger chamber. About fifty soldiers stood in the middle of the room. From where Iwala stood, the room looked like a dead end.

Then the ground shook. The soldiers cowered. Out of the shadows emerged enormous shapes, twice the height of large horses and three times the width of cows. Gigantic tusks protruded from dozens of long, menacing heads. With each three-toed step, the beasts tightened the circle around the soldiers.

Iwala watched in fascination, almost forgetting the danger. *What are they? Some type of cave rhino?* Panicking, one of the soldiers launched a spear at the nearest animal, but the spear just bounced off the scaled skin without denting the armor. *Maybe we can just wait here for these rhinos to kill all five hundred soldiers and then go back up.*

But Iwala knew they couldn't wait. Kwee had diverted the earlier soldiers, but sooner or later, one of the soldiers would see them as they passed. The commanders would realize that it was unlikely their prey had survived the rhinos; they would search the corridor more carefully.

Another soldier launched a spear and the rhinos charged. Iwala winced as she heard bones trampled and tusks ripping through flesh. She held on to the wall to keep her feet steady as the cavern shook. She hugged the girl close. No wonder no one had made it back. As she watched the rhinos trample the last of the soldiers, she wondered what hope they had. Maybe they could find a place to hide in the corridor, or in the ceiling until the rhinos killed the remaining soldiers. The rhinos could no doubt defeat the five hundred soldiers, even five thousand soldiers.

Then, before she could stop her, the little girl walked out toward the rhinos. Iwala tried to pull her back on the rope, but it was too late. The rhinos had already seen them. *Hyenas take me! How do I always get myself in these situations?*

The rhinos stared at the girl, and at Iwala, who still had Him Too on one shoulder and Kwee back on the other. The girl reached up to the nearest rhino and pet his knee.

Iwala stared, but the girl kept massaging the rhinoceros.

The girl said, "They attacked only after the soldiers attacked them. They're not even eating the soldiers. Look. One of them is eating plants."

As if he could hear her, the gigantic rhino lowered his tusks, sliding the needle-thin end past her until the side of his tusks massaged her shoulder gently.

Was that why no one had returned? All who had ventured forth were adults, and adults would have perceived the rhinos as a threat.

Iwala heard Tefono's words again: "Have the Old Ones not taught, 'The young shall lead the old?'" Poor Tefono. In the end all his Old Ones sayings hadn't saved him.

Now that she looked again, Iwala saw that some of the rhinos had faded to the shadows, where they ate some sort of fast-growing cave vegetation. She could see the vines growing back almost as quickly as the rhinos ate them.

Well. Iwala wasn't going to be left out. *Wait until I tell people that I touched a cave rhino.* Iwala touched the smooth, cold tusk, bringing her hand to the point, wincing as she thought of the tusk slicing through her body. The sounds of soldiers rushing above jarred her back to reality.

Adjusting Him Too on her shoulder, Iwala led the girl past the rhinos to a passageway on the other end. She stopped and lowered Him Too's body. Dropping down, she grabbed several packs of food that the soldiers had carried and positioned the packs on her back.

She searched the bodies until she found seven daggers. Hoisting Him Too back on her shoulder, she pulled the girl away from the cave rhinos who seemed to have taken to her. A soldier's torch in hand, she ventured through the passageway.

They had only walked a few hundred yards when the events of the day overwhelmed her. Iwala fell to the ground, almost dropping the torch. Pulling the young girl close, Iwala wept deep, unmitigated tears. *We added misery to your misery, massacre to your massacre. Whoever you are, enemy, evildoers—you will suffer for this. You will suffer for all thirteen villages.*

# Twenty-One

Twid had heard stories of Delgam since childhood. Delgam towered eight feet tall. Delgam walked with the precision of a panther. Delgam's legs dwarfed most men. Delgam's blond hair hung like a thousand lions' manes.

Twid looked at the giant walking before them. The stories were all true. Delgam made Zinna look like Him Too. Twid steadied his arm, holding the blade close to Delgam's side.

To his right, Zinna walked unperturbed, her dagger pressed against Delgam's right kidney.

Twid strained his eyes in the evening light. Soldiers materialized, dressed in Dream King garb. They stopped and Zinna called out.

"We wish neither you nor your leader harm. We desire only to pass. Once we have passed, two things will happen: You will take your army and head south immediately, stop ten miles below this village, and wait for two days before moving. At that time, we will free Delgam, unharmed. This I, Zinna, daughter of Abraha the Bold, promise you."

Zinna had to be the only person alive who could issue orders while surrounded by one thousand enemy soldiers.

A man stepped forward. He wore the insignia of a captain. After struggling for a few moments, he spoke. "Prince Delgam commanded us before he left. He gave us specific instructions on what should happen if you captured him and held his life in your hands."

As he spoke, dozens of soldiers pulled out their arrows and pointed at the three.

Delgam spoke, "I can't let you escape again, Zinna."

Zinna grimaced as the realization set in. She should have seen it. Delgam had always had his pride. He would rather die than have the world know that he had lost Zinna again.

Zinna looked at Twid. Eight hours a day she had trained him, even on the two-month long journey to reach Baria. The boy never complained, and she knew he had even continued training at night. He was good. There was no doubt of that. But was he good enough? All it took was one misstep, one miscalculation.

As she called Twid to her side, she could see the hesitation in his eyes.

Keeping her blade intact on Delgam's side, she whispered for Twid's ears only, trying to keep her voice from cracking. "You need no more from me. Keep practicing the basics and you will reach mastery. Remember: In the end, the master wins with their mind; the master can kill with a blade of grass, much less a sword."

She held herself together as tears sprang in his eyes. He understood.

"Do not look for me. Attempt no rescue. Go to The Source of Harmony and unlock the Harmonies. Come back, find a way into The Cursed Lands, and find The Golden Eagle. You will do it. I have faith in you, Twid. Say you will do it."

Tears stung Twid's eyes. Why did it have to be like this? Why did life always mean loss? Why did one gain only to lose? He found a way to say the words, "I will do it."

Zinna raised her head, addressing Delgam and the soldiers. "Above all, you seek my life. I offer you this: I will go with you willingly and I will spare Delgam. You in turn will spare the boy. Give him your fastest horse. Let him ride from the camp in any direction he sees fit. If he comes back to attempt a rescue, kill him on sight. But you shall not pursue him. We will wait for one hour to ensure no one moves to pursue the boy."

She paused, looking at the captain again. "In exchange, you will have captured Zinna, the First Prince Defender, and pre-served the life of Delgam, the Second."

Twid didn't feel the horse pounding beneath him. He couldn't feel anything. His body disappeared and he felt himself floating up, looking down on himself as he rode across the wilderness. It was strange. He knew it was him riding across the desert. But why wasn't he in his body? Why was he looking down?

He rode for hours, not looking back, not directing the horse. The horse rode straight east, deeper and deeper into the desert.

His life would be different forever. He knew that. A sacrifice had been made. And not just any sacrifice, but Zinna, the First Defender. Why hadn't she fought to save her life? Her life was worth so much more than his.

Find the Harmonies, she had said. Find the Golden Eagle. She was so confident in the bloody fox. In Hibu's prophetic poem. But how could he do it. He'd be hard pressed to make the finals, much less find the Source of Harmony. And the Golden Eagle? How did one find a myth?

Wind buffeted his face and his senses returned, the horse still pounding beneath him. He slowed. He was killing the horse. South. He had to go further south to ride along the desert's edge. He would never make it straight across.

Were Him Too and Iwala alive? Where had they gone? Iwala he could understand. But Him Too? How could he be so irresponsible?

Twid held his anger at bay. It was better they weren't with them or they would have been captured too. But who knew. Maybe they were captured.

Think. He needed to think. He had received a gift. The greatest gift. He could not fail. He had learned from the greatest teacher. He could not fail.

# Twenty-Two

**Z**eru groaned. His body ached everywhere. What had happened? He had gone searching for his companions. He had been walking. And then…

Was he losing his memory again? How long had he slept? As he creaked up, he found that dried mud clogged his shoes, plastering his cloth and even his hair.

Then he remembered. A small mudslide had erupted out of nowhere, smashing him off his feet. He must have hit his head because he couldn't remember anything else.

He had survived. But what about his children? What about Zinna? Forcing himself up, he started hobbling. He hoped he was going the right way. He'd know soon enough. If he walked into The Cursed Wall, he would just turn around.

Zeru quickened his pace. What if they got caught by that same mudslide? Zinna wouldn't have let herself and Twid be caught, but maybe Iwala and Him Too. Up ahead, behind some tall grass, he saw the village.

Then he stopped; an inexplicable tremor ran down his spine. Something was wrong. An Old Ones saying ran through his head, "Travel the path of health even if takes a dozen years."

Finding a patch of tall grass, Zeru crept low and waited. But the only movement was wind blowing dust between the adobes. Near the well, someone had left a flipped wheelbarrow.

Zeru tried to wet his tongue but his mouth was dry. His left eye twitched. There was no movement. Nothing. Maybe approaching from another direction would be better. Zeru crawled out and approached the village from the north.

Was he overreacting? He could think of no one he'd rather have in a tough situation than Zinna. Even if Him Too or Iwala hadn't returned, surely she and Twid were safe.

Zeru stopped at the northern outskirts, hidden from view

by tall grass. With any luck, food awaited, and a warm bed. Looking out again, he contemplated the stillness.

No movement, no sound of any kind. Not from the villagers, not from the livestock. Nothing. The twitching spread from Zeru's left eye to his left jaw. Even in the rain, Zinna had forced Twid to run for an hour every morning.

Zeru crept closer, moving from adobe to adobe until he reached Twid's sleeping quarters. As he stepped inside the dark room, small cobwebs broke over his face. How long had Zeru slept in the mudslide?

He stepped over to Twid's bed. It was made now but had been unmade when Zeru last looked for Twid. Had Twid returned then left again? Twid's pack and his change of cloth still sat next to the bed.

Zeru's anxiety grew as he went through Him Too's room. It was impossible to tell if Him Too had returned. What was clear was that Zinna and Twid, and maybe even Him Too and Iwala, had departed unexpectedly, leaving almost all their possessions behind. He'd even found Zinna's smaller practice staff.

He searched inside the large adobe. Nothing seemed out of place. The room was as empty as he had left it.

Yet something *was* off. As he walked, his eyes settled on a small table in the corner, with a black cloth over it. Where had the table come from? He approached it and took the cloth off – below was a pile of dirt and straw thatch. Zeru scratched his beard. They had enough tables already. Were they trying to hide the dirt and straw…? Why?

Walking to the central support beam, he looked up, straining his eyes. The roof looked thinner, maybe even a bit off center. Could it be? Over the decades, Zeru himself had escaped through more than one roof.

Had someone trapped Twid and Zinna in the room? Zeru put himself in their shoes. *They heard strangers outside. They suspected the strangers meant them harm.*

Putting his hand on the beam, he saw light indentations

where someone had climbed. *Zinna climbed up and looked outside.*

Zeru straddled the pole and dragged himself up. He pushed himself through the opening. Yes. Someone had cut through the roof. Zeru sat on the roof and looked out. His hand touched something hard—it was a long piece of rope tied around the pole. *They saw enemies. Zinna pulled Twid up because Twid couldn't climb fast enough with his one arm.*

Zeru walked to the side of the roof. The rope led to the back of the adobe, to the opposite side of the door. *They climbed down using the rope and then tossed it back up.*

He threw the rope down to the ground and tugged on it, ensuring it was still tied well. He climbed down. *Knowing Zinna, they snuck back to the front and waited for their captors to enter.* And then they escaped. They fled.

Zeru stood before the front door and then stepped backwards. Where would they have hidden? *In the well!* They waited across from the adobe, in the well, then either trapped their captors or escaped. He walked to the well and looked down, praying he wouldn't find their bodies below.

Zeru didn't smell anything. Lowering the well's bucket, he brought some water up for himself, all the while keeping his eyes alert. He drank in small gulps, pausing to clean the mud off his face.

*Why did you not wait for them here? You could have helped them.* Zeru slapped the bucket in frustration, flipping it. *What was the point of living for hundreds of years if one couldn't help when help was needed?*

Then his body froze, needles coursing throughout. Even his face stopped twitching. The bottom of the bucket had letters scrawled in it, letters that were a lighter color of wood than the bucket.

There were four words: The Source of Harmony.

# PART III
## The Source of Harmony

*"To become more, become less."*

Tirhas the Light

# Twenty-Three

**T**he man known as the Knowledge Thief scanned the massive arena, assessing the fighters. Who would be the next Prince Defender? The girl who killed with her hair? The one they called the Endurance King? The Worm?

It didn't matter. He would make money regardless of who won. It was just a matter of how much money.

He knew that not all the fighters would come ahead of time to spar in the Dream Training Center. In fact, the most cunning fighters wouldn't spar publicly at all, and if they did, they would understate their strengths and overstate their weaknesses. Ruses within ruses. The Knowledge Thief smiled.

Most people trained at the main arena, but there were hundreds of smaller sparring centers all throughout Dream City. Maybe the winner would be someone no one had heard of, a complete nobody. No one had heard of Kahn before the games.

He had scouts watching every sparring center, but still, one never knew. If he had learned one thing, it was to expect the unexpected. He watched a few moments more and then left, fighting the crowds as he headed home. Dream City had always been crowded, so heavily populated that some said you could throw a stone in the air, and the stone would always hit someone.

But with the Games set to begin next month, one might not have the elbow room to throw a stone, much less see where it landed. Still, the visitors didn't bother him. For him and the Thieves' Guild, bigger crowds meant bigger opportunities. And this time, with his new position, he would make one hundred times what he had made during the last Games.

He entered a small stone home. According to legend, the enlightened one had lived in a small hut. But he couldn't bear to live in a hut like the peasants in Wirba.

Books covered every wall in his home, the shelves stretching

as high as the ceiling. His favorite learnings came from conversations in taverns and inns, from talking with Dream City's
residents and visitors. But one could not deny that much of the
world's knowledge lay hidden in old tomes.

Money was money. No one could deny its power. With money one could buy food, horses, labor, sex—anything. But with
money *and* knowledge, one could control entire guilds, entire
cities, entire governments. Reaching up, he selected his favorite
book, *A History of the Thieves Guild in Ancient Ras.*

# Twenty-Four

Four months ago, the young man had knocked on her door and asked to work on the farm. He had promised to work six hours a day doing whatever the old woman asked. All the young man wanted in return was lodging and food.

The old woman hadn't believed it. Youth didn't want to work anymore; anytime they lifted a finger, they acted as if they deserved a Dream Medal.

Freedom and Dreams. Winning the Dream Lottery. Winning the Dream Mansion. That's all youth thought about. Even her own sons had abandoned her to search for the Map of Legends.

The old woman puffed on a maple pipe she had carved herself.

She had set the young man to weeding and then tilling the soil. He had volunteered his horse and constructed a plow. As the crops rose, he created support fences made of fallen branches to keep the tomato plants and corn straight. He had even fooled the raccoons by planting a perimeter patch of green corn that ripened late. Six hours, he had said, but he had really worked closer to eight.

During the other sixteen hours, the boy disappeared into the barn, eating his meals alone. He refused to sleep in the farmhouse.

The old woman had snuck in late one afternoon to see what he did. Balanced on a thin beam, the boy had practiced for hours with a short blade and some sort of whip attached to his arm. His feet danced on the hand-wide beam as if it were the stable floor. The boy had cracked the whip and launched himself from beam to beam, eventually landing on his horse where he continued his swordplay standing on the horse's back.

Either the boy was joining the circus, or he was fighting in the

Prince Defender Games. The old woman refilled her pipe and
smiled.

It all amounted to the same thing anyway.

✺ ✺ ✺

Twid slept on the ground, his ear against the dirt floor. Ever
since he saw Zinna anticipate Delgam's arrival, he had slept on
the ground. His first week staying with the old woman, Twid
had also cut an exit out of the barn's back.

He had almost gone back. To rescue Zinna. To find the others. But he had promised; a promise paid for with Zinna's life.
He would go to the source of Harmony. He would return to the
Cursed Lands. He would find the Golden Eagle, whatever she or
it was.

As Twid lay on the ground, sweat covered his body and a
numb sensation crept down his spine. Twid knew that sensation. He had felt the sensation when he lost his mother and sister. He had felt it whenever he had met anyone who reminded
him of his family. And he felt it now, creeping everywhere and
nowhere, all at once.

He would survive. That's what orphans always did. Survive. If
he never saw his friends again, he would slowly eliminate them;
he would even forget Him Too. Not because he wanted to, but
because he had to. Sure, he would think about his best friend
from time to time, laughing as he remembered the time they
had raced goats down the big hill or stolen Iwala's tobacco. He
would remember Zeru chasing Iwala out of the house with a
broom, and Zinna's relentless training. But such times would be
rare. He had learned that remembering too much would only
cause pain.

But for now, it was still okay to remember. Maybe they had
survived somehow. Maybe they had found the message on the
well's bucket. Maybe they would meet him in Dream City for
the Games.

His ears perked as he felt light tremors from the ground. Someone approached. And it wasn't the old woman. He knew she had watched him at least once. Heart racing, Twid grabbed his sword and tiptoed to the back of the barn. He melted into the cold night. Then he heard voices and three men approached with a lantern.

"These fools are wasting the horse on farm work. Hagos will give us at least fifty birr for it."

"We can't steal from an old woman."

"It's not hers. She can't even ride it. I'm telling you, that new hired hand brought it. It's his."

Twid's teeth dug into his gums. He forced himself to remember one of Zinna's favorite sayings: "The rich man kills without leaving his seat, the master warrior without lifting a finger."

Twid called out to the men when they were several feet from the entrance. "I applaud you for not wanting to steal from an old woman."

The men sprang back; one fell; another grabbed his sword hilt.

Ignoring the wind's howl, Twid took a step forward. "But you are mistaken. The horse does belong to her. In exchange for lodging and food, I have given her the horse."

Twid whistled, and the horse bounded out, standing next to him. He turned the horse and motioned for the men to lift the lantern. The lantern's soft hue outlined a brand of the sun shining over three clasped hands. The men started as they saw the Dream King seal.

"In truth, even I don't own this horse; he belongs to the Dream Kings. The Dream Kings commissioned me to study soil and farming practices for two years. You do know that the Dream Kings have greatly improved agriculture in the Three Lands?"

As the men nodded, Twid heard Iwala in his head: "When outnumbered, appeal to a power your enemies fear."

"I have neared the end of my commission. Tomorrow, I will

leave to make my report to the Dream Kings. Dream City is just
a week's walk so I will leave the old women the horse as a token
of the Dream King's appreciation. We will return to check on
her and the crop rotations every two years."

Twid patted the brand, "Freedom and Dreams to you and
your households."

The men nodded, confused and relieved at the same time.
They had almost made a catastrophic mistake, almost attacked a
representative of the Dream Kings.

As he watched them leave, Twid wondered how many others
in the countryside had seen the horse. Rubbing the horse's neck,
he led him to a beam and tied him.

After surveying the stable one final time, Twid grabbed his
things and left. As he passed the field, he stopped and poked at
the dirt. Like sentinels, the shoulder-high corn stalks guarded
the tomatoes and squash, the green peppers and carrots, the
green beans.

Twid reached down and pulled out a carrot. If only old Zeru
was there to see the crops, even in the moonlight. Zeru would
never believe that Twid had grown such a garden.

As Twid continued to the main road, he considered the
weeks ahead. Not only would he have to pass the preliminary
qualifying round, he would then have to win eight straight
battles. Even if he won the eight battles, he'd have to find the
Source of Harmony, sneak in, and unlock the Harmonies.

The Harmonies. It all came back to the Harmonies. Where
did they get their power? Were they magic? If they were so powerful, how come no one knew them or sought them?

Twid brushed dirt off the carrot. It wasn't ripe. He took a bite.
The loud crunch and sharp taste reminded Twid of radishes.

Then, there was the question of who could use the
Harmonies. Anyone who learned them? If only a select few
could harness the Harmonies, how were the few selected?

He thought back to the First Harmony. *Freedom: You choose
your actions.* It was such a simple idea, but hadn't it been powerful

enough to help him a few minutes ago; even if he'd had to lie?

Was that it? Was that the power of the Harmonies: You could avoid harmful situations and create more positive situations? Could that simple idea match up against the hundreds of thousands of Dream King soldiers?

Twid tossed the carrot stem into the night.

# Twenty-Five

The light breeze scattered the sand to the desperate, knee-high desert shrubs spaced every ten paces. Dust spread to the hunched camels, resting after weeks of waterless toil; to the adobes, adding sand and dirt to the hardened grime already there.

A wooden sign hung before one of the adobes, *The Copy Cat*. Zeru pushed the tavern's door open. For the last month, he had traveled as fast as he could. He had stolen two camels, riding each of them to death across the endless Hasara desert. Three times, he had almost died in sandstorms.

Zeru plodded to the bar and sat at the counter. A thin middle-aged barkeeper was talking, wispy hairs clinging to the sides of his bald head like leeches.

"Go fool someone else. I've raised dozens of camels. And I'm telling you, camels have a memory. Pinch the udder too hard when you are milking, and wait, wait about a year, when you're not looking and the camel will slam your head with..." The barkeeper snapped his bald head forward, showing off a scarred imprint of a camel's foot.

Without asking, the barkeeper slammed a tankard of ale before Zeru. "If you wanted to see the filthiest, dirtiest, cesspit in Nisha, welcome. Our dirt roads are filled with camel dung. Our huts are made from camel dung. Our women are uglier than our camels, and our camels are smarter than our men..."

Zeru smiled as the barkeeper continued to denigrate his town and tavern. You had to be careful with people like this. They loved to deride their town, but woe to any outsider who did.

Leaning back against the bar, he surveyed the room. It was a strange crowd, not at all what he expected from the barkeeper's description.

On an elevated table sat four short young men, hairy feet exposed. One of them played with a small nondescript ring. Next to them sat a tall man, with a hard, weathered look, his dark eyes striding from right to left.

Directly behind, on a lower table sat a gigantic man, face hidden behind a dark cowl, and a short man with pointed ears next to him. The short man pulled out three blue gemstones, rotating them in his hand. Somehow, it seemed to Zeru that the second table copied the first, drinking whenever the first drank, eating whenever the first ate.

The barkeeper tapped Zeru. "Yes. We have strangers, too. Stories have spread that the Map of Legends can be found in these parts."

The Map of Legends. For decades, young and old alike had searched in every desert and forest, every mountain and molehill, seeking to find the mysterious map and the riches it promised. The Dream Kings themselves had provided money and supplies for many of the expeditions.

Zeru sneezed. Had they brewed the ale from hot peppers and radishes?

As he took another swallow, Zeru thought back to Baria. He couldn't get the well bucket out of his head. The bucket had been dark brown, but the indentations light tan. So the indentations had been fresh.

But who had left the markings? Twid? Zinna? Him Too? Iwala?

Zeru steadied himself and took another deep draught, sloshing the sharp ale around the toothless side of his mouth like a gambler shuffling cards. He would have spit if he weren't inside. He looked at the ground. Not that the inside of the tavern was any nicer than the desert outside.

Who would scout the warriors for Twid? Who would help him find a way into Himlee? Zinna herself had said she couldn't enter...

The tavern door slammed open. Zeru turned and set down his tankard. Pulling his mutton pie close, he hunched into the bar. The left side of his chin quivered.

It was a dozen Dream King soldiers. They didn't bother to wipe the dust from their faces or their obscured uniforms. As they gathered around the bar, Zeru caught the animalistic scent of layered, hardened sweat.

Remnants of ale dripped out of Zeru's toothless side. Zeru had chosen the most direct, arduous route to Dream City. In the absence of rare need, travelers always went south or north to avoid the endless Hasara Desert. Surely these soldiers weren't searching for the Map of Legends.

He watched them out of the corner of his eye. They ordered stew, bread, and water. *Don't get involved in anything new. Finish your meal. Go to the inn. Sleep. Wake at midnight and start walking again while it's cool out. You only have two more weeks if you maintain your pace.*

Not one of the soldiers ordered ale. They were in a desert, but still… What self-respecting soldier ordered water after weeks of travel?

He shifted in his chair, trying to read their stoic faces.

The man who seemed to be in charge, a tall Nishan, ordered more stew and meat. Enough for fifty men. The barkeeper nodded, saying they would have to charge extra for the bowls since the soldiers would not return them. The soldier threw a pile of gold pieces on the table.

Head down, Zeru paid and left. As he stepped into the night, he knelt and looked at the ground. Like him, the soldiers came from the west. Rising, he followed their tracks. He glanced behind him. Who demanded extra plates of hot food if they didn't have someone nearby to feed?

After a half-mile, he heard light noises ahead. Slowing, he curved around, angling towards a small sand hill. Dozens of campfires blazed, surrounded by several hundred soldiers, a caravan. In the middle was a tent.

Two hundred Dream King soldiers in the middle of the Hasara, surrounding one tent? The soldiers from the tavern returned and carried the food into the tent.

Zeru knew he should leave. Twid and Zinna needed him. Him Too and Iwala needed him. But who was in that tent?

※ ※ ※

Donkeys brayed, heralds for the humble owners who plodded beside them. Carts rumbled. Merchants waved their wares at anyone who would look and even those who wouldn't. Twid walked to the side, taking in the chaos, having long since ceded the road to braver travelers.

He heard a short, stocky man comment to his companion. "Is this not an example of the Dream Kings' freedom? Here we are on the main road to Dream City, and donkeys and sheep walk as freely as any man."

Twid stepped around a rock. He still couldn't believe how many people walked the roads. Or the loads some carried on their backs. Earlier, Twid had seen six men lift a gigantic pack onto another man's shoulder, placing the load on the small of his back. Yet the man lumbered along at the same pace as Twid.

Twid fingered his beard. It had grown so long that he had braided the lower part. And his skin, once brown, shone a near-black.

He shifted to avoid a roadside shop. With Dream City's massive walls just a hundred yards away, merchants milled like bees. To the right, a woman hawked firewood that cost less but lasted longer. A man proclaimed that his potion could make any woman fall in love.

A red-haired woman on the side of the road had a cherry wood sign that read "The Secret." Her smooth voice rang out across the road:

> *Come, good people, unlock the secret.*
> *For what wings are to eagles, the secret is to men.*
> *Come, soar to dreams unimagined.*

*Come, seize your freedom.*
*Only 20 birr, and The Secret is….*

As he drew closer to Dream City's walls, Twid found himself unable to look away. Tall white walls sparkled in the sun. Parapets adorned with circular and triangular designs punctuated the walls. Soldiers lined…

Suddenly a gigantic man loomed before Twid. He waved a potion:

*All that you seek, yours.*
*All that you dream, realized.*
*All that you desire, now.*
*All you…*

Twid moved to avoid the man only to find himself accosted by a beautiful blond woman who waved a parchment and proclaimed:

*Young man — have you not heard?*
*Young man — have you not learned?*
*Stop — for no longer must you toil.*
*No longer must you march like the ants.*
*Lost for centuries, at last it's yours!*
*The famed Map of Legends…*

Women hawked exotic pastries made from raf, the Dream King's new white grain. Merchants offered instant wealth. Everything got louder and faster, until Twid felt the crowd, the merchants, the Secret—whatever it was— crawling under his skin.

And then Twid was walking past Dream City's gigantic gates. Past the intent eyes of the hundreds of soldiers who scanned every entrant. Past the insurmountable iron gates, thrust-wide open. Past the perfect white stones that formed the walls.

Twid fought to keep his face straight. He'd made it! Dream

City! Despite his disguise, despite the massive crowd, despite the many months that had ensued, Twid had feared that Scout-boy and a Dirg would jump from the walls and shackle him.

Just inside the walls, a massive, spectacular statue towered, arresting Twid's attention. Twid jostled closer. Atop a massive horse, a bearded warrior extended his left arm as if he could push the horizon itself. Drawn back by his head, his other hand held a long spear, triceps flexed in mid-launch. With the horse in mid-gallop and the warrior arched forward, the statue carried a sense of movement, of purpose that sent Twid's heart racing.

Walking closer, Twid read the caption engraved into the statue's base, written in the ancient Giiz. "Talia can rule in my land if I can rule in his." Twid stared at the warrior's face again. Ras Alula the Unconquerable, considered by many the greatest warrior to ever live. Two hundred years ago, he had slain the Dirg Talia, and turned back Idgistu's hordes, preserving freedom for the Three Lands.

Twid angled his neck and took in the jutting cheekbones, the intense eyes.

Feeling as if he could battle Idgistu himself, Twid kept walking. Hunger pangs cut his stomach. He had looked for food made from tef, but the merchants only sold food made from raf. After Zinna's story of how the new Dream King grain caused addiction, Twid had stopped eating raf.

Despite his hunger, Twid smiled at the irony. Here he was surrounded by more food than he had ever seen but none that he wanted. It was probably best to just find an inn first. Then he could find suitable food and scout his competition at the Dream Training Center. On the road in, he'd already heard people talking about a girl who killed with her hair and someone they called The Worm.

Suddenly, a shriek rang out. A woman's head scarf covered her eyes, blinding her. Her hands fumbled at her purse but it was already gone.

Without thinking, Twid unfurled and snapped his whip. The

thief, a boy of about thirteen, tripped to the ground. Twid leapt forward and pinned him with his foot, but Twid almost took a step back when he saw raw defiance in the boy's eyes.

Twid said, "Isn't the penalty for thievery in the Three Lands fifty lashes?"

The boy snarled. "Imbecile! Release me now or the Thieves Guild will have you dead within the hour."

Twid's head browed. The city actually had a guild that protected the rights of thieves! If only Iwala could hear this.

"Well, maybe I should finish you here then." Bending to his knees, Twid popped the blade in his left arm and pressed it against the young man's side.

"Fool. My uncle is Guild Master. You've heard of him: the Knowledge Thief." The young man spat on Twid's foot. "Release me now or you will die. I swear it. At least ten thieves watch you right now."

Twid scanned the passersby. Farmers bringing in crops, merchants, street vendors. He didn't see any thieves watching. In fact, everyone ignored them, including a donkey that stepped over the boy.

"Knowledge Thief. Never heard of him."

Twid resisted an urge to cuff the boy. Someone needed to teach him manners but the last thing Twid needed was Dream King soldiers asking questions.

Twid retrieved the stolen purse and rose. Instead of running, the boy stood and stared at Twid like an archer marking a deer.

Without turning his back, Twid walked to the woman. She had readjusted her scarf over her head, revealing jutting cheekbones and light, brown skin that marked her a Rasan. Her warm, crinkled eyes shone with genuine gratitude. Twid guessed she was about sixty years old.

Twid tilted his head, as was customary when speaking to one's elders. "Freedom and Dreams to you, mother." He handed her the purse.

The woman's voice was as deep as a ram's horn. "Blessings to

you my son. May you always have shade above your head and
sandals beneath your feet. May you always be the giver and not
the beggar."

Twid bowed his head again.

Looking up, he saw the woman shiver. She said, almost to
herself, "I was warned that the thieves here blind women using
their own head scarves... I thought I had my scarf on tight."

She opened the purse to give Twid a few coins. Twid shook
his head. "Your blessing is enough. And don't judge yourself too
harshly, mother. Have the Old Ones not said, 'The wily thief will
steal your eyebrows even as you stare at him, your teeth even as
you chew?'"

At his reciting of the Old Ones saying the woman looked at
Twid anew. Twid asked her, "Are you near your home?" She motioned across the street to an inn called The Flying Hare.

Twid nodded and walked her to the inn. As they walked,
Twid scanned the crowd for any sign of the boy, but he had
disappeared.

The Thieves Guild. What was next? The Liars Guild?

# Twenty-Six

Anticipation swept the Dream Training Center. Twid could see it in the eyes of the hopefuls who sparred below, could feel it tingling in his own heart—excitement at the opportunity to compete, but fear of what could go wrong.

And much could go wrong. In each of the previous Prince Defender Games, more than thirty warriors had died. Greater than one hundred had suffered wounds that left them blind, lame, or otherwise maimed for life. In the last games, Inj alone had killed three of his ten opponents.

Twid's gaze shifted below, to the sparring area and the woman from Wirba. The two short swords he could handle. But her hair? Zeru's name! Her two braids ended in studded steel balls that whipped around with frightening speed. They would smash bone and flesh alike.

Then there was the man they called the Shepherd. Twid wouldn't ordinarily fear anyone with a staff. Not after Zinna. But his staff, it had a curved end used to hook people's feet, arms, anything. Even without the hook, the Shepherd was good with the staff, almost as good as Zinna.

Twid glanced back to the front corner, where the one they called The Endurance King had fought for hours. Different fighters had shuffled in and out, trying to land a blow on the thin Wirban, but he wore them all down with his dizzying footwork and elaborate feints. The ultimate defense until the offense collapsed. Zinna would be proud.

Twid massaged the skin above his eyes. He wondered what the fighters were hiding. That they were hiding something was clear. They wouldn't let themselves be scouted unless they could somehow turn it to their advantage. The girl with the hair—did she have another weapon? The Endurance King—did he shift into attack mode in unexpected ways? The Shepherd—was there more to the staff than he was letting on? How about the other fighters who weren't sparring? Twid had heard of a Nishan they called the Needle and…

"Thank you for helping my mother yesterday."

Twid's eyes snapped up. A husky man stood before him, exuding the strength of a bull. Warmth shone from his dark eyes, his smile revealing top teeth that jutted out like the staff he carried. Twid started as he realized he was looking at the one they called the Shepherd.

The Shepherd pointed fifteen seats to the left. A smiling woman waved. Twid waved back at the woman the Knowledge Thief's nephew had robbed.

The Shepherd said, "My mother can't stop talking about you. Not just because you helped her. She said you cited some Old Ones saying native to our homeland of Tembien."

Twid smiled. "It was nothing. As to the saying, my father had more Old Ones sayings than a monastery."

The Shepherd extended his hand. "They call me Berhane. Berhane, son of Ahferom."

Twid shook the Shepherd's calloused hands. Twid asked, "Isn't Ahferom ancient Giiz for 'He who embarrasses others?'"

Berhane stamped his staff. "Lightning pierce me! You know Giiz, too. Are you trying to oust me as my mother's son?" He smiled. "As to the meaning of Ahferom, why do you think I'm here? Wouldn't you rather embarrass a few fighters than win?"

Twid laughed. "Not sure what it says about me, but they call me Wolde, son of Tayle." The Shepherd's husky shoulders shook as he laughed and Twid joined him. Tayle was the common tongue for goat.

Twid said, "I watched you earlier. Wolves and hyenas must have starved in the areas that you shepherded."

Berhane said, "But you're wiser than I. You choose not to spar at all."

Twid smiled then stopped; his eyebrows arched. How did Berhane know that he was entering the Games? Noting Twid's consternation, Berhane explained, "My mother has been watching you watch us. She says you will enter the Games."

Berhane moved over as his mother approached. "Here she is now. Mother, his name is Wolde and he knows ancient Giiz, too."

Twid bowed his head, trying to hide his smile. Her head scarf was so taut that the Knowledge Thief himself couldn't remove it, even with the entire Thieves Guild to aid him.

"Giiz. Next you will tell me that you know the ancient shoulder dances of northern Ras."

Twid didn't tell her that Zeru had taught them the dances since childhood. Instead, he said, "Berhane said that you are from Tembien. I don't know that land."

Berhane said, "Tembien is the ancient birth land of Ras Alula the Unconquerable, son of the farmer, Engda Qubi, who was the son of Abba Nega before him. After Alula killed the Dirg Talia, Idgistu and the other Dirg razed Tembien. Now, for the last hundred years, Hyek vermin have overrun Tembien and even the Dream Kings dare not send their soldiers there."

Berhane drew himself straight and smiled at his mother. "Once I am Prince Defender, I myself will lead the soldiers north to restore my people's homeland."

Twid exhaled. Zeru's name! He had never considered that other fighters would have their own, deeply held reasons for competing; reasons that went far beyond money or fame.

They talked for several more minutes. Twid learned the mother's name, Senai, and more about Tembien, which lay about fifty miles from Idgistu's stronghold in the north. Twid would have kept talking were it not time for his evening workout.

As Twid rose to leave, Senai asked, with a smile around her lips, "Other than my son, which fighter would you most avoid?"

Twid hesitated. "It's like asking a goat to choose between a tiger and a bear. But I'd have to say the woman with the hair. The steel balls could come out of nowhere and if they smash you once, she'll follow up with her short swords."

Twid returned the question. "How about you?"

The Shepherd smiled. "Me? The lions of Tembien fear neither man nor beast. I'll embarrass the Endurance King and the girl together."

Twid laughed and bowed good-bye to Senai. He made his way from the arena out into the soft evening air. As he walked, he kicked several pebbles.

These last six months on the farm, Twid had purposefully avoided getting to know the old woman. And here in Dream City, he had planned to keep to himself, to stay focused on his end goal: The Source of Harmony.

But he had to admit. He liked Berhane and Senai. He hadn't laughed that much since he and his friends had parted. As Twid turned onto the small street that led to his inn, he thought of the day ahead. He had only…

Suddenly, Twid stopped and glanced around. The street was bare. Neither light nor noise emanated from the surrounding homes. Twid swallowed.

Feet shuffled. Two men bounded from nearby roofs. Three men sprang from the shadows. All five drew their swords. Twid heard a short laugh then a loud crack.

"I think you owe me your money pouch." The Knowledge Thief's nephew stepped forward. He brandished a horsewhip. "And the Thieves Guild owes you fifty lashes."

As the men circled Twid, the Knowledge Thief's nephew spat. The saliva clump struck Twid's forearm and slithered like a rotten fig. Nausea overwhelmed Twid like over-fermented ale on an empty stomach. He called out. "I have no quarrel with you."

The boy smiled. "Nor I with you. I'm actually here on your orders. Earlier today, you decreed that the penalty for thievery was fifty lashes." The boy snapped the whip. "Then you stole my money pouch."

Twid's back quivered as if it could already feel the lashes. As the soldiers laughed, despair rocked him. Even if he somehow defeated the six men, he'd have the whole Thieves Guild after him. And if he let them whip him, he'd barely walk, much less fight in the Games.

The nephew cracked the whip at Twid's head. Twid dodged with a slight movement to the left. Twid tried to concentrate on the soldiers but somehow found himself thinking of old Zeru. If only he was there with him, old Zeru would grab them each by the ear, grown men or not. "Tell me. Who is your father? Tell me. Who is your mother? Let us go talk to them now. Do they know what you are..."

Twid heard a clanging and looking down. He blinked to ensure he saw right. Somehow, without realizing it, he had unrolled his own whip, and yanked two of the soldier's swords out of their hands.

The other three men attacked. Twid darted between them, his whip cracking. Within moments, he had the other three swords on the ground before him. He still hadn't drawn his sword.

The soldiers fell back, eyes wide, knees bent, ready to flee. Twid drew his money pouch out and tossed it at the boy who now looked at him with awe. "I say to you again: I have no quarrel with you. Take the gold and leave me in peace."

※ ※ ※

Twid realigned his body on his room's wooden floor, trying to find a more comfortable position. He had replayed the scene with the soldiers and he still didn't know what had happened.

Sure, he had practiced eight hours each day, practicing the same moves day after day for a year. But earlier, when he had moved, it had felt like someone else. Like something else. Like magic...?

Was it Zinna? He hadn't fought anyone other than her for the last year. Had training with her thrown off his perspective? He shuffled his body again then paused. Had he heard someone approach? He kept still for a moment then relaxed. It was nothing.

Maybe he was ready for the Games after all. Who knew, maybe he could even win.

Light tremors resonated through the wooden floor again. Someone approached. Twid crept to his feet and tiptoed behind the door. Releasing the blade on his left arm would be too loud. He unsheathed a dagger and waited.

The lock jiggled, and the door opened. Whoever it was remained outside.

A soothing yet commanding voice spoke. "Your bed is unslept in. Hence you were probably sleeping on the floor to better hear intruders. Your whip is too loud to unfurl and less useful in close quarters or you'd use that. If you're half as good as they say you are, you heard me approach and are waiting behind the door with a dagger in your hand."

Twid almost fell over.

"May I enter?"

Twid stepped out from behind the door. Before him stood a middle-aged blond man. His smiling teeth radiated in the moonlight.

Twid motioned for the man to sit in the small chair in the corner.

"Who are you?"

The man looked around the room and walked to the corner where the sword from the tree lay. The man's eyebrows arched, the only sign of surprise. "You are wise not to wear a sword from the Ancient Tree of The Five."

Twid frowned. He tried to regain his senses. What did the Old Ones say, "The fool reveals his ignorance when he opens his mouth?"

The man put the sword down. "Not in this city at least, if in any city at all."

As Twid remained silent, the man sat. "I'm not here to force you to talk. Tell me to leave, and I will do so immediately."

Twid considered his words. "You are the one they call the Knowledge Thief." The man nodded.

"You're the head of the Thieves Guild." The man nodded again.

"Right again. Let's play my favorite game. Tell me something I don't know and I'll tell you something you don't know."

Twid thought for a moment. He only wanted the answer to one or two questions. How would he find the Source of Harmony if he made it into Himlee? What were the Second, Third, Fourth, and Fifth Harmonies?

Twid started. "There are more than two Harmonies."

The Knowledge Thief nodded. "There are five Harmonies."

Twid continued. "The Dream Kings betrayed Zinna. Zinna did not betray the Dream Kings."

The Knowledge Thief continued. "And Delgam captured Zinna six months ago."

Twid's brow furrowed. Zeru's name…!

Twid tried again. "The source of Harmony is in—"

"Himlee, the innermost chambers of the Dream Palace."

Twid said. "The First Harmony is Freedom: You choose your—"

"Actions."

"And the Second Harmony is not Dreams, as the Dream Kings have taught us. The Second Harmony is—"

The Knowledge Thief cut in again: "Discipline: You become your actions."

Twid stopped; his breath caught. Tremors rocked his spine.

The Dream Kings had taught that you could have anything you wanted, be anything you wanted. Not next year. Not tomorrow. Today. Now.

But hadn't he felt the Second Harmony earlier? Hadn't he become the countless small actions he had taken for the last year and the eight years preceding? Little by little, hadn't he felt himself moving faster, with more balance, more skill? Until today, the power became supernatural?

Twid closed his eyes, overwhelmed with the magnitude of the

Dream Kings' lies.

So simple, yet so easy to hide. Clear as day, but invisible as air. That was the second harmony. Dream as you might, you didn't become your biggest dreams; you became your smallest actions.

The Knowledge Thief said, "I pursue knowledge every moment through books, conversations, reflection, experiences. And now, I have become my consistent action. I have become more knowledgeable than but a handful of people alive. So knowledgeable, that you cannot offer me even one piece of new knowledge."

The Knowledge Thief stood. "I revealed to you what you already sensed about the Second Harmony. So now, you owe me one piece of knowledge. I always collect my debts. Make the finals of the Games. Gain admission into Himlee. Find the Source. Once you are inside, study every detail for when you return, I expect you to tell me what lies at the Source of Harmony."

Reaching into his pocket, he withdrew a small pouch and threw it at Twid.

"If you figure out any of the remaining Harmonies, or find the Golden Eagle, or anything about the River of Life, those pieces of knowledge are acceptable as well."

Twid fingered the money pouch he had given the boy earlier.

"What if I get you more than one piece of information?"

The Knowledge Thief smiled. "Then you'll be in a rare and enviable position."

He walked out, his words floating back to Twid.

"The Knowledge Thief will be in your debt."

⁂ ⁂ ⁂

As he waited in line, Twid assessed the soldiers around him. Some towered over seven feet tall, others made even Him Too look like a giant. Twid knew size didn't matter. Zinna had warned him. *"Some of the small ones are stronger than the big ones and the big ones are often quicker than the small ones."*

First things first, he had to qualify. He wished he could watch the qualifying rounds. But the Dream Kings had forbidden any fighters from entering the arena, instead requiring them to wait in the cavernous holding area, where they were called out in groups of twenty.

A soldier motioned Twid forward. As Twid walked through the corridor, he suddenly felt like vomiting. His bladder contracted. He entered the Dream Coliseum with his head pounding like war drums. The crowd's euphoric screams careened around the arena like a chariot pulled by rabid horses. A wild sensation overran his senses. Forcing himself to stop and breathe, Twid closed his eyes. He wondered if the spectators might rush the fighting area.

When he reopened his eyes, a line of Dream King soldiers faced him, separated into twenty groups of three. The judge, a gruff, barrel-chested man, bellowed, "To qualify, you must last for thirty seconds with two out of the three soldiers. If you land a hit on a soldier before the time is up, you win that battle automatically; if a soldier lands even the tiniest blow on you, you lose that battle automatically."

Twid picked up a wooden sword. He kept his whip hidden and blocked out the crowd. Stepping forward, he surveyed the three soldiers. Two could have been twins. Of medium build, they wore light armor and carried long spears. The third soldier dwarfed them, his muscles rippling in the sunlight.

Twid bowed then settled into the defensive Ras fighting style. At the sound of a bell, one of the smaller soldiers dropped his spear and grabbed two short swords.

He charged Twid. His swords blurred like butcher knives. Twid circled back, parrying each thrust, keeping his knees poised. Balance. He had to keep his balance.

Before he knew it, a bell sounded, signifying that thirty seconds had passed.

Twid bowed to the soldier and settled into the defensive Ras again. At the sound of the bell, the gigantic soldier charged, wielding a sword as big as Twid's body. Twid kept his distance. Wooden sword or no, if the giant landed a blow on him, Twid was dead. Twid saw an opening where he could have struck the giant's knees, then shoulder, then arm, but Twid held back.

"Think defense," Zinna had told him. "Reveal as little of your offense as possible."

The bell rang again and Twid bowed. The giant nodded. "Freedom and Dreams to you little brother. We will see you tomorrow at daybreak for the opening ceremonies and the first day of fighting."

He pulled up Twid's right sleeve and slapped a seal on Twid's shoulder. Pain shot through Twid, but he didn't care. He looked at his shoulder: 17. He had made it. Only eight more battles and he would reach The Source of Harmony.

# Twenty-Seven

A faint light revealed three tattered figures strewn on a rocky corridor floor. Two appeared no more than children; the third, a gaunt woman, wore disheveled braids covered by grime. A thin rope connected each of their thin arms. On a narrow ledge above, a small animal stood guard.

Iwala looked at Him Too and the young girl, Rua, the sole survivor from the 13th village. Without Rua, they would have died long ago. Rua had shown them edible corridor plants, water vines, and even beetles, ants, and spiders. The spiders. It helped if you killed them first. Iwala had learned that the hard way.

And the light sticks. Rua had shown them small sticks that stayed lit for several days at a time. Not that the light had helped them find their way. Even Rua was hopelessly lost.

Had it been two months or two years? All Iwala knew was that it wasn't two weeks. They had had half a month's food when they left the rhinoceros. Now, Iwala couldn't remember what bread, even unleavened pack bread, tasted like.

Iwala felt a tingling on her leg and tossed an ant up to Kwee. She heard a crunch; something squirted her face.

She tugged on the rope. "Wake up. We have to keep moving."

Him Too helped Rua to her feet. "Go kid someone else, Iwala. You sit here snoring like a donkey and you tell us to awaken. As if we could sleep. Rua and I have been waiting for hours. Right, Rua?"

Rua nodded as she rubbed her eyes. Iwala shot Him Too an appreciative glance. Him Too and Iwala had agreed that despair as they might, they would never let Rua know; not after what they had put her through. If not for themselves; if not for their friends who waited aboveground; if not for Tefono and the massacred Thirteenth Village; they had to survive to ensure Rua did.

Without her to motivate them, they would have despaired long ago.

As she trudged behind her companions, Iwala felt like a blind woman with a cane: The light stick provided just enough guidance to hobble forward, but not enough to show what really lay ahead.

Him Too called over his shoulder, "We're heading back to the cavern."

Iwala massaged her forehead, moving her fingers to keep them from cramping.

She stopped before the wall …the end of the corridor had the square markings. The entire last week….however long it had been, they had been going in circles. Again! She resisted an urge to scream. The friends had carved markings on both sides of any new corridor they entered but that hadn't stopped them from looping.

They emerged into a large cavern. Without counting, Iwala knew that ten corridors branched out. She also knew that nine had markings.

The one that was left…the hairs on Iwala's neck stood straight. The smell. They had avoided the last corridor because of its stench, if stench was the right word. Not quite the smell of rot or dead bodies. Iwala had tried to place the nauseating stench. She had decided that the smell was like a flying turtle— turtles didn't fly. And smells…even the worst smells, couldn't feel like this.

※ ※ ※

Him Too called backward, "The trail is getting slicker." He tried to improve his footing by pushing the soles of his feet harder into the uneven corridor ground. The jagged edges scraped his feet. But Him Too didn't mind—if nothing else, the pain distracted him from the foul stench that had somehow worsened, even as they grew accustomed to it. Even as it covered their cloth, hair, mouths, tongues.

Him Too coughed. His throat burned, and he thought again of the voices. Ever since the massacre, the voices had disappeared, as if the Dream King soldiers had slaughtered them, too. Him Too didn't want to admit it, but he felt more than a bit betrayed, finding his fate much like that of an average girl, who having been promised a prince, found herself betrothed to a beggar. But hadn't Old Mogus warned them in Metka's prison? Hadn't he had told them that even Minja— the *real* Minja —had failed? Him Too grunted.

Iwala said, "Stop moaning up there like a calf in mid-labor. Rua and I are trying to listen ahead."

Him Too smiled and called back, "Ignore her, Rua. Iwala's hearing is worse than the stench in this corridor."

Iwala said, "What? Your breath is fouler than this corridor?"

Rua's laughter washed over Him Too like cold water on a burn. Even more than Iwala, he felt responsible for the girl's fate. She had approached him and his staff outside the cursed Dream Wall; she and her village had thought him a hero. But when the fighting started, he had proven himself a burden to be carried, not a warrior.

Kwee's claws tightened along his shoulders. Him Too came to a halt and motioned for the others to stop. Leaning forward, he closed his eyes. A rhythmic rumbling echoed ahead, like the breathing of some gigantic animal.

Him Too exhaled and slipped the rope from his wrist. "I have to see something up ahead. You two wait here and—"

Iwala interrupted him. "Don't even try it. Kwee and I will go. You—"

Him Too said, "No. You stay with Rua."

But then Rua interrupted, "Listen! It's a river."

Him Too paused and listened again. The rhythmic rumblings, the slippery ground, the soft mist — maybe it *was* some sort of underground river. Nodding, Him Too reattached the rope. He crept forward. Him Too always led because earlier, Iwala had fallen off a ledge while leading, and with her heavier weight, almost dragged the other two with her.

Vines grew along the ground, making it even slicker. The sound grew into a mix of rhythmic pounding and rapid gurgling. Him Too's shoulders relaxed, and he loosened his grip on his staff. The sound was too layered to be an animal's breathing. But the stench—somehow it worsened. Him Too gripped his staff tight. The corridor walls widened.

Then his staff dropped; his hands suddenly numb. The light stick's glow danced around a gigantic cavern, shining with the brilliance of the noonday sun. Crystals twinkled along the walls and ceiling, radiating over and around the golden waters like happy dreams of childhood. Him Too dropped to his knees. The water's gurgling and brightness reminded him of a harp's deep melodies.

To his left, Rua touched a protruding crystal. Iwala stumbled to the water's edge and crumbled. It took Him Too a moment to realize he had stopped breathing and when he raised a hand to his hollow cheeks, he found tears streaming.

The sparkling waters cut the cavern in half, and across the water, Iwala saw a corridor opening. Rua whispered, "They used to tell legends sometimes, of a crystal river." She sat next to Iwala, "Father Tefono said that somewhere in these tunnels, there was a great river, narrow yet deep, rapid yet gentle, guarded by crystals. The River of Life."

They took in the wondrous cavern like a desert traveler in an unexpected oasis. Iwala said. "Maybe Tefono meant 'The River of Heaven.'"

Lying back, Iwala looked up to the crystals in the ceiling. Rua gazed at the waters. Even Kwee didn't make any noise. Iwala pointed up, "Look up at the ceiling."

Up above, from between the crystal in the ceilings, little drops of yellow fluid dripped into the water. Now that her eyes had adjusted, Iwala saw that they released a light vapor that floated throughout the chamber.

Rising, Iwala unfurled a long piece of rope and snapped it out over the river, toward the dripping fluid. The rope hissed and disintegrated where the fluids touched. Iwala pulled back the charred rope end and held it close to her nose. While the rope was still a hand-length away, bile rushed from Iwala's stomach, cutting her throat and mouth like Nishan hot peppers. Her head slammed into the ground and Rua and Him Too leapt to hold her down.

The smell! It slithered inside her like a snake, clawing as if it had fangs and talons, slicing and tearing with the ferocity of a lioness protecting her young. Somehow...the smell was alive. She retched and then hurled the rope from her. She rose. "That smell is...alive! It's squirming inside me...everywhere." She coughed. "We have to get out!"

Iwala turned and found a large piece of crystal. She swung herself onto it. She called to her friends, "Swing on this with me." Rua, Him Too, and Iwala gripped a piece of the protruding crystal and tugged. It didn't move.

Iwala turned and walked several paces to the left, across from the corridor door on the other side. She looked up. No dripping fluids. She made a lasso out of the rope and tossed it across the cavern, past the river, and missed a crystal high on the other side by a few feet. She tried again. And again. Inside, she felt the smell squirm like a spider. If this was the River of Life, some-thing was poisoning it.

She landed the rope. She called to Rua. "Hold on tight." She gave the rope a final tug and sailed over the river, her heart pounding. She let go just as they crossed and they rolled into the corridor door.

"Him Too. You need me to come across and get you?"

Him Too gave her a withering look and grabbed the rope as it came back across. Kwee on his shoulder, he swung himself across the narrow river, scraping his arms as he landed. The friends retrieved their rope, took one last look at the golden river, and disappeared.

# Twenty-Eight

**B**erhane turned and waved at his mother, who sat fifty rows up from the arena. They had spent most of their remaining gold to get her that seat.

Ten. Win ten times and he was the next Prince Defender. Ten times and his mother could rest. Ten times and he could free Tembien. No longer would vermin conquer the home of the Unconquerable.

He maneuvered past countless fighters as he made his way to stage nineteen. Reaching into his ear, he withdrew the small strips of cloth he had used to block out the crowd. As he passed stage seventeen, he heard someone call out.

"How fares the lion of Tembien?"

Turning, he smiled, "Better than the goats."

Twid laughed. He hadn't seen the Shepherd during the qualifying round but hadn't doubted he'd make it. Twid pulled up his sleeve and pointed at the 17. "For Tembien's sake, I hope you are not on my stage."

Before the Shepherd could retort, Twid angled his head toward a short figure by the elevated stage. Though she sat motionless, her long neck arched forward like a viper. The girl who killed with her hair.

The Shepherd didn't hesitate. It wasn't just that he liked Wolde. No. He owed Wolde for helping his mother.

Leaning forward, he whispered. "Be careful. She's more than short swords and spinning hair. She has metal blades in her shoes."

Before Twid could ask him how he knew, a chorus of trumpets rose above the crowd's din. Across the arena, gigantic banners unfurled, reading "Live with Freedom," "Dream Forever," and "Freedom Forever."

Twid and Berhane climbed the wooden stage to get a better

view. A line of children marched wearing resplendent multi-colored clothing, carrying banners of three clasped hands under a sun. Tambourines clattered. Long metal pipes blared.

Behind the children, a figure crept like a panther, clothed head to toe. The maniac, Inj. Behind Inj, a thin woman flashed short swords. Twid exhaled as he saw his mother's killer. His heart thundered; light seared his head. When Twid opened his eyes, Kahn's lithe form had joined Tah and Inj. There was no sign of Delgam.

The crowd pounded their feet with such force, clapped so hard, that Twid feared the coliseum would collapse. Behind the Defenders, on raised daises, wearing robes that made the children's look plain, stood Wirla, Ran, and Nin, hands outstretched to the crowd.

They passed so close Twid could have struck them with his whip. Wirla was tall and thin, like the herders of Wir. Ran had jowls. Nin's bony face was as hard as his desert homeland.

Twid imagined Wirla salivating at raf's addictive nature; Ran betraying Zinna in the Hall of Kings; Nin sending Tah to murder villagers.

"Wolde?" As he looked at Berhane's concerned face, Twid realized that he alone in the stadium was not cheering. Twid forced himself to smile and clapped his good hand on his thigh.

The Prince Defenders and Dream Kings circled once and then settled in their booth over the arena. The three defenders lifted a gigantic flag featuring the familiar clasped hands and sunrise and placed it on a stand.

Inj swept his hand in an arc, silencing the crowd.

Then King Ran spoke. "Gathered esteemed, on behalf of King Wirla and King Nin; on behalf of Freedom and Dreams themselves, I welcome you to the sixth Prince Defender Games."

The crowd erupted again. After minutes of deafening applause, Ran continued. "As you know, these Games bring together the finest warriors in the land. All who qualify earn a privileged rank in the Dream Army, should they seek it. And to the winner, goes fame, wealth, and most of all, duty beyond measure, for on their broad shoulders shall rest the title of Prince Defender, Defender of Freedom and Dreams in the Three Lands.

"There are thirty-two battle stages around the arena. Thirty-two warriors will compete at each battle stage. After fighting five rounds, there will be one remaining soldier at each battle stage to represent his stage tomorrow. Today, then, we shall narrow the field from 1024 warriors to just thirty-two. A warrior can win by forcing his opponent to submit, by maiming his opponent, or in extreme cases, by judge's decision. In rare…"

Twid closed out the rest, trying to remember Zinna's words. *"Do not be like the man who bought a new mattress and slept on it on the road home. Be patient. The only battle that matters is the current battle."*

Ran finished and the crowd cheered again. Twid whispered to the Shepherd, "May Alula himself be with you." The Shepherd clasped Twid's hand, gave Twid an iron smile, and headed to his stage.

Twid surveyed those who gathered at stage seventeen. The girl with her hair hadn't moved. A few staff-wielders. Several tall Wirbans who carried spears.

Twid licked his lips. At least the Endurance King wasn't there.

A tall, thin man with eager eyes announced himself as the judge. He lifted a ram's horn. "We've determined the match-ups by pulling your names out of this battle horn. The first battle is between Luah of Doha and Wolde son of Tayle."

As he heard his fake name called, Twid scanned the stage to see who Luah was. No one moved. And then, he saw her. The girl who killed with her hair.

Twid trembled. Did the Dream Kings know who he was? Were they trying to kill him in the first battle? Sighs of relief escaped the other fighters.

Twid joined Luah on the wooden stage. He pulled out a narrow piece of cloth and bowed down on his knees, holding the cloth over his head as his head touched the ground. Then, using his stump for support, he tied the cloth across his head, letting the ends stream down beneath him.

Twid popped the blade in his left arm. He couldn't use the short blade to reverse a frontal attack, but he could alter momentum, deflect, parry. Twid squinted in the sunlight, trying to see any signs of the blades in her shoes.

But then the bell rang and Luah leapt at Twid, short swords whirling. Twid leapt forward to meet her, parrying her first wave with his own sword. He could see the surprise in her arched eyes. She had expected him to back away from her hair. But Twid sprung forward, parried her left thrust and smashed his elbow into her chin.

Luah whirled and retreated. She spit blood. Twid heard Zinna in his head. *"Do the opposite of what your enemy expects."*

Beads of sweat glistened on Luah's olive skin. Her eyes tightened. Bending her knees like a mountain lion, she circled Twid. Twid refused to engage her. He circled left when she circled left, right when she went right.

As she leapt forward, Twid watched her neck for sudden movements. Blade met blade. Her neck arched and Twid ducked as the studded balls screamed by. Twid thrust at a small opening with his short blade; Luah's left sword met his. He nicked her right arm. Her short sword grazed his leg.

They fought for ten minutes, then twenty, then thirty. The crowd zeroed in on their battle. Twid tried to maneuver so the sun was in Luah's eyes.

The first creepings of panic struck. Her swords. Her hair. It was too much to watch and she hadn't even used the blades on her feet.

A faint clicking was Twid's only warning. Twid arched his head, knowing he was too late. A glinting object struck above his eyebrow. Blood erupted and pain flooded his head. Twid screamed. A Nishan throwing star! Cursing, he tried to wipe the blood from his right eye but Luah was already coming to finish him. She sprang the blades in her feet. Through Twid's bloody eye, the blades gleamed like red raindrops in the sun.

Twid darted back. Blood trailed him. Then a drifting sensation swept Twid and he felt himself rise above the battlefield, looking down on it, as if he weren't connected to his body. Left blade up. Parry low and to the right. Without thinking, Twid blocked each attack, ducking, feinting. The pain in his right eye numbed but the eye no longer saw anything.

Twid thought of Zinna's words. *If you are evenly matched with an opponent, conditioning will determine the outcome.* Luah was panting. Twid was breathing evenly. It was incredible. The first battle would be decided not by skill but by Zinna's unforgiving training schedule.

Luah lunged at him with her right sword. Twid leapt forward to meet her then ducked. Her hot breath scalded him as her momentum carried her forward. Even as he ducked Twid bent his legs and swung his elbow with the full force of his body. His elbow crushed her right ear with a violent crunch. Luah crumpled. Before she could move, Twid smashed his sword hilt into her head. A loud crunching sound cut the arena. Luah lay motionless.

The bell rang.

Twid collapsed. Like a ship escaping fog, he descended into his body. Massive gyrations rocked him, and then he realized that the gyrations were the crowd's pounding and screams.

※ ※ ※

None of the other battles were nearly as tough. Twid fought an axeman, two spearmen, and in the finals for stage twenty, a swordsman from Ras. He had worn each of them down, attacking only when he had clear openings.

His eye. Twid used an ointment that Zinna had given him and with a narrow strip of clothing, closed the wound.

Most of the fighters on stage seventeen had stayed to watch the final match and after Twid won, implored him to continue winning, "We want to tell our kids that we lost to the Prince Defender."

Luah had awoken after a half hour and been carried away. Remorse struck Twid. He didn't want to be the next Prince Defender. He just wanted to enter Himlee. And yet he had ruined her chances. He had ruined the chances of everyone on stage seventeen.

Between battles, Twid had wanted to walk to stage nineteen, to see how the Shepherd had fared. But Zinna had instructed him to watch every battle on his own stage, every warm-up.

The Shepherd had won his stage early, however, and after congratulating Twid, gone to speak with his mother. As he left the arena, Twid didn't want to think about what would happen if he met the Shepherd in the next round. Twid rubbed the skin above his eyes. The soft massage relaxed him.

He waded through the crowds and arrived at his inn. Twid found several sheets of paper on his bed, signed KT. The papers described each of the thirty-two finalists, their strengths, their weaknesses, and the Knowledge Thief's advice for defeating them. Twid flipped through the pages and stopped when he got to his own description. He swallowed as he read about himself:

**Assumed name: Wolde son of Tayle**
Real name: Unknown.

**Strengths:** Superb defense. Unparalleled balance and conditioning. Managed to keep whip a secret through first day's fighting. Head scarf ritual may mask ruse.

**Weakness:** Lacks killer instinct. Wastes opportunities to end matches early if doing so means maiming opponents.

**Best Approach:** Do not attack. Force to become aggressor.

Twid exhaled. Even with Luah, at the beginning, he could have smashed her throat, instead of her chin. But he had feared to kill her and in the end she had almost taken his eye.

Twid tossed the paper aside and laid flat on the ground. The pulsating cut on his thigh didn't matter. His bloodied head didn't matter. The nervous tingling along his spine didn't matter.

Tomorrow was the day. The day when a year's training would be tested, the day when he would earn an invitation to the Source of Harmony.

✳ ✳ ✳

The morning sun blazed over the Dream Coliseum and the gigantic stage in the center. Around the arena, murals had sprung up overnight with the faces of the different stage champions. The Endurance King. The Worm. The Bearded Barber. The Weaponless Wonder. The Mountain. The Needle. The Shepherd. The Panther. The Whirlwind. The Blade.

Trumpets sounded and the Dream Kings rose.

King Wirla spoke, his northern accent cutting each syllable as if it were a foe. "Honored guests, Freedom and Dreams to you on this second day of combat. To advance to the final four, each warrior must today win three battles. You know the rules. Let the Games begin."

Behind the stage, away from the other competitors, a bearded warrior rolled on the ground, patting his body with the palm of his hands. Blood quickened through his arms, legs, neck, and feet.

He rose, and with a swipe of his good hand, cleared his beard of sand and pebbles.

He didn't bother to wipe the dust off his grimy clothing but he did check his shoulder strap.

Twid of Adwa walked to the stage and approached a tall husky man. Twid hesitated. Was he just confirming what The

Knowledge Thief had said about his weakness?

"Berhane, I need to show you something."

He pulled out two scraps of paper and handed them to the man they called the Shepherd. Berhane read through them. His eyes arched and his brow furrowed. "Who gave these to you? Do you have them for the other warriors?"

Twid said, "I didn't want to read your profile unless you had read mine. That's all I can say." Berhane gave him a look and nodded. The friends walked toward the stage and the opening round.

※ ※ ※

Twid faced a giant they called The Mountain in the first round. The Mountain had sustained leg wounds from the day before that left him hobbled and Twid had worn him down with endless circling.

Early in the second round, Twid heard his name called out, "Wolde the son of Lab to face Ishko the son of Nigus."

Sweat covered Twid's neck and he licked his cracked lips. Ishko, the one they called The Needle. According to the Knowledge Thief's report, the Needle carried a sword in one hand, and tossed thin, needle-like daggers with the other.

**Ishko son of Nigus**

**Strengths:** Explosive offense. Carries two dozen hand-length, finger-wide, razor-sharp needles. Missed just two out of eleven launches in first round. Sword is primary weapon.

**Weakness:** Has yet to demonstrate adequate defense in close quarters.

**Best Approach:** Launch immediate, all out attack. Must win in opening minutes to avoid needles.

**Warning:** Killed second and fourth opponents with needles to throats.

Twid walked atop the large, single stage. On this second day, battles were one at a time and fighters had the attention of everyone in the stadium.

The crowd roared. Some shouted "Needle!" Other answered, "Barber! Barber! Barber!" It still didn't make sense to Twid: The crowd had dubbed him the Bearded Barber because he had defeated the girl who killed with her hair.

Twid readied himself by repeating his ritual. Bowing, he attached a thin narrow head scarf around his neck. The Needle towered with a nose that jutted like an errant tree branch and long limbs that hung like reeds. His wide afro itself could have hidden several needles.

Knees bent, Twid settled back into the defensive Ras style. The bell rang and Twid shifted into the Nishan style, attacking with sword and dagger.

But the gigantic stage gave the Needle ample room to maneuver and whenever Twid got close, the Needle circled away. Knees bent, shoulders hunched forward, the Needle swung back and forth with the ease of an orangutan. Twid grit his teeth. Had the Needle read the Knowledge Thief's assessment?

Minutes passed. Thrust met parry, feint feint. The sheen of sweat covered both their temples. They traded light nicks. The Needle continued to circle.

The wound above Twid's right eye opened. Droplets of blood obscured Twid's vision. Something sang and Twid swerved, but then the air hissed again, and pain exploded in both of Twid's legs, a wetness, a sharp pounding.

The needles! He was going to lose…maybe die! Blood spurted from Twid's thighs. The Needle moved in for the kill. Twid stumbled back and somehow kept his footing. He forced himself to follow Zinna's advice: *"Keep your hands on your weapons, never on your wounds."*

Swerving left, Twid avoided two more needles but slipped on his own blood. He parried late and the Needle's sword nicked his shoulder. Blackness descended; panic swelled.

Twid attacked wildly with both sword and dagger. He had to get close. But the Needle circled Twid like a hyena that sensed its prey would die on its own. Blood drenched the entire lower half of Twid's pants.

Twid's head whirled. The stage spun. He couldn't keep track of the Needle. The whip. Twid had wanted to save the whip until the final fight. His sword felt heavy. Zinna's words rang: *"Contained chaos is the best mask for a ruse."* Twid attacked wildly, feinting hard with his sword, and then curled out with his whip.

The Needle jumped. Twid snapped the whip downward. The tip bounced off the stage and curled around the Needle's foot. With a hard yank, Twid slammed the Needle to the ground. Before the Needle could move, Twid swung his arm and smashed his elbow into the Needle's nose, crushing it in a mass of blood and cartilage. Twid slammed another elbow to the Needle's ribs. Bones cracked. The Needle screamed. Twid whipped his blade toward the Needle's neck. But then the judge was pulling Twid off... and Twid collapsed.

He had almost... Twid grabbed his own head. He had almost killed the Needle! Feeling the pain heighten, if that was possible, Twid looked down. Two needles protruded from his thighs; blood gushed in rivulets. Twid stared like a farmer who had spotted locusts during harvest.

Gritting his teeth, Twid steadied himself and yanked the needles one at a time. He screamed. The world exploded red and black and disappeared.

Then the Shepherd's husky arms were around him, carrying him from the stage.

The crowd screamed Twid's new name, "Three Arms! Three Arms! Three Arms!" But only one thought rang clear in his head.

He had won the battle but lost the war.

The smell of drying blood nauseated Twid. His head whirled again and he forced himself to focus on a fixed object. The stage. Not the stage! A mural. It read, "Your Freedom, Your Dreams." Twid looked away again, to the ground. To the thick cloth wrapped around his legs. To the dark crust of blood.

He forced his gaze back to the stage. The Endurance King had worn down The Worm. The Shepherd had outdueled The Blade. The Whirlwind had tamed The Panther.

It was maddening! Just eight warriors remained. Just one battle from the Source of Harmony! Another tremor rocked his leg; he leaned back on his elbows as if that could reduce the pain.

He braced himself as the judge called the next match: "Wolde son of Tayle to face Berhane of Tembien." A sudden quietness crowded out the arena. Time stopped. Breathing stopped. Images sprang in Twid's head. The Shepherd's mom, her kind words, her tightly wound scarf, her hopes for her son. Alula. Tembien. The sun striking Zinna's gleaming face. Zinna standing next to Delgam. Twid riding away after Zinna's sacrifice. Him Too and Iwala. Old Zeru.

Was Twid's search for the Harmonies any more important than the Shepherd's desire to free his homeland? Tears bit Twid's eyes, and not from his physical pain. What if one person's good destroyed another's? Was that the Third Harmony, that life was never as easy as one thought, never as simple; that good and evil couldn't be compartmentalized into convenient buckets? If the Shepherd hadn't bandaged Twid after the battle with the Needle, would Twid even be conscious to fight the Shepherd?

Twid heard his name again: "Wolde son of Tayle to face Berhane of Tembien. Son of Tayle, take the stage or forfeit."

Twid leaned on his sword and forced himself up. Blinding pain pierced his legs. A small trickle of blood wove down his right calf. He hobbled up the steps. The Shepherd wore a sad smile. "Are you sure you are not from Tembien?"

Twid whispered, "Win or lose, by my mother Nigiste's grave, I will help you free Tembien." Without kneeling, Twid forced himself to repeat his ritual. He tied the head scarf tight around his head and bowed his neck.

The bell rang and the Shepherd circled Twid. "I have no desire to hurt you, Wolde. For Alula's sake, please just leave the stage."

Twid shook his head. The Shepherd jumped forward, staff whirling. Twid leaned left, then bent his neck under. The staff's wind passed over his neck hair. He heard Zinna's words, *"The master parries with the most minimal of movements."*

The Shepherd swung at Twid's midsection. Twid parried. The Shepherd swung again. Twid leaned back and avoided the blow. Surprise registered on the Shepherd's face. His eyes narrowed and he locked his jaw. Leaping forward, he feinted to Twid's thighs, then hurled a powerful blow at Twid's right leg. Twid leaned, then parried again, all the while moving as little as possible. The Shepherd intensified his attack, using increasingly dizzying sequences. But Twid had trained against the greatest staff-wielder in the Three Lands.

Wetness dripped down Twid's legs; the salty smell of his own blood was everywhere. His vision blurred. Sweat and blood stung Twid's right eye. He lost sight of the Shepherd. Something struck Twid's jaw hard, but Twid blocked the follow-up blow that would have ended the battle.

With each passing minute, The Shepherd became more aggressive, less forgiving. He liked Wolde but this was bigger than Wolde or the Shepherd. Hyeks ravaged Alula's homeland. As a Prince Defender, he would have the authority and resources to free Tembien.

But try as he could, the Shepherd could not penetrate Wolde's defenses. He attacked low, high, tried to snare him with the hook. It was as if Wolde had already seen their battle, already knew what the Shepherd was going to do.

The Shepherd had no choice. He didn't want to hurt Wolde, but he had no choice.

Twid stepped back. The Shepherd had retreated to the far side of the stage. The Shepherd twisted his staff and the hook dropped off the stage. The Shepherd twisted the staff again and sharp metal spear-ends sprouted from either end of the staff. Twid swallowed. Whatever it took to win. If the Shepherd had to kill Twid, he would.

The Shepherd jumped at Twid and the blades hissed. Twid unfurled his whip and stepped back. Then, as with Luah, Twid ascended and looked down on his body like a traveler seeing his home from a distant mountain. Twid saw blood gush from his wounds, his legs wobble. His sword and dagger rose to meet each attack.

The Shepherd lunged close and head butted Twid. The wound above Twid's eye exploded. Twid hobbled back but the Shepherd swung a sharp blow at his neck. Twid blocked then sprung back again. His legs wobbled. He would only last another minute.

The Knowledge Thief's assessment of his own weakness flashed through his head: "Lacks killer instinct."

Twid feinted hard with his sword, then with his whip, and with a shout, slammed his dagger into The Shepherd's left thigh. The Shepherd screamed. Blood spurted onto Twid's whip, arm, everywhere. Twid swung down with all his remaining strength. The Shepherd's leg shattered; white bone protruded from the skin.

The bell rang but all Twid could hear was the Shepherd's wild screams. All he could see, the Shepherd's protruding bone.

Then darkness came and Twid knew no more.

# Twenty-Nine

Four spindle-shaped towers arched high and leaned into each other, connecting at the abdomen by circular walkways. The light-brown stones curved left and right, dotted by spores like honeycombs, as if the towers actually breathed and could at any moment shake the tightness from their legs and lumber like some mammoth emerging from a millennia-old cocoon.

A dozen monks carried a resplendent dais on their shoulders. On the dais, Twid and the other finalists stared at Himlee, unable to look away from the grotesque yet beautiful structure.

The dais disappeared into the gaping entrance. A vast chamber opened like the maw of some colossal creature. Ornate carvings lined every wall. Curves within curves, even the floor seemed sinuous. A light breeze rustled from an oval window and cooled Twid's neck.

The dais lowered. The Endurance King helped Twid to his feet. The other finalists, the Whirlwind and the Weaponless Wonder, surveyed the chamber.

Twid leaned against a staff. He had made it. Himlee. After sixteen months of planning and training, he had made it. But the cost had been high. The Shepherd. Zinna. Maybe Him Too, Iwala and Zeru. Too high.

The Whirlwind and Endurance King smelled of layered sweat. What would happen if Twid faced them? Could he win? Twid hobbled forward. When the time came to fight, he would just forfeit.

He had no desire to face anyone else. Not after the Shepherd. The Knowledge Thief had been right. Twid lacked the killer instinct; he had hesitated to hurt his opponents. And the Prince Defender Games had no place for hesitation. Eight of the thirty-two finalists had suffered serious injuries that would leave them bedridden for life. Three had died.

Twid was glad that he hadn't seen the Shepherd's mother after the battle. Tembien. Alula. The Shepherd's protruding leg. Twid turned his head.

A thin, imperious monk interrupted Twid's thoughts, "Tonight, rest where few mortals have rested. Ahead, you will find food and private sleeping chambers." He paused. "Tomorrow, the Dream Kings themselves will greet you."

※ ※ ※

Twid surveyed Himlee's main chamber again. He had crept from his small room two hours earlier. His body ached with every step. But adrenaline had energized him and he had used the wall's curved edges to support his legs. Himlee had helped, too, with its cool breeze and promise of life. Twid's legs had not yet bled and it was already past midnight. The other three finalists were asleep.

Himlee had four towers that connected to the main chamber. Towers that would each take a day to search, if he were healthy. As it was, Twid had circled for two hours and he still hadn't finished half the main chamber.

Why hadn't he asked the Knowledge Thief about the entrance to the Source? Was the entrance below, through an opening in the floor? Was it outside the walls?

A sparkle caught Twid's eyes. Defying the night, two gigantic words sparkled from the nearest wall: "Dream Kinms." Twid did a double-take; the sudden movement shot pain down his legs. Then Twid remembered. Old Zeru had warned them of Giiz's strange rules; "M" was sometimes substituted for "G."

The monks had locked them in, telling them that Himlee was theirs. Theirs to enjoy. To enjoy what few alive had ever experienced. The others slept in their own quarters, on extravagant silk beds that the Dream Kings had prepared.

Why so easy? Why leave them alone? Was it a trap?

After everything, what if there was no Source of Harmony? What if there was a Source, but he couldn't find it? Twid pushed the thoughts away.

The wall. Twid had seen this section of the wall before. Inlaid carvings depicted a rolling landscape that featured hills and bridges, caves and what appeared to be sand dunes. A mountain loomed. Where had he seen the carvings?

The voices stirred in Twid's head.

Along the cavern, curves straightened.

A point appeared on the stone before Twid. A line. A square.

Sudden chills coursed along Twid's back as he remembered Him Too's words with the old man in Metka: "The power of the Third Harmony is unto a square, with infinite lines."

Hands trembling, Twid pushed against the square. It moved. A small light appeared, growing in intensity and then the wall shifted before him. Face flush, hands raised to shield the blinding light, Twid stepped forward.

❈ ❈ ❈

A peace washed over Twid. Thoughts and emotions ceased; the burning in his legs ceased. He opened his eyes and saw an empty wall.

A bright point appeared on the wall before him, and Twid heard a soft voice in his head. "The power of the First Harmony is like a point."

The point extended into a line and Twid heard the voice again. "The power of the Second Harmony expands the point into a line, with infinite points and infinitely more power."

The line expanded, adding three more lines, forming a square. "The power of the Third Harmony is unto a square with infinite line. A new dimension, leading to revolution."

Another square appeared, with one vertex at the center of the first square. One by one, the vertices connected, forming a cube. "The power of the Fourth Harmony mirrors a cube, with infinite squares."

The voice paused. The wall paused. Twid held his breath. What was the fifth harmony? He didn't see how the cube could expand again.

But then another cube formed at the exact midpoint of the first cube, extending out past the original cube. The corresponding vertices connected again, creating a supernatural object containing infinite cubes, an object impossible to carve. "The Fifth Harmony is unto a mystery, transcending all understanding."

Wind lifted Twid through the wall. When he stepped forward, he found himself inside a room with a pool of water so immobile it looked glass.

Stepping forward, he looked into the water. An old house appeared. Carrying a small bucket, a boy stepped out, tripping on a small bundle. The boy picked up the small bundle and left it at the orphanage across town.

The house came back. Again the boy stepped out. This time, the boy laid the bundle on a cart next to the house. Later that day, the cart rode off with the bundle.

The house came back. This time the boy ignored the bundle and kept going to the well. The house came back. Again, and again, whirling around the pool.

While the myriad images of the house and the boy whipped around the pool, Twid saw another image, this time, of a darkskinned woman speaking at a small gathering in a forest. He saw a one-armed man rush to the stage and shake her hand.

He saw the forest again and the one-armed man rushed to the stage and offered her deer meat. He saw the forest again and the one-armed man shot an arrow at the woman from the trees.

More images from his life joined the whirling images of the house and the forest. Twid before the tree; Twid with his mother and sister; Twid with Zeru. The images sped until Twid closed his eyes.

He exhaled.

Endless choices. Choices he had never thought he had,

infinite choices, so many choices it made his brain hurt. That was the problem with the first harmony: You had many more choices than you wanted to acknowledge, more choices than you could comprehend.

Yet how often did people grasp the full range of their freedom?

Twid nodded. The old man from Metka had known; he had challenged Twid. *"What do you know of freedom's pain?"*

When he opened his eyes, the pool of water had returned to its original immobile state. Looking across the room, Twid saw a small door. He couldn't look at the pool anymore. Walking to the door, he passed through, and descended down a narrow set of stairs. Somehow, his legs did not ache.

He reached the bottom then cringed and fell. A gigantic lion rose on haunches, claws curved, ready to pounce. After cowering for a moment, Twid realized that the lion couldn't move.

Picking himself up, Twid hurried past the lion, examining the rest of the room. Nothing. He looked at the ground. Had the Dream Kings removed the rest of the objects in the room? Did they have the power to alter the Source of Harmony?

Returning to the lion, Twid tiptoed close and touched its nose. An icy sensation overwhelmed him. Images flashed through his head. He saw himself as a child, stealing a mango, then a melon, then money pouches, then moving to Dream City and working for the Thieves Guild. He saw himself cutting wood with his good hand, carving little by little, practicing each day, until he had a carpenter's shop. He saw himself lying, each day, the lies growing bigger, smaller, bigger, until he no longer knew the difference between lying and telling the truth. He saw himself screaming at everyone near him, day after day, until no one approached him because he was a screamer. The images whirled, faster and faster, and he saw himself become different people, all based on little, repeated actions.

Letting go of the lion, Twid hunched over. Infinite choices leading to infinite becomings. Dreams created, nightmares created, one moment at a time.

The Dreams Kings had taught that the Second Harmony was all about dreaming. Everyone deserved to have a dream, to reach a dream. Yes, dreams for everyone and everyone for dreams; dreaming alone enough to make dreams come true.

To their credit, the Dream Kings did do more than talk. They had provided raf, a grain affordable to even the poorest; they had given away the Dream Mansions; they had talked of freedom and dreams at every opportunity; they had sponsored expeditions to find the Map of Legends; they had created the Prince Defender Games that anyone, even the poorest, could enter. Dreams for everyone. Freedom for everyone. And not someday, but today. That was the genius of the Dream Kings. Everything you ever wanted, right now, at no cost.

As he leaned on the lion, Twid realized the lion didn't have real fur. Twid drew closer. *What in Zeru's name?* The lion was made of thousands of little mice, their heads removed, their bodies sewn shut, their skin painted to fit the right color. *What in isolation is mouse skin, can collectively become a lion.*

He nodded to himself–it was a lesson worth remembering. That was the power of the second Harmony.

He turned and saw a new passageway leading to the next room. His heart raced. The Third Harmony. After countless challenges, it was time to claim his prize.

He tripped and fell to the ground, jerking back as something crawled up his finger. Spiders! There were spiders everywhere, weaving their webs all throughout the corridor. Where had the spiders come from? He could have sworn they weren't there earlier.

As he pushed himself up, his hand touched something hard. A human skull. Twid yelled and jumped back. His legs wobbled. Twid felt dampness by his wounds.

The floor, which had been smooth and empty before, was now scattered with swords and spears, daggers and arrows. It was impossible to move forward without stepping on some sort of human bone.

Something had lived and killed here, in the Source of Harmony. *How can it be The Source of Harmony if people die here?*

As he crept forward, trying to avoid the bones, Twid had the feeling that he was a sheep leading himself to his own slaughter. *Travel across the world, fight in the bloody games, all to reach the Third Harmony, and now there are bones leading to the door. Nothing is ever easy.*

He was fifteen feet from the door when he heard it. Raging like a hurricane, it shrieked like a whirlwind of tears, a thousand screams reverberating throughout the chamber. Twid covered his ears but he couldn't keep out the shriek.

It had no eyes. Just a mass of thick green appendage darting in and out. And it was still rising, growing taller and wider every second, a hundred tentacles lashing in every direction.

What in Zeru's name! Was it some sort of plant? He remembered that Iwala had once told him of underground plants that lived for millennia.

The creature finally stopped growing, standing a head over Twid. It was impossible to reach the door without passing the tentacles.

Twid reached to the ground and pulled a dagger. Aiming low, he launched the dagger, slicing a tentacle in half. But before the tentacle hit the ground, another tentacle grabbed it, and reattached it as if nothing had happened.

Twid howled a guttural grunt. No wonder no one knew The Third Harmony. It had an invincible guardian. As he stepped back, Twid wondered if he should just head back. Leave. Find some other way to figure out the Third Harmony. If nothing else, he could tell the Knowledge Thief about the guardian.

But when he looked back, the door had disappeared. The lion had disappeared.

As if reading his thoughts, the tentacles picked up intensity. "You're trapped," they seemed to taunt. "There's only one way out."

He had cut several tentacles. He had hurled burning wood. He had searched every other wall for an exit. Nothing. If he didn't return soon, the other fighters and the soldiers would miss him and wonder where he had gone. And his legs. Sharp pains shot through his legs.

He had to think. Think! Mogus from Metka wouldn't have sent him if there wasn't a way out. The Knowledge Thief wouldn't have helped him if he didn't think it was possible for him to survive.

His mind wandered and he thought about Him Too and Iwala, wondering if they were alive, if he would ever see them again. What he wouldn't do to have Iwala here. Iwala would probably challenge the plant to a game of cards and leave the chamber owning all the plant's tentacles. Yes. Iwala would beat the plant in cards, learn the Third Harmony, and then forget it before she could tell anyone. That was Iwala for you. Even when she did everything right, she'd find a way to undo it.

Sitting back, Twid balanced himself with his good hand then stopped when he felt his fingers get tangled by a sticky substance. It was the dratted spider webs again.

Chills raced down his spine, and he shivered, his body shaking. That was it! The lion had been his clue. Use the Second Harmony to get to the third.

He sat and gathered as much spider webbing as he could, weaving it together, making strong impenetrable strands, all the while careful not to get himself tangled. Strand by strand, little by little, each chord grew stronger.

Hours passed. His stomach rumbled. Blood crusted along his leg.

The words ricocheted through his mind. JIGNA. THE FIVE HARMONIES. JIGNA. He kept weaving until his fingers cramped.

He made a wide loop with the rope, creating a type of lasso and walked to the plant. Thrusting the loop over the plant, he trapped some of the tentacles and pulled the rope tight. He created another lasso and trapped more tentacles and more tentacles and more tentacles.

It was so simple. So simple it was stupid. If a mouse could become a lion, then a spider web could become an iron rope.

That was why the Second Harmony was so hard to see. It was nothing spectacular, nothing sensational, nothing that could be accomplished in a moment. It was the power of little things becoming big things.

He watched the plant squirm for a few minutes. Would it break free as he darted past? Would the spider rope hold? But then Twid was already moving past the plant. He took a final look at the plant. *Who's trapped now?*

He sprang through the door, his heart quickening, his body shaking. After a year of training and endless pursuit, after months of separation from his friends, after intense battle at the games, he had made it. The Third Harmony! *Zinna, I did it! Your sacrifice meant something! I'm entering the Third Harmony...*

He stopped.

He was back in the main hall. Twenty soldiers surrounded him. A familiar voice rang out.

"It's good to see you again, Twid."

Scout-boy.

❇ ❇ ❇

On the other side of the world, Iwala paused. "You found a way into Metka," Zinna had said. "You found a way into the monastery. And you will find a way into the Cursed Lands. You will find a way."

Iwala looked at the stone door. She could see faint slivers of light streaming in through small cracks.

If only Zinna, Twid, and Zeru could be there with them to see it.

Iwala took a deep breath. What awaited on the other side? Would they find the Golden Eagle? Would they find the monsters that the Dream Kings had walled away?

She looked at Him Too and the girl, Rua, the last living member of the Thirteenth Village. They had walked and crawled for months, maybe even a year.

Unless they had gone in circles, they would emerge on the other side of the Wall. They would see what no one in the Three Lands had seen for centuries.

Her companions nodded.

Iwala flexed her thin legs and pushed the door upward. Him Too and Rua followed Iwala. It took several minutes for their eyes to adjust to the morning sun. They had emerged on a hill covered by small shrubs. The morning dew sparkled on the short grass.

Him Too raised his hand in excitement. "Look! The sun is rising on the other side of the Dream Wall! We're west of the Wall!"

Iwala squinted at the Wall, hand raised to block the sun. She jumped and raised her hands. Kwee dug into Iwala's shoulders and Iwala found herself in an uncharacteristic embrace with Him Too. They pulled Rua into the embrace.

The massacre of the Thirteenth Village would mean something! They would track down the Golden Eagle wherever she or it was. They would find Zinna, Twid, and Zeru and exact retribution on the Dream Kings.

As her eyes adjusted, Iwala pulled away from her companions. She walked further up the hill. Sudden chills ran down her back. Her breath caught.

It couldn't be.

Iwala heard Him Too gasp.

It was impossible. Insane!

No!

No wonder they needed the Wall.

No wonder the crops were so cheap.

No wonder the Dream Kings had endless raf.

Waves of guilt mixed with shock, and Iwala crumbled to her knees.

As far as her eyes could see, fields sparkled with white grain. Tilling the fields were folks with red hair and weathered, white skin. Overseers dressed in Dream King garb patrolled the fields, whips ready, striking the men, women, and even children if they paused from their toil. An overseer kicked a woman's face. A man swung from a tree branch. Flies covered his bloodied back.

Iwala collapsed.

The Twelve Villages hadn't been wiped out.

They hadn't disappeared.

They had been enslaved.

# Thirty

**T**wid tried to quell the panic. What happened? Had he taken the wrong door? Had it all been a trap? Was the whole thing a ruse, a way for the Dream Kings to sniff out their enemies?

They had him in a circle. There was no way out.

Hadn't the old man tried to warn him? Hadn't he said the Harmonies would betray him?

Twid wanted to scream. It had all been for nothing! All a ruse.

No! He refused to believe it. Not after coming so far. He felt someone push him from behind; a fist rushed at him from the left. He ducked.

A blow rocked him and when he turned a staff smashed into his ribs, creating a loud crunching noise. He gasped. They had broken his ribs.

Another blow smashed into his head and he almost blacked out.

Then he heard another familiar voice. "I love the arrogance. Thought you could just walk into the Source and no one would know?" A massive figure materialized. Delgam. "You had your chance. You could have disappeared." Delgam swung with his right hand, and blood erupted from Twid's left eyes. Another blow smashed his mouth, loosening most of his upper teeth.

Then Delgam kicked him in the face and everything went black.

※ ※ ※

The crowd's roar woke him. Twid struggled to breathe, each gasp heightening the pain from his broken ribs.

Was he blind in his left eye? He reached up with his good arm and touched it. It was swollen shut.

The questions assaulted him again. Was it all a trap? Were the Dream Kings right? Was there really no such thing as a Third Harmony? He had been so sure; he had felt the power of the Harmonies, had felt the Second Harmony click in his head; had heard the voices.

The crowd quieted. Nin spoke. "Brothers and sisters, as we have long warned, traitors roam the land. Evildoers who would do anything to destroy Freedom, to betray Dreams."

"Yesterday, Wolde the Son of Tayle, whose true name is Twid of Adwa, betrayed your trust and our trust. With defiance never seen before in these games, he defiled the Dream Palace, entering secret, forbidden passages, attempting to harm those who hosted him."

Nin raised a gavel and smashed it on the wooden stand before him. "For his crimes against Freedom and Dreams, Twid of Adwa must die."

Two soldiers grabbed Twid and hoisted him to his feet, leading him to the stage where the arced blade of a guillotine shone. Twid teetered.

In Twid's head, Zinna's common refrain echoed: "When all else fails, the master wins by using his head. The master can kill with even a blade of grass."

But the words seemed weak now, useless.

Hundreds of soldiers surrounded the stage. Two hundred thousand spectators watched. There was no escape.

*I don't care. I know what I felt. I know the First Harmony is real. I felt the Second Harmony. That lion was real. That plant was real. I used the Second Harmony.*

Twid straightened his back, the pain from his ribs so searing that he dropped to one knee. Blood erupted from his thighs. The First Harmony taught that you always chose your actions, that even when you didn't like the choices available, you still had a choice.

He surveyed the crowd. *You don't always choose your actions, but you still have a choice. There's got to be power in that.*

As if lifting a boulder, he raised his hand over his head. The crowd quieted. He turned and faced the Dream Kings.

Nin spoke. "Confess your crimes and go with dignity."

Excruciating pain blinded Twid as he projected his voice. "I call upon the Dream Code, the highest law in the land. That when a citizen has been accused of crimes against Freedom and Dreams, he may choose the right of trial by combat against a Prince Defender, whose greatest duty is to defend Freedom and Dreams."

What had Zinna said? Delgam always had his pride?

"Yesterday, I was pummeled and attacked by the coward Delgam, when he had thirty soldiers to help him. Now I challenge the pathetic son of a dog to a duel for my freedom. I will enter the fight with nothing other than my clothes and my body. Delgam may wield whatever weapon he desires. Should I defeat him, I will claim my freedom and innocence, as declared by the highest laws of the land."

Before the Dream Kings could protest, Delgam was on the stage, his face red, veins bulging, removing the guillotine with just one hand when it had taken three men to place it on the stage.

No one in the crowd moved. It was unthinkable.

Twid stood on the stage, the pain from his thigh and ribs clouding his mind. Reaching down to his tattered tunic, he tore a long strip of cloth and waved it above his head.

He would have once chance. One chance for freedom. One chance to live.

It had to be true. He didn't care. He had known the Second Harmony before he had even stepped into Himlee. He had felt its power.

The Second Harmony taught that you became your actions. That you became what you did and thought, not once, but over time. Before each of his matches, Twid had tied a cloth around his head. With each harmless use of the cloth, Twid's opening had become more and more routine, the cloth just a harmless ritual. Now Twid tied the tunic around his head one final time.

Bowing to the ground so no one could see him, Twid reached into his mouth. He found his upper saber tooth on the right side, a tooth Delgam had loosened the previous night.

The bell rang. Twid leapt to his feet, ignoring the pain in his legs and ribs, ignoring the blood in his mouth. He hobbled toward Delgam. He grabbed the cloth from his head, folding it in half the long way, using it to wipe the blood spurting from his leg.

When he was just several feet away, Twid felt himself leave his body, saw himself snapping the cloth straight, spinning it. Once. Twice. On the third spin, he snapped the makeshift slingshot, ignoring the blood spurting from his thigh and the blinding pain emanating from his ribs.

*Fly true. Please fly true.*

Blood erupted from Delgam's left eye and Delgam dropped his sword, his hands shooting to his eye.

*You've forgotten Zinna's teachings, Delgam: Don't move your hand to the wound; keep it on your weapon.*

Leaping onto Delgam's right thigh, Twid sprang up, his arm cocking back as he soared. His right elbow smashed into Delgam's left temple. Delgam's head whipped around, and in one fluid motion, Twid's left elbow struck Delgam's right temple. As Twid descended, Twid flattened his right hand into a blade and with every remaining ounce of strength, crushed Delgam's Adam's apple.

Delgam slumped. Crumpled. And fell.

No one breathed. No one talked. No one moved.

It was unthinkable. A Prince Defender slain at the Prince Defender Games.

Reaching down, Twid grabbed his tooth and placed it in a pocket. He hobbled off the stage. The pain rocked him as the adrenaline subsided. He tied the cloth around the wound in his left leg.

*Take that, you sons of dogs. Murdering, lying, cheating sons of dogs.*

No one spoke as he limped toward the exit. The phalanx of soldiers parted.

He had to hide. Had to find a hiding spot. They would kill him as soon as he left the arena. He knew that. The Dream Kings would never let him live, whatever their law said.

Surveying the crowd, he tried to find the Knowledge Thief, but it was futile. There were too many people. *Knowledge Thief! I have information for you. I've seen the Source of Harmony!*

A booming voice stopped him just as he reached the exit. "Halt." Twid turned. Ran stood, one hundred feet away on the stage.

"You have earned your freedom, young warrior, and you may leave should you so desire. But first, we would ask for your aid with one final task." Twid turned and watched as the soldiers placed a double guillotine in the middle of the arena.

"We have two traitors charged with crimes far greater than yours. Delgam was to execute them. Since you have incapacitated him, we invite you to execute them in his place."

Twid's heart plunged through the arena ground. His blood pounded so hard he thought his head would rupture.

Hands bound and faces swollen, two prisoners hobbled toward the guillotine. Zeru and Zinna.

※※ ※※ ※※

He could do nothing to save them. He had barely saved himself. His legs quivered and he crumbled to his knees. Blood squirted to the ground, darkening the dirt.

Nothing! There was nothing he could do. He had to escape. Even Iwala had never pushed her luck this far.

But how could he abandon Zinna? His teacher. Without her, he never would have survived the Games. And Zeru? His father. Zeru had cared for him since childhood.

He had learned the first two Harmonies. Hadn't they just saved him? Now, he had to remember his promise: To go to the Cursed

Lands and find the Golden Eagle. Nothing else mattered. Zinna had already sacrificed her life and Zeru would have done the same. He could not save them. Better that two die than all three.

Time stopped and Twid looked around the stadium, at the tens of thousands of faces. Did any of them even know why he was there? Did the Harmonies even matter to them?

The banners around the arena proclaimed the Dream Kings' most consistent message. You deserve to live YOUR dreams. You deserve to have YOUR freedom. YOU deserve an amazing destiny.

YOU. YOUR. YOU. YOUR.

It was all about you.

Twid hobbled toward his friends.

The voices screamed. THE FIVE HARMONIES. JIGNA.

Twid stood before the guillotine's lever and said. "As you command, I will execute them."

Two soldiers pushed his companions down, locking their heads.

Twid checked their heads. He wanted to say something to them but the soldiers watched with intense, merciless eyes.

*Come on, Knowledge Thief! Come through for me. I have put our lives in your hands. I have risked all trusting you.* Nothing. No explosion. No commotion. No distraction. Where was the bloody Knowledge Thief?

Twid moved to the lever and then suddenly, swung up with his elbow, slamming a soldier's head. Grabbing the soldier's sword, Twid cut down the other soldier then sliced through his friend's bonds. He ignored the soldiers running toward him—he had to free Zinna and Zeru before the guillotine severed their heads!

Out of nowhere, an arrow screamed by, striking King Ran's shoulder. Chaos erupted as the Prince Defenders leapt to protect the kings. The Knowledge Thief!

As Twid cut the final ropes, he heard a click. Another soldier had released it, and the guillotine's glinting blades descended!

Fighting with his stump to get a grip, Twid shoved the headlocks up then pushed his friends' heads out of the way. But then ice-cold steel sliced; numbness struck.

Twid's right hand fell to the ground, severed, and his left forearm crashed next to it. His arms! Both arms! Twid screamed.

Blood spurted from his two stumps, and in the background, the crowd erupted. Standing guard over him, Zinna defended with two swords, screaming, tears flying down her face, felling soldiers. Behind her, Zeru fought with a short sword. Soldiers circled.

Light exploded in Twid's head; words burned: *You can choose your actions. You can become your actions. But as long as you focus only on you, on your own freedom, on your own dreams, you will never TRANSCEND your actions.*

In his head, a line morphed into a square and the Third Harmony blazed like lightning across a wet field. *Connection: You transcend your actions.*

A tingling erupted in Twid's arms. Looking down, Twid saw his blood turn gold then black. JIGNA! THE FIVE HARMONIES! JIGNA! The words quaked.

Light flashed through his swollen left eye. The smell of burning flesh overwhelmed him. Twid tried to scream but nothing came out. His arms smoldered then ripped apart.

Zinna yelled, her eyes shining madly, a wild glow on her face as she thrust her staff toward Twid's arms and then smashed the staff up into a soldier's throat. Zeru's entire left face twitched and he yelled something Twid couldn't hear.

Twid convulsed, unable to comprehend what he saw. His arms! His hands! They had grown back! And they glowed midnight black like Zinna's skin. Twid thrust his arms to the sky.

Tattooed on each arm, with one wing starting near the hand, and the other ending near the elbow, with beak opened wide in fury, and black eyes narrowed in pursuit, a Golden Eagle soared, talons arched, scintillating in the sunlight.

The words seared his mind. *Connection: You transcend your actions.*

Power surged through Twid like wildfire that had caught new

wind. Injuries forgotten, he seized two swords and cut through soldiers. Chaos escalated. He joined his friends and the enemy fell before them like grass before a stampede.

JIGNA. THE FIVE HARMONIES. JIGNA.

It was him.

JIGNA. THE FIVE HARMONIES. JIGNA.

The Third Harmony had done it.

It was him.

The Golden Eagle.

They reached the exit.

And disappeared.

❖ ❖ ❖

Herein ends *The Third Harmony,* Book One of **Harmony Wars**.

❖ ❖ ❖

In Book Two, *The Map of Legends,* Him Too and Iwala will fight to liberate the Twelve Villages; Twid, Zinna, and Zeru will attempt to unlock the Fourth Harmony; and the companions will finally know their true enemies.

# EPILOGUE

The tall man ignored the exotic flowers that lined the winding road. But he couldn't ignore the twitching along his taut cheekbones.

His mother would blame him — he knew that. He had assured her that he had eliminated the Jignas and that the disappeared fox would be of little consequence. But who could have predicted? Who could have known that the fox would live for two hundred years? Who could have known that the Cursed Lands weren't west of the Wall, where the slaves huddled?

He bit his lip and spat warm blood onto the path. They had posted spies in every slave quarter. Monitored every child's birth. Ignored the Prince Defender Games because they were on the other side of the wall. All to watch for the Golden Eagle's rebirth. All to prepare. All because the Great Mirror had told them the time was nigh.

His sister's voice interrupted him. "Calm yourself, Nekom. Even mother couldn't have predicted this. Now that we know, we will finish him."

Nekom nodded as they approached a home made from symmetrical, triangular stones.

His sister was right. They would find the boy, Twid, or whatever he called himself.

They would kill him before he found the Map of Legends.

They would kill his troublesome friends.

They would end the war before it started.

# GLOSSARY of TERMS

Much of *The Third Harmony* is derived from Ethiopian/Eritrean culture, language and history. Below is a concise glossary.

**Adwa:** A city in northern Ethiopia, site of the famous Battle of Adwa in 1896 where Ethiopia defeated the colonial armies of Italy, becoming the only African country to decisively defeat a colonial power.

**Birr:** The currency of Ethiopia.

**Dirg:** The brutal army of the Ethiopian dictator Mengistu Haile Mariam, who was convicted by the Ethiopian High Court of genocide. According to some sources, Mengistu was responsible for the seventh worst genocide in modern history.

**Giiz:** A root language of many East African languages, much like Latin for Romance languages.

**Jigna:** A Tigrinya word describing a legendary hero who can never be conquered.

**Ras Alula:** A legendary Jigna from Tembien, Tigray, who helped drive the Italians from Ethiopia in 1896. The statue of Alula described in this book can be found in the airport of Tigray's capital, Mekele, in northern Ethiopia.

**Tef:** A grain native to Ethiopia.

# ABOUT the AUTHOR

Mawi Asgedom is an award-winning author who has been featured by the Oprah Winfrey Show, *Chicago Tribune, ESSENCE,* and many other media. He has spoken to over 700,000 students and is the founder of Mental Karate, an organization that trains real-life Jignas.

As a child, Mawi fled civil war in Ethiopia and survived a Sudanese refugee camp. After being resettled in the U.S., Mawi overcame many challenges to graduate from Harvard University.

To learn more about Mental Karate, visit MentalKarate.com where you can also receive a complimentary monthly newsletter.

**MENTAL**™
*think. act. attain.*

## DO YOU WANT TO TRAIN JIGNAS?

Learn how at MentalKarate.com

OF BEETLES & ANGELS:
A BOY'S REMARKABLE JOURNEY FROM
A REFUGEE CAMP TO HARVARD

———————

Mawi's inspiring memoir shares his harrowing journey
from a refugee camp to Harvard University.

Winner of awards from the American Library Association
and The Social Studies Council of America,
*Of Beetles and Angels* has inspired
tens of thousands of students.

———————

**Visit MawiBooks.com**

# BOOK MAWI TO SPEAK

---

A nationally recognized educator, Mawi Asgedom
has spoken to over 700,000 students and educators.
He has trained educators at the Harvard School of
Education and many international conferences.

---

To learn more about Mawi's speaking,
**visit www.MawiSpeaks.com**